THE FOREST BRIDE

A FAIRY TALE WITH BENEFITS

The

FOREST BRISÉ

JANE BUEHLER

Published by Emily Jane Buehler
PO Box 1285, Hillsborough, NC 27278 USA
https://janebuehler.com

Publisher's Note: This is a work of fiction. Names, characters, businesses, places, events, locales, and incidents are either the products of the author's imagination or used in a fictitious manner. Any resemblance to actual persons, living or dead, or actual events is purely coincidental.

The Forest Bride (Sylvania Book 1) / Emily Jane Buehler
ISBN (print): 978-0-9778068-4-3
ISBN (ebook): 978-0-9778068-5-0
ISBN (PG version, print): 978-0-9778068-6-7
ISBN (PG version, ebook): 978-0-9778068-7-4
This book is the PG version.

Library of Congress Control Number: 2020920416

*To all the late bloomers,
and everyone who's still afraid to try something new*

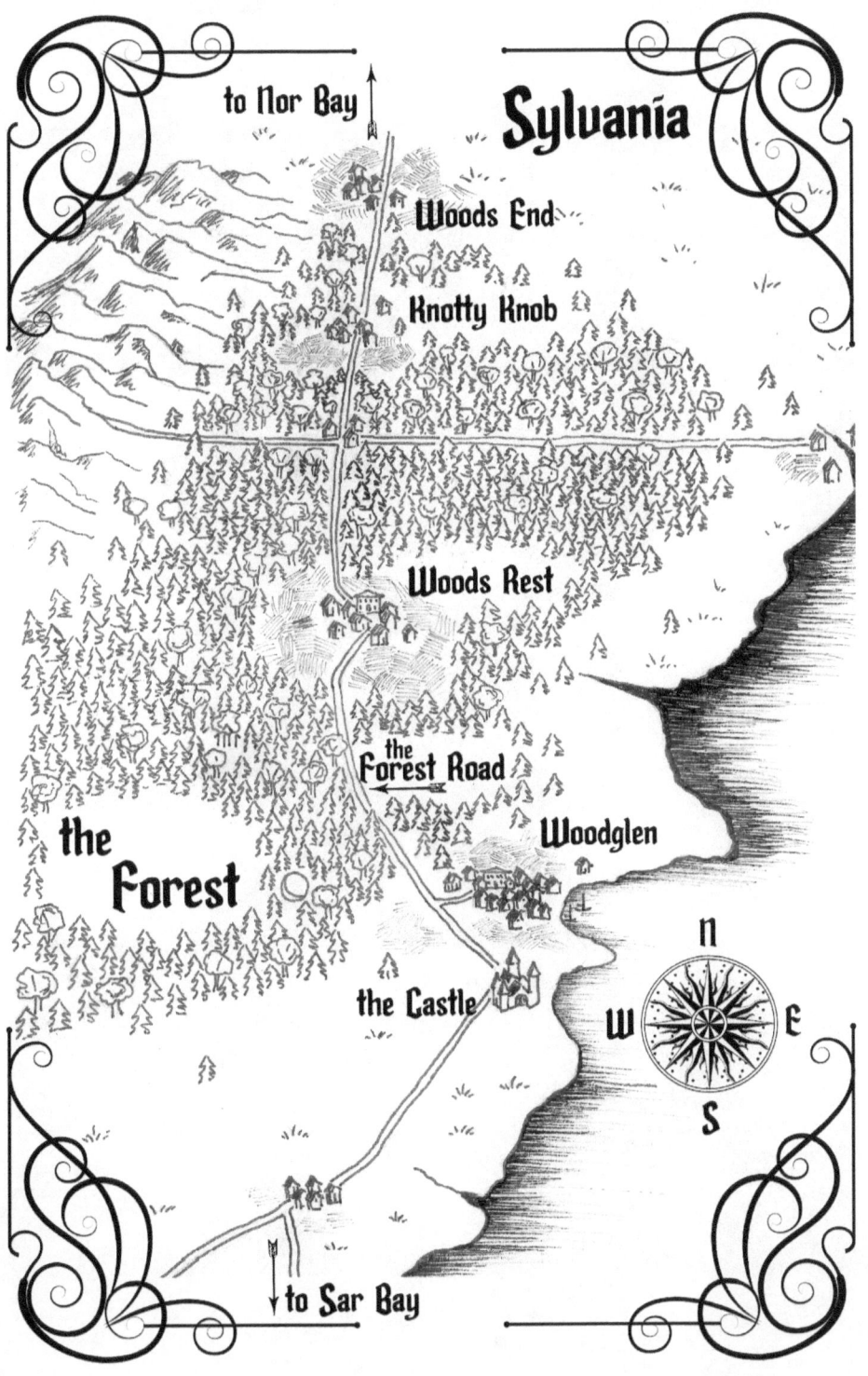

THE FOREST BRIDE

PART 1
THE PRINCESS

Chapter 1

ℒ

ROSE JOLTED UPRIGHT. SHE BLINKED as her eyes adjusted to the daylight reflecting off the sandy beach. How had she fallen asleep with the day so bright, and where was everyone? Her la-dies-in-waiting usually jabbered like crows, suffocating her with their pointless gossip.

Her vision began to clear, and she glanced down. The ladies lay wilted on the cushions and rugs around her chaise, the sound of their breathing eclipsed by the waves breaking on the shore. They were asleep, all of them, as if the court magician had tricked them into it, or a spell had been cast—like in the old book of fairy stories her mother used to read her. Not that fairy spells existed anymore. The ladies must have sneaked whiskey into their midmorning tea. As usual, they hadn't included her in their mischief.

Overhead, the canopy shuddered in the wind blowing in from the ocean. A feeling lingered that Rose couldn't place. Another salty gust hit the canopy, and the curtains flapped and blew a dust-ing of sand across her bare feet. With a lulling shush, waves rolled onto the beach in thin curls. Well, if the ladies were going to sleep, Rose would enjoy their silence. Quietly, she stood and slipped out from the tent.

Up the beach, toward the gate to the castle, her guards had disappeared.

No guards! Her morning was getting better and better. They must've stepped behind the dune for a break from the wind. Her father would have their heads if he knew they weren't watching her. Not that she was going to tell him.

Out of habit, Rose scanned her surroundings for escape routes. The beach was walled in by a tall cliff. She'd tried to scale it once, but it had been painstaking work. There was no chance she'd make the top before the guards returned. She couldn't swim, and waves crashed against the base of the cliffs, blocking her from going around them. The only way off the beach was through the castle. There was no escape.

But she was on the beach unguarded. She had a chance to do something, anything, without anyone else knowing. She might as well enjoy her moment alone.

Something whined, startling Rose. She glanced about and there, in the deep shadow cast by the tent, a dog watched her. The dog wagged his tail and began to pant.

She crept toward the dog and knelt, reaching out her hand. He was a medium-sized mutt with matted brown fur, one ear perked up and the other hanging down, nothing like the king's hunting dogs. He stopped panting to sniff her fingers and then laid his head on his paws.

"Where did you come from?" Rose asked. "Did you fall off a fishing boat? That would be a long swim. You probably *can* swim, though, can't you?" She tentatively scratched behind his ears, and his tail thumped. "You're a tough boy. Maybe you swam around the cliffs from the village."

He nuzzled his face into her hand.

"The king won't like you being here," Rose said. "He'll get rid of you." She glanced around one more time to make sure the guards were still absent. "Just like he's getting rid of me. Although you wouldn't have to bond with some awful prince." The thought of her impending life-bond gave her a sick twisting in her gut. Her hand stilled, and the dog nudged it back into motion.

Rose patted the dog and watched the waves roll onto the beach. The ladies slept on. If only it could always be like this, with no fussing, no attendants ordering her about, and no guards watching. And while she was at it, no Adela as a warden, no king for a father, and no wretched life-bond hanging over her. One of her few clear memories of her mother was when she'd explained the life-bond—how it should happen between two people who loved each other with pure hearts, who cared for each other's happiness, and who wanted to be together until they passed on from the world. Her mother hadn't had such a bond, but she'd sacrificed a bond based on love to bring peace between Sylvania and Sarland by bonding with Rose's father.

Now it was Rose's turn. Only her life-bond wasn't bringing peace to anyone. As far as she could tell, the only things her own sacrifice would bring were riches to the king and a new prison for her. She would travel to the kingdom that paid the highest price for her, but she'd never *really* travel, not the way she dreamed of—talking to merchants in village marketplaces across Sylvania, meeting the artisans who blew glass and wove cloth, seeing the treasures from the vast continent of Norland arrive at the trading post in Nor Bay. Maybe even crossing the treacherous sea to visit Norland someday, or Sarland to the south, where her mother had been born.

She should make the most of this moment of freedom while she had it. Go to the water and dip her feet in. She pictured herself stepping across the sand and into the waves. No one would see. The guards hadn't returned, and the sleeping ladies hadn't budged. But if her skirts got wet, Adela would know what she'd done and punish her.

Somehow, she didn't care.

She stood, forcing the doubts away, and the dog scrambled to his feet. She lifted her skirts clear of the sand and marched to the waterline, waiting for the next wave. It rushed in, bigger than the last one, and crashed, sending water up the sand toward her toes. The water washed over them, cold and exhilarating, and she smiled, stepping into it with a splash. Beside her, the dog darted near, then away as the next wave came. Rose lifted her skirts higher and walked out, tasting the salt in the wind, until she'd reached the line where the waves crashed against her calves. The wind blew fiercer, and she laughed and clutched her skirts close to keep them dry.

What had come over her? She never broke the rules. There was no point. She'd tried every escape she could think of, from climbing up the cliffs to hiding in an empty ale cask leaving the castle, planning to hide among the peasants and disappear into the throng of village life—not Woodglen, of course—but maybe distant Nor Bay or Sar Bay, as far away as she could get. She'd had no idea how she'd support herself, but the pull of freedom had made her try to escape. But she'd always been caught.

Now she did as she was told to avoid Adela's rod rapping her knuckles and only imagined escaping them all—cruel Adela, her greedy father, and her noisy ladies-in-waiting.

Today felt different. Some force urged Rose to do as she wished.

Behind her, the dog growled, and her heart lurched. Still growling low, the dog stared at the water. He leapt into the waves and stood before her, barking at the sea. He backed up a step and bumped her knees, and she was forced to step backward or risk falling.

"It's all right," Rose said. "I'll go back."

Under the shady tent, the ladies slept on. Rose returned to her chaise. She leaned to brush off the sand crusted to her feet and stopped dead.

A pair of cream-colored gloves lay folded on the sand next to her chaise, where—just minutes ago—she'd been sleeping. A tingle of fear and excitement shot through her. She glanced around, but the beach was still deserted.

Rose reached for the gloves. They were soft—softer than velvet, yet plainer. And they felt warm, although they'd rested in the shade of the canopy. Warm, as if someone had recently worn them. She unfolded one glove and held her hand against it. Her fingers were tiny compared to those of the glove. It was a man's glove.

Where was he? Rose scanned the dunes and the cliffs on either side. The flapping curtains of her canopy hid no one. Her ladies had trod all around when they'd arrived, and the swells of dry sand around the canopy didn't hold any new footprints. On the wet sand nearer the water, only her own steps, and those of the dog, showed. The man was gone without a trace, except for his gloves.

And who was he? Not a villager, with gloves like that. A pirate? Or a new prince, one who didn't follow the castle rules? Had he watched over her as she slept? Fear crept up her spine—fear that a man had been present while all the ladies slept. But he hadn't hurt them. Still, Adela would be horrified. Adela would want her to tell the guards about the gloves immediately.

But Rose didn't want the visitor captured and locked in her father's dungeon, not without knowing more about him. He could have harmed her and he hadn't. What if this man was her chance at a new life? She'd been stuck for so long. She followed Adela's orders. Stayed in the castle. She dreamed of being free to explore the world, to meet new people and try the things forbidden to her. But she no longer tried to escape. She had so little hope of success.

But what if the mysterious visitor could help her succeed?

Avianna stirred and rubbed her eyelids. Rose couldn't let her see the gloves and tell the guards. She folded them quickly and stashed them down the front of her dress, smoothing it over so they didn't show. Several of the ladies twitched, like a den of slow-moving snakes in winter. Avianna opened her eyes. Rose braced herself for whatever biting words she would say. But the other woman's eyes widened and she let out a shriek.

"What?" Rose asked. "What is it?"

Avianna sat up, gulping in panicked breaths. Her mass of curls was mussed from sleeping, but she still managed to look ready for court. She pointed out of the tent, at the dog.

Rose relaxed. "Hush, Avianna. It's just a dog."

"Where in the skies did it come from?"

"Maybe he fell off a fishing boat and swam to shore."

"It would be a long swim," Avianna said, turning to shake Elspeth awake.

Odd that the shriek hadn't woken Elspeth, or any of the others. Rose knelt beside the dog.

"Oh, don't touch it!" Avianna said. "It's so dirty."

But Rose patted the dog's head. His tail thumped.

And then the shouting began.

Chapter 2

∅

HER FATHER'S VOICE RANG UP the stone steps to her tower. "How did this happen?"

Ever since guards had swarmed onto the beach, jerking Rose to her feet and dragging her back to the castle, he'd been bellowing on and on. Now she sat on the divan in her sitting room, her hands folded primly in her lap while the gloves she'd tucked into her dress pressed against her chest with each breath. Where could she hide them? Nowhere in her sitting room or the adjacent bedchamber was safe from Adela.

If only the door to her rooms had been left open. The king repeated his demanding questions, and a voice mumbled in reply. No doubt this guard was echoing the others, sharing the same information she'd overheard earlier. The heavy gates had been locked, the thick, towering hedges intact—there was no sign that anyone, other than the dog, had entered the castle grounds. The only access to the beach was through the castle gardens. Nothing was wrong at all.

Nothing except that all the guards had fallen asleep in the middle of the day. And no one remembered a thing about it. One moment they'd been standing on duty, and the next moment they'd awoken, lying on the ground.

Just like she'd awoken on the beach.

"What if they came by boat?" her father shouted. "They could have taken her! And you lot dozing on the beach."

A kidnapping by boat. If only she could be so lucky.

Her father had unwittingly hit on Rose's most replayed daydream—of a fishing boat with a young man aboard, sailing near the beach. She never knew how to picture his face—she only knew that he was handsome and when she saw him, something in her quaked and drew her to him. No one would be watching when she stepped into the surf, tugged free the laces to shed her heavy gown, and swam toward the boat. Only then would the guards notice, but she'd reach the boat with a delicious thrill as the man pulled her aboard. He'd swing the boat around, sails flying, and take her away from life in Sylvania and out into the waves, maybe headed to a sunny island in the eastern sea.

She touched her dress where she'd hidden the gloves, and a shiver tingled down her spine. Would she find the owner? At least she hadn't let the guards see the gloves. She still couldn't believe she'd taken them. If anyone found out she'd kept them secret, she'd be in trouble.

Another shout from her father wrenched her attention back to her rooms. Escape was impossible. Even if a boat came near while she walked on the beach, she couldn't swim. And every moment, someone was watching her, even when they'd locked her in her suite at night. Even now, Adela knitted in a chair near the wall, her graying hair pulled into its usual tight bun behind her austere face.

Escape was impossible—unless she could find someone to help her.

"Are you feeling all right, m'lady?" Adela was watching her, her knitting needles frozen over a pile of yarn.

No matter what Adela said, her voice made Rose squirm. Usually it cowed her into submission. But today, the voice made a sly thought creep through Rose's mind. She could trick Adela. Maybe she could avoid tonight's supper.

"I'm feeling a little weak," Rose said, keeping her voice faint. "I'd like to keep resting."

Adela nodded and resumed her knitting. Rose sank back on the divan, sniffing the buttery aroma of the biscuits Adela had ordered from the kitchen. They filled a basket on the low table before Rose. The truth was, she felt just fine. In fact, she felt more than fine, as if she were more alive than usual.

Footsteps pounded on the tower steps.

Adela stood, eyeing Rose one more time as she stepped to the door. She walked out and closed the door behind her. Adela's voice was a mumble through the thick wood, saying something about Rose.

"Of course she's attending the supper!"

Rose jolted in surprise. Her father never came up to her tower rooms.

His voice lowered. "Three new princes have arrived, and one of them, we're told he has splendid gifts. He might be the one."

Her stomach sank. Each new prince filled her with the dread that this time, she'd be sold. It hadn't happened yet. But three at once? And one that had already impressed her father?

His voice dropped further, and Rose strained to hear him. She pushed herself off the divan and stepped lightly across the room to press her ear to the door.

"She's not getting any younger," her father said. "We need to finish this now. I know you're ready to be done with it." There was a pause. "See that she's ready."

Rose's stomach twisted in fear. Her father was going to do it this time, she just knew it.

Adela began discussing the details of the supper with her father.

Rose stepped away, anticipating the afternoon ahead of her. Her hair would be combed, washed, combed again. They'd rub stinking oils into it. She'd sit without moving for an hour while it dried. Her skin would be scrubbed and painted, her hairs plucked, her nails filed and painted with gloss. No doubt she'd be chastised again for biting them.

Suddenly she realized that she was alone. The gloves! She'd already scanned the sitting room, so she hurried up the steps to her bedchamber. Other than the bed that dominated the room, three trunks were lined up against the wall near the wash basin. Maybe she could hide the gloves in the trunk with her oldest dresses, the ones—

"Rose!"

Rose jumped. She checked that the front of her dress was still smooth before turning back to the sitting room.

Adela stood in the doorway with Avianna and Elspeth. Adela's lips pursed. "You should be resting, my dear, if you're still feeling weak."

Avianna smirked, before transforming her expression into a glowing smile as Adela glanced her way. "Yes, Rose," she said in a sweet voice. "Sit and rest, and Elspeth and I will keep you company until it's time to dress you."

Adela nodded and left, pulling the door shut. Rose didn't need to hear the click to know they'd been locked in.

Avianna's smile twisted back into a smirk. She and Elspeth had matching blue eyes, typical of southern Sylvania. But while Elspeth had the straw-blonde hair and pale skin to go with them, Avianna had the darker skin and hair of the north.

"Is the princess feeling weak?" Avianna asked, adding a whimper to the final word.

"Leave her alone, Avi," Elspeth said, moving to the divan. She reached for a biscuit from the basket and leaned back, breaking a piece off. "Skies, I wish we had these biscuits in the parlor."

"The cook loves the princess," Avianna said, sitting beside Elspeth.

"They're not for me," Rose said, stepping forward, although it was true Kate was kind to her. "It's only when Adela is here that we get them, and half the time she won't let me have one. I think she forgot they were here." Kate's biscuits were delicious.

"Well go on," Avianna said, nodding at the basket.

Rose reached for a biscuit, and Avianna snatched the basket away.

"You can only have a biscuit if you promise not to repeat what we say."

"Fine," Rose said. "You know I don't care what you do."

Avianna returned the basket, glaring at Rose as if to threaten her.

Rose took a biscuit.

Avianna turned to Elspeth. "The prince of Merlandia is here tonight."

"Merlandia? Where's that?"

"How should I know? But El, he is so fine."

Fine? Somehow Rose doubted that. He might look nice, but underneath, they were all the same. She took a bite of the biscuit, and the buttery sweet flavor almost made her feel better about being stuck with Avianna and Elspeth.

"How do you know?" Elspeth asked. "Where did you see him?"

"There was no one to escort me to the village . . . after the fuss on the beach, but Adela told me to go on alone anyway."

"I can't believe it." Elspeth leaned in, her biscuit forgotten.

"You know she needs her fix. And on the walk back, a carriage passed. This man leaned out and offered me a ride. Of course, I didn't know who it was, and I started to refuse, but I wanted to go so badly. He was so striking, I didn't care if he ravished me."

"Don't say that!" Elspeth said.

"Well, he didn't. But he wasn't entirely well behaved." She pursed her lips in a smug smile.

Rose's heart sank. The prince of Merlandia sounded dreadful. What if he were the one with all the gifts and her father chose him?

Avianna turned as if she'd heard Rose's thought. "You'd be

lucky to land him, Rose. A man like that would keep you up all night."

"Don't be crude, Avi," Elspeth said. "You know she's never tumbled anyone."

"Well she's got to start sometime. There's no sense being scared of it."

Rose's face burned. "At least I'm not scared of a dog."

Avianna huffed. "I can't believe you touched that dog."

"What happened to him?" Rose asked. "Did you see?"

"You mean after Adela ordered him killed?"

Rose cried out.

Elspeth smacked Avianna's arm. "Stop it, Avi." She turned to Rose. "She told the guards to get rid of it, and that old one took it. The one you like."

Aidan, it must have been. He wouldn't have killed the dog. Maybe he'd taken the dog to his home in the village. Maybe the dog was sniffing the corners of his cottage, or teasing his cats, or was playing with his grandchildren now, or with his youngest daughter—the shy one who made him think of Rose. Rose wished she could be there, too.

The lock clicked, and the girls turned to the door.

Adela's head poked in. "Girls, come help me."

Avianna and Elspeth stood and scurried from the room. No one needed to explain that Rose wasn't included. The door shut again.

Rose stood and dashed to her bedchamber. This time she went straight to the window and pulled up the latch, pushing open the glass. After being shooed away by Adela season after season, the birds had given up hope of nesting on the wide stone window ledge. At the far end of the ledge, as the tower wall curved away from the frame of the window, there was a small gap between the stones. Leaning out, Rose tucked the folded gloves into the gap, far enough in that they almost didn't show.

She leaned back in and watched the guards training on the grassy plain outside the castle walls, as the breeze ruffled her dark hair. Beyond the plain stretched tilled fields where the villagers worked, and farther still loomed the edge of the forest. She inhaled, but instead of the salty, humid ocean air, she breathed in the dry, sweet scent of the fields and an earthy hint of forest. If only she could be outside, walking on the grass like the guards, or working at something meaningful as the villagers did. Even being in the forest would be better than being trapped in her rooms.

Adela called from the sitting room. Rose sighed and pulled the window shut.

Chapter 3

℘

FOUR HOURS LATER, ROSE WAS combed and scrubbed, oiled and perfumed, and squeezed into the tightest of corsets. In the chamber where they'd prepared her, the clouds of cloying scent smothered her. She tugged at the top of her dress, trying to hide more of her breasts, but Adela removed her hands and stood back, as if admiring her work.

"I suppose you want to walk in the garden?" Adela asked.

Even though Rose had reached Adela's medium height many winters ago, she could never get over the feeling that Adela towered over her. "Yes, please."

Adela led Rose out and along a hall to a parlor where the ladies-in-waiting sat, fanning themselves or doing needlework. The ladies stilled at their entrance, looking up to await orders.

"Shall we take some air?" Adela asked. A scramble of motion followed.

As Rose exited the parlor onto the terrace, the noise of the ladies dispersed as they fanned out into the garden, pairing off with their friends to gossip. The day was still clear, cooling now that the sun was low. The distant crash of the sea reached her ears, and she tasted the faint tinge of salt in the air. Rose stood still, waiting on Adela to move, careful to keep her neck straight. Her dark hair rose so high that it might topple if tilted.

"Let's get you out of this sun," Adela said, and headed down the main garden path. Rose followed. It was no use reminding Adela that her skin never burned in the sun, in spite of its Sarlian pallor. Rose followed her as she turned down a path that led under a row of plum trees just starting to blossom.

Birdsong filtered down through the branches—a small joy, as if the bird were a friend. The boughs swayed, and a faint flowery scent drifted across the garden. A small boy stumbled into the path ahead, chasing a butterfly as it tried to land on a daisy. Rose had a sudden memory of her mother picking a bouquet for her, daisies and baptisia and irises, with herbs hidden among the flowers. "Rosemary to remember," her mother had whispered into her ear.

A nanny chased after the boy. Rose shook her head, returning her thoughts to the present. What was the boy's name? He was one of her half brothers. The king had bonded again, of course, after Rose's mother died, but her stepmother and siblings lived in a different part of the castle. Other than at supper, she rarely saw them.

Adela was almost to the end of the plum trees when her footsteps faltered. Rose stared as Adela staggered sideways. Rose hurried to her and helped her sink onto the nearest bench.

"Adela?"

Adela's head sagged as her body slumped sideways. "I'm fine," she muttered, "just need a nap." The last word stretched into a yawn. Her head fell forward.

"Adela?" Rose whispered. Was she all right? Her behavior reminded Rose of what had happened at the beach—a sudden slumber. Maybe whatever had happened that morning was starting again. Rose should alert the guards. But around the gardens, no one else had fallen asleep.

And without Adela, Rose could walk alone.

The ladies who hadn't disappeared into the hedges sat on benches or watched the fish in the pond. Only one guard was in sight, far across the gardens and examining his fingernails. No one had noticed Adela.

Rose slipped into the nearest path between tall hedges. She was enveloped by shade that was cool with the deep fragrance of earth. The hedge muted the laughs of the women and the splash of the fountain. Rose let out a sigh. It was blissful, being alone.

Without looking back, she set off between the hedge walls. At the first turn, she took the path away from Adela. She made another turn, and another until she was across the main garden. She headed for the small gate. When she entered the herb garden, she froze. A man knelt in the path, facing the bushes along the walk. His dark hair stood in unruly peaks. He hadn't seen her yet.

Men were never in the gardens, save the guards. When the ladies went out to walk, the gardeners were hustled out.

But this man didn't look like a castle gardener. His clothes were plain but not the rough cloth of the castle workers. They looked finely made, and clean. And his hands were bare—was he the owner of the gloves?

Adela would want Rose to report the man to the guards. But she stood, rooted in her spot, some new force overpowering her lifetime of being trained to fear anything out of the ordinary. She held her breath, waiting to see what would happen.

The man knelt by a rosemary bush and was brushing it with his finger. "Come on," he said to the bush. "Onto the branch."

Rose stared.

He drew back his hand and stood, dusting off his knees. When he looked up, surprise flashed across his face.

Rose wanted to assure him she wouldn't call the guards, but she couldn't seem to speak. His face was so handsome. Her gaze went to his shock of dark hair, and he immediately ran a hand over it, as if trying to smooth down the spikes. His skin was the same birch wood color as that of the local villagers, but for a moment, it seemed to glow. Like moonlight, she thought. But she blinked and the glow was gone. His features were fine, not rough like those of the villagers. He stood still, but his presence filled the path. He nodded in acknowledgment, and Rose automatically dropped into a curtsy.

"I hope I haven't startled you," he said. His voice was low and quiet, and it curled around Rose's spine and tugged her toward him.

She stepped forward and shook her head. They stood for a moment in silence. "Were you picking the rosemary?" Rose asked. Surely he hadn't been talking to it.

"No." He pointed at the plant, and Rose stepped closer. The pungent scent of the herb drifted toward her. "There was a lady-bug. She landed on my shoulder, and I didn't want her to get hurt." Where he pointed, a small red dot clung to the rosemary, climbing over the sprigs.

Rose smiled. "Adela always kills the spiders in my room. She gets angry when I try to carry them to the window." She looked at him.

He was studying her, and she had the sensation that she'd surprised him. He shook his head slightly and smiled back. When he smiled, her insides warmed. His eyes were tinted emerald green, like hers. She'd never met anyone else with the same defect.

"Are you a gardener?" she asked. "I'm Rose." She couldn't quite bring herself to ask, Did you forget your gloves on the beach earlier, after watching me sleep?

"I'm Dustan," he replied, extending his hand, "and I am a gardener, but I don't work for your father."

She stared at his hand. Handshakes were for men. But he waited, watching her, so she extended her arm. His hand was warm, and she didn't want to let go of it, but she didn't want to seem improper.

A bird sang overhead.

"Do you grow vegetables?" she asked. She quickly added, "For your family. Your wife?"

"I have no wife," he said. "I grow vegetables, and herbs, and flowers, and more. Sometimes I grow wishes."

"What does that mean?"

"Just what I said. Wishes. They take a long time to ripen, but they're so useful."

Now he was teasing her. He must think her a child. But she didn't want him to leave so she played along.

"What do you use them for, these wishes?" she asked.

"I won't tell you about the ones I've used," he said. "But I can tell you what I'd wish for next time." His gaze stayed on her face.

For some reason, she began to blush. The heat rose up her neck, and she remembered her low-cut dress and blushed harder.

"What is it you'd wish for?" he asked her.

How should she answer? Love, or happiness? Neither seemed possible.

"A moment alone," she said. "I am never alone. Even now, there's probably someone lurking in the bushes—I can't understand how they've left me to talk with you. And the people I'm with, they're not friends. They're like prison wardens."

He didn't laugh as she expected. His brow furrowed. "These ladies who surround you, they are always with you?" She nodded. "Even at night?"

"Sometimes I can't sleep, but I dare not make a noise. The slightest thud will wake Adela, and she'll start fussing. Her pallet is in my sitting room."

Dustan put a finger on his lips. "You need a sleeping potion," he said. "To make her sleep through the night."

Rose stared. "A potion?" Potions were bogus, for gullible people.

"Not like the ones they sell in the village," he said. He lowered his voice. "A real potion."

Their eyes locked, and she trembled.

"Where would it come from?"

"I know places to get one." After another moment of silence, he held out a hand again. Was this another handshake, as if they'd made a pact? When she placed her fingers on his, he simply squeezed them. This time, he continued to hold them. "I can tell you why they let you talk to me," he said, "but I fear it will make you dislike me."

"I can't imagine disliking you."

"You see, I'm a prince. Here for tonight's supper."

A prince! He didn't look like a prince, or behave like one.

"I arrived early," he continued, "so they sent me out to walk in the garden. Only it was supposed to be that garden over there"— he gestured toward the wall—"and not the garden filled with the delicate ladies." He nodded to indicate her, but he smiled like it was a joke. "I should get back before they find me and toss me out as a scoundrel."

"But I'll see you tonight?" she asked.

"Aye, you'll see me tonight," he replied, and he grinned.

Rose blushed again. He didn't seem to notice; he merely bent to kiss her fingers. He dropped her hand and strode away. Rose watched him go, his shirt hanging loose over tight britches. He passed under an ivy-covered arch and disappeared behind a hedge.

Rose pressed her kissed fingers against her face. Dustan. A prince.

Usually each new prince filled her with horror. The life-bond was a sacred vow, and her father expected her to make it with someone she didn't even know. And the men he'd paraded her in front of . . . obviously they didn't care about the vow—if they'd make it with an unwilling mate. What she didn't understand was why they wanted her. The kingdoms had been at peace since her mother's life-bond ended the incursions by Sarland. Sylvania didn't need a treaty, nor did any of the smaller kingdoms. Why did these princes travel across the sea for a chance to pay for a bride?

Thankfully, none had been rich enough. At least that's what Rose assumed. Why else wouldn't her father have chosen one by now? Everyone said he was after a good price.

Would her father consider Dustan? Her hopes sank, remembering his simple clothing. Usually the princes wore richly embroidered clothing, sometimes jewels, which seemed to impress her father. He wouldn't look twice at one in such plain clothes.

Would she want to bond with Dustan if her father chose him? He seemed kind. He was handsome. And his hands were warm. She glowed with delight when she remembered him asking what she wished. No one ever asked what she wanted. How could she trick her father into choosing him?

Chapter 4

⟡

As Rose approached the dining hall, the din of voices and the clattering of dishes reached her ears. Her father always insisted she arrive fifteen minutes after dinner had begun—to make an entrance. He'd then bawl about the vanity of women, always primping and arriving late, while she stood mortified before the crowd.

When the first prince had come, she'd been excited for the inaugural supper. She was to meet someone new, and a man! A man who was interested in her, from the gossip. Instead of sitting at the women's tables, she'd been ushered to the main dais, where the servants poured wine into tall goblets made of clear glass and served heaping platters of food. The prince from Perland had sat next to her father.

Her heart had fluttered when she saw him dressed in his regal attire, with his thin mustache, and his sparkling eyes that stared as she'd entered. He'd stood to kiss her hand and push in her chair. Her mind had raced ahead to life in Perland, imagining love and freedom.

But then supper had begun and the prince had doted on her father. They drank goblet after goblet of wine, their talk growing lewd as the night progressed. That was when the prince had begun to glance at Rose again, and her stomach had turned.

The prince of Perland hadn't impressed her father, though, and there had been over a dozen princes since, all wealthy by the look of them. What was her father waiting for? Now she saw past the rich clothing and handsome faces, the phony civility. Her heart no longer fluttered. By the end of each supper, every prince had acted just as the others had.

But Dustan hadn't seemed like the others.

She reached the dining hall and peered through the doorway. Twilight had come, and torches lit the otherwise gloomy space. On the dais, at the center of the head table sat her father. Dustan sat a few seats closer to her, his white linen shirt bright in the guttering light. He was looking to her father, who nodded heavily, his mouth gabbling. The smell of roasted meat wafted down to her.

Two men flanked her father. One looked very young. He had ridiculous puffed sleeves that stood out so far one knocked into the servant pouring his wine. He glared at the servant and fixed the dented sleeve. The other prince was big, with greasy, dark hair that hung in limp curls over his shoulders and a dark, tight-fitting tunic. When he lifted his goblet, heavy rings sparkled on his fingers. Her father's advisers filled the rest of the table, save for the empty seat on the end. Below the dais, long tables stretched the length of the hall. Nearest were the current queen and the king's mistresses and all their children and nannies.

As Rose entered, all the faces in the room turned to her, including Dustan's. She flushed. The greasy prince licked his lips. But looking into Dustan's eyes calmed her. He winked and gave her a hint of a smile. She lifted her face and stopped herself from smiling back in front of the entire court.

She moved forward. All she had to do was reach her seat and the crowd would stop staring. She neared the dais steps and lifted the edges of her skirts, and everyone stood as she ascended. She stepped carefully, as she always imagined herself tripping on her hem and sprawling onto the floor. How the courtiers would laugh.

When she reached her place, the herald announced the three princes. The young one, who looked about sixteen winters, was Prince Herbert of Carltonshire. The greasy-haired one was Prince Murkel of Merlandia. So that was the one Avianna had flirted with. She could have him. Dustan was the prince of Skye. Rose had never heard of Skye, but she liked the name. It made her think of soaring, free of the castle.

At last she sat, and the roar of talk resumed.

Usually Rose ate as much as they'd allow. The ample food at the head table was the one benefit of being required to sit there. But tonight, she barely noticed the platters the servers set down. Her salad wilted on the plate as she strained to hear her father's conversations. Prince Murkel dominated, waving his hands like a marionette, and she caught snatches about the unceasing wealth of his homeland and the hard-working people who happily toiled in his mines. Prince Herbert kept trying to speak, but each time was cut off by Murkel or her father.

Dustan simply sat watching, faintly smiling. What was his plan? If he didn't speak, didn't brag about his wealth, he'd never win over her father. And Rose wanted her father to choose him, she felt sure of it. As the supper progressed, Rose's anxiety grew. But in the middle of an exchange about the relative value of metals and gemstones, Dustan stole a glance her way, smiled, and lifted his eyebrows. His smile melted her worries. Rose covered her own grin with her hand.

The servers poured more and more wine. The air reeked with the smell of it. Murkel grew ever more talkative as her father listed toward him. Herbert became sullen, downing goblet after goblet, and one time banging his knife against his glass and yelling for the server to fill it. Dustan sipped at his wine. Rose wished he'd look at her again.

After two hours, the eating and drinking slowed, and her father waved his hand vaguely in the air, his drunken signal for the servers to remove the plates. Everyone rose and crowded out through the main hall, heading to the gardens. Rose pushed toward Dustan, but Adela appeared and pulled her away. Ushered along by her handler, she lost sight of him in the crowd.

The balm of the evening air greeted Rose after the heat of the dining hall. The sunset had faded and stars twinkled overhead. Adela hovered near Rose as guards lit torches and the court spread out over the lawn, the noise of the crowd dissipating in the large space. Rose caught sight of Avianna looking over her shoulder as she slipped behind a hedge. Usually, Rose envied her ladies-in-waiting as they disappeared into the bushes with their sweethearts or walked away in pairs, while she was expected to entertain the princes, and she wished she could disappear into the hedges, too. But tonight, she didn't want to hide. Maybe it would be Dustan who appeared at her side, and not the aggressive Murkel.

Herbert of Carltonshire staggered up beside her. A pale fuzz coated Herbert's sweaty upper lip as he blinked to focus on her. Rose's hopes sank.

"M'lady," he said, giving an overly deep bow and reaching for her hand. He stumbled as he righted himself, gripping her fingers. Rose pushed back to keep Herbert upright as she looked about the gardens. Herbert was bobbing his head, talking about the supper. He swayed slightly as he tugged Rose away from the crowds and onto the lawn.

Rose scanned the clusters of people, hoping to see Dustan's bright shirt in the evening light. Adela had dawdled behind and now had a middle-aged courtier whispering in her ear.

Herbert was rattling on about his three older brothers. As children, they'd locked Herbert in basement rooms and fed him slugs. Now they caroused and helped themselves to women. "But I'll show them," Herbert said. His body swayed sharply, and he stumbled, grasping onto Rose's arm.

Rose pulled him up and led him to a fountain, where he sank onto the stone edge. She pulled her arm away and sat, leaving a good space between them. She did another sweep of the gardens looking for Dustan.

"I can be one of them," Herbert said, pointing his finger and waving it. "Just need a whoa-o-men." His words slurred, incoherent.

Rose leaned away to avoid his pointing hand as it reached toward her breasts.

Herbert slumped on the fountain's edge, trying to continue. "Jus' one, then'll get mowr," he muttered. He turned to the water and retched.

Rose leapt up and backed away as Herbert's attendants hurried over.

Adela was so engrossed with her admirer that she hadn't looked up.

Rose was unguarded. Hope surged through her. She'd find Dustan. She darted for the hedges, her spine tingling with anticipated capture. She glanced back. Herbert was having another go in the fountain, and Adela's eyes were closed as the courtier kissed her neck. Rose slipped into the bushes.

She hurried down the deserted path, her heart pounding, but no one came after her. She moved parallel to the main garden and emerged at the far end. From here, she could see the entire space and should be able to spot Dustan. She settled onto a bench recessed in the hedge, hidden in darkness. Figures drifted along the paths, but no Dustan.

A short, muted shriek came from the bushes behind her, startling Rose. A woman giggled, followed by a man's sultry laugh.

"Oh, oh, do it again!" the woman said in a breathy voice.

It was Avianna. More shrieks followed, and a rhythmic moaning began. Rose blushed for Avianna. Maybe she should move away, but she didn't want to leave the sheltering darkness. Besides, Avianna was in the gardens, not the privacy of a room. It wasn't Rose's fault she could hear.

As the moans increased in speed, Rose surveyed the garden. Two ladies sniffed a hanging blossom, and Prince Herbert staggered to a bush to be sick again. Dustan still hadn't appeared. Maybe he was with her father, winning her hand.

The tumult behind Rose ended with another small shriek, followed by a crying moan. This time, the man joined in with a deep groan that went on and on. Rose suppressed a giggle. Perhaps it was genuine. What did she know about such things?

The moans fell silent.

A few moments later, a figure emerged from the hedge to Rose's left. As it swaggered toward her, she recognized Murkel, the prince of Merlandia.

It was too late to hide. She shrank back, on the chance he might pass her by, but he paused—he had seen her in the shadows. He straightened his tunic and continued toward her. He was unusually tall, with a hooked beak of a nose and protruding lips. His hair looked even shinier in the dim light of the garden. Sweat beaded on his brow, and his clothes were disheveled.

He bowed his head. "M'lady."

Rose stood to curtsy. "I'll let you pass, sir," she said.

"Pass? How can you think I'd pass, while you're here alone?" He stepped in front of her, pinning her against the bench and blocking her view of the garden.

She kept her chin high and hid her disappointment. "Very well." His gaze began to make her uncomfortable. His pupils were unnaturally dilated, rimmed with yellow irises.

After an awkward pause, he said, "I got lost among the hedges. They are quite impressive."

"Our castle gardeners have been caring for them for generations," Rose said. She couldn't believe they were talking about the bushes. "Did you enjoy the supper?"

"It was passable," he said, shrugging his shoulders. "But not like the splendor of the food in Merlandia."

"What do you eat in Merlandia?"

"Merlandia is . . . on the sea," he said, "so we eat all manner of fish and shellfish. Dolphins are particularly tasty."

Rose didn't know what a dolphin was, but she pitied it.

"And our chefs make marvelous creations out of seaweed," Murkel continued.

"Seaweed? How do they manage that?"

Murkel smiled. "No doubt you've seen it blowing about the beach, dry and sparse. Under the water, it grows thick and green. You're seeing the dead remains of seaweed."

"I've never been in the water," Rose said. "I've not learned to swim."

"That can be corrected."

"Do the women swim in Merlandia?"

"Everyone swims in Merlandia," he replied with a smile, and for some reason, chills crept down Rose's back.

A bell tolled from the castle. "That is Adela," Rose said, eager to escape, "calling us back." The prince didn't move, so she used her elbow to nudge him aside, and he slowly stepped back to let her pass. She tried not to brush against him as she did.

Rose didn't see Dustan anywhere. When the court and the guests had gathered near the castle, her father appeared and mumbled some parting words. Rose ignored the speech as she scanned the crowd. Had Dustan left? Had he decided he had no interest in her, or that he stood no chance against the prince of Merlandia? Murkel had followed her and now pressed against her in the crowd, although she kept moving away.

When the speech ended, Murkel grasped her fingers and whispered in her ear, "I'll be seeing you again, m'lady." He kissed her hand with clammy lips, leaving a wet spot.

She swallowed her disgust, waiting for him to turn away so she could pull her handkerchief from her pocket and wipe it off.

Dustan had never appeared.

Chapter 5

ℒ

EARLY THE NEXT MORNING, ROSE spotted Prince Herbert's party on the guards' training field below her tower. Attendants dismantled the elaborate tents they'd raised only the day before. Maybe Dustan was camped nearby, out of sight of her tower windows.

Rose tried the door. Locked. She'd known it would be, with Adela gone and no one left to mind her. Of course, she could pick the lock. She'd taught herself to do it as a child, but she'd only managed to sneak out a few times before they'd caught her. Since then, guards were always stationed in the tower.

She knocked on the door.

Someone moved on the other side. She knocked again. And waited. A key scraped in the lock. The door opened and a guard peered in.

"M'lady? Are you all right?"

"I'm to meet the ladies in the garden," Rose said. "Adela told me last night."

The guard scrunched up his face. "That can't be right."

"She said so." Rose scrambled to find something believable. "To catch the early sun. For my complexion. Please, if I'm late she'll punish me. She must have told you. Maybe you don't remember?"

The guard pressed his lips together. Rose guessed he was imagining the demotion he'd receive if he forgot one of Adela's commands.

"I'm not supposed to leave my post for anything."

"That's because you're guarding me," Rose said, struggling to keep the excitement from her voice. She dipped her head and looked up at him the way Avianna did with men. "You'll escort me, so there won't be anyone here to guard."

The guard thought for another minute before relaxing his grip on the door. "All right."

Rose rushed past him, but he grabbed her elbow and yanked her to a halt. "Pardon, m'lady, but you need to stay by my side."

She was out without Adela! Rose followed the guard down the curving tower stairs. When they reached the first landing, she strained to hear any sounds from below. Her guard nodded at the guard on the landing, and they continued down. At the second landing stood another guard. One doorway led to the back stairway and down to the kitchens, but they turned to the other doorway that followed a corridor into the parlors and the front of the castle.

Adela stepped out from the kitchen doorway. Her lips pressed tight and her nostrils flared, but only for a moment before her face morphed into her emotionless mask. "What's this?" she asked. Behind her, Elspeth stood rooted, holding the tea tray.

"I was to be in the gardens," Rose said, hoping Adela couldn't tell her voice was shaking. "You said so last night, that we'd be out early so I could try to get some color in my cheeks before the sun rose too high."

Adela watched her closely. But all she said was, "You must've dreamed it, my dear. I'm going to the village today, and Elspeth will keep you company. In your rooms."

Beside her, the guard swallowed. "Come, m'lady, let's go back."

Reluctantly, Rose turned and climbed the tower steps. Behind her tramped the guard, and Elspeth puffed in and out as she climbed. Adela was silent as a stone, as always.

Back in the room, Adela poured the tea. "Drink your tea, Rose," she said, handing her the cup. She turned to Elspeth and showed her the embroidery Rose would stitch that afternoon.

Rose drifted up the step to her bedchamber and moved to the window, sipping at the bitter tea. She stared at a wavy countryside through the thick glass windowpanes. When would she see Dustan again? The outdoors called to her. She glanced through the doorway. Adela continued to lecture Elspeth.

Rose quietly undid the window latch and pushed on the glass. The window swung open a hand's width and a fresh breeze stole in, rifling her hair. The sky had clouded over, bringing out the vibrant spring green of the forest treetops. The impulse to pour her tea out the window seized her, but she knew how important it was to drink it every morning. At least, Adela had stressed its importance time and again.

She pushed the glass farther, and the window opened wide. Rose leaned on the sill, inhaling all the freshness of spring. Even at this height, the melody of birds reached her. She peeked sideways to see the gloves she'd hidden.

A delicate vial now rested in the center of the folded gloves.

Rose trembled. Dustan had said she needed a sleeping potion. And that he knew places to get one. Had he gotten a potion and left it for her? Was that where he'd been last night, while the other guests walked in the gardens? She'd hoped he'd been with her father, impressing him with tales of wealth more extreme than Prince Murkel's.

But this was better.

Rose looked to the sitting room doorway. The two women were out of sight. She leaned out to retrieve the vial. It was as thin as her finger, crafted of glass in the shape of an elongated teardrop. Inside swirled a blue liquid that sparkled like stars in the night sky.

The top narrowed to a point, but the vial had no cap. Rose tipped the vial upside down. The liquid stopped just shy of dripping out. She tapped the bottom, and a single drop formed. Carefully, she righted the vial, and the drop of potion slid back inside.

Rose pocketed the vial and pulled the window closed. She breathed deeply to compose herself and stepped down into the sitting room.

"Rose, we've laid out a new project for you," Adela said. She motioned Rose toward the embroidery frame by the window. "See the fish? And the castle over the sea? I thought it fitting after last night's events."

Rose knew what Adela implied but didn't care. Dustan had managed to sneak her a sleeping potion. He must have a plan to win her father's approval.

Elspeth stared at the panel of fabric, pouting as she sullenly eyed the sketch of a castle and fish. She twirled a lock of her hair in her fingers. Maybe she wished that Prince Murkel were courting her—or tumbling her in the castle hedges.

"I'll be back by dinner," Adela said.

A thought seized Rose. Maybe it was the faint blush creeping up Adela's neck, or maybe it was the way she avoided looking at Rose. Adela wasn't going to the village to shop. She was up to something, maybe sneaking out to meet her courtier, the one who'd flirted with her last night. Rose held back a smirk.

After Adela had gone, Rose seated herself at the embroidery frame and threaded her needle. Elspeth settled into a chair with her own sewing. Rose began to stitch at one of the fish. She made its eye a short dash instead of a circle, as if it were dead. She counted the minutes in her head, waiting until thirty had passed to be sure Adela had left the castle.

"Elspeth, would you fancy a cup of tea?"

"You just had tea," Elspeth said. She didn't look up from her work. "And it's just another hour till I ring for lunch."

"My throat is parched. And the morning tea is so bitter. Please?"

Elspeth huffed out a sigh and put aside her sewing. She stood to pull the rope and opened the door, leaning out until someone arrived a minute later. "The *princess* wants tea," Elspeth said into the stairwell. "Don't dawdle." She left the door ajar and returned to her sewing.

A few minutes later, Maybeth crept into the room with a tea tray, moving silently past Elspeth. Beneath her cap, Maybeth focused her big eyes on the table where she set down the wooden tray with its delicate cups and steaming pot of water. Rose stood and went to the low table, sliding the old tea tray out of the way.

"Thank you, m'lady," Maybeth whispered.

"I'm sorry to interrupt your morning."

" 'Tis no trouble."

"Is all well downstairs?" Rose asked. Elspeth stopped sewing and stared at Rose.

"Yes, m'lady, only Burne's had to join the guard. You know Kate tried to keep him out, having him work in the kitchens. But they made him start training. The maids have to carry the water in from the well now. And of course, we all miss Burne being here."

A stab of sadness struck Rose. Kate's son Burne had always been shy and anxious, not fit to be a guard. "Will you send Kate my greetings?" Rose asked. "And tell her the supper last night was delicious."

"That's enough," Elspeth said, rising from her seat.

Maybeth nodded quickly at Elspeth, looked back at Rose, and scurried for the door. She gave another quick nod and half of a smile before disappearing.

Elspeth stared at Rose before turning to the door. Rose swallowed her nervousness. As Elspeth closed the door, Rose pulled out the vial, turned it over one of the cups, and tapped. A single drop formed at the vial's tip. She tapped again and the drop fell into the teacup. Rose stashed the vial back into her pocket as Elspeth turned. She picked up the teapot, steadied her shaking hands, and poured the tea as if her heart weren't racing with excitement.

Elspeth sat on the divan. Rose handed her the teacup with the potion, took the other, and sat beside her. Elspeth blew daintily, and Rose watched her, waiting. Elspeth had a sweet face when she wasn't using her sharp tongue. Rose tore her gaze away and took a hasty sip from her own cup, hiding a reaction when the tea burned her tongue.

"It's perfect," she said.

But Elspeth looked to the tray. "I don't know what's with this girl," Elspeth said, lowering her cup. "Imagine bringing tea with no honey."

"It's plenty sweet," Rose lied, taking another hot sip. "And the perfect temperature. They must've sweetened it in the kitchen. Try it, I think you'll like it." Her heart threatened to burst from her corset.

Elspeth snorted, but she raised her cup and sipped. As she lowered the cup, her nose wrinkled at the taste, and her eyelids fluttered. Rose reached for the teacup as it slipped from Elspeth's hand. Elspeth slumped sideways on the divan and her arm flopped to the floor.

Rose stared. Elspeth's body rose and fell with her breaths. Air whispered in and out of her slightly open lips. She was fast asleep. Rose poked Elspeth. Nothing. She shook Elspeth's shoulder. Elspeth slept.

The potion had worked.

How long would Elspeth sleep? Would she wake before Adela returned?

Rose watched Elspeth another minute, and looked around the silent chamber. Peace descended on her. She leaned back on the divan and sipped her tea, loving that no one warned her against scalding her tongue, or commented that she was drinking too fast, or too slow, or sniped that she was wasting time and should get to her embroidery. She slumped farther back, sipping until her teacup was empty, and still Elspeth slept.

Rose placed the cup back on the tray and stretched. She went through the rooms and opened all the windows. With the bright sun shining, the breeze had warmed in the past hour. She hid the vial of sleeping potion, tucking it safely into the gloves. Once she'd secured it, she leaned far out of her window, breathing the fresh air, watching the peasants in their fields and the birds flittering over the treetops of the forest.

The birds didn't fear the forest. And Rose had seen squirrels and deer emerge from the trees. But the fairies had always been friends with the animals, the stories said. It was only the humans who needed to fear the fairies.

Adela had lectured her more than once about the dangers of the forest. And her ladies-in-waiting repeated fantastic tales they'd heard in the village, of fairy men who forced human women to be their lovers, of children who strayed too close to the edge of the forest and disappeared. Rose had tried to argue once that the fairies in her mother's storybook had not been cruel, but Adela had scoffed and called her mother foolish.

Everyone she'd ever asked about the fairies had shared Adela's fear. Not that anyone had ever seen the fair folk. Some people thought they had gone from the world, taking their cursed magic with them. But others thought they still lurked in the forest. And no one was willing to wander among the trees, or willing to stray even ten paces from the road that cut through the forest to Woods Rest.

The bones of Rose's corset dug into her ribs as it rubbed against the windowsill. She loosened the laces of her dress and reached inside to undo the hooks down the front of the corset. Her body reacted, expanding with relief each time she undid a hook. As the last hook came undone, the scratchy garment slid down to her hips. She shook it down through her skirts and stepped out of it, and left it lying on the floor.

Her thoughts turned to Dustan. Where was he? Would she see him again soon? He wouldn't have made the effort to grant her wish, to bring her the potion, if he didn't have any interest in her, would he? How had he done it? She'd have to ask him.

Thinking of Dustan being there, in her bedchamber as he hid the potion, shifted something inside her, as if birds were fluttering from her breast to her legs. She wanted to be still and imagine more. She glanced into the sitting room where Elspeth still slept, slumped over the arm of the divan. Rose drifted to her bed and parted the gauzy curtain, kicked off her slippers, and crawled onto the coverlet.

Away from the warm breeze at the window, her room was chilly, the stone not yet warmed from the winter. She pulled a quilt over her body and leaned back into the pillows. She imagined Dustan there, lying beside her. Of course, he would never presume to touch her. He was too polite. But what if she wanted him to? Asked him to?

What if they were bonded?

She closed her eyes and snuggled down into the quilt. She pulled her dress down her shoulders and trailed her fingers along her skin, pretending it was Dustan who touched her. She skimmed them over the top of the dress, and danced them down across the fabric. She began to feel something new inside, like an ache of longing. She kept thinking of Dustan being with her, until all at once, the ache seemed to release.

Rose lay still, savoring the feeling. It was like she'd momentarily escaped the castle and found somewhere safe. Her whole body had relaxed. She'd forgotten about Dustan for a moment, but now she imagined him lying beside her. He'd wrap his arms around her, nuzzling into her neck.

HOURS LATER, WHEN THE DOOR to her chambers opened, Rose was sitting by the closed window, embroidering her fifth fish. Hopefully Adela wouldn't notice how little embroidery she'd accomplished. The empty dishes from lunch were stacked by the door. Rose had eaten Elspeth's portion.

Adela entered holding a few parcels. Her face hardened as she spotted Elspeth, still slumped on the divan. Adela strode across the room. Rose winced as Adela slapped Elspeth across the face.

Elspeth's eyes popped open. Her fingers rose to her cheek as tears filled her eyes. She sat up, staring around the room.

"What are you . . . Sleeping?" Adela shouted. "I should . . . Go!"

Elspeth stumbled off the divan, tripping and catching herself. She swept up her sewing and ran from the room.

Rose returned to her fish, swallowing her guilt about getting Elspeth slapped. Adela grumbled and opened her packages, pushing aside the tray of cold tea. Rose thought back over her delightful day, the best day she'd ever had. Dustan had made it possible. Her father had to choose him.

Chapter 6

ROSE WALKED THROUGH THE NEXT day with heightened awareness, always thinking of Dustan, looking for him around every corner in the gardens. Trapped in her rooms, she imagined him coming to her in all sorts of impossible ways—disguised as a guard, wrapped in an oversized package, flying to her window on a giant bird.

A message came. Rose was to entertain someone in the gardens that afternoon.

When her ladies began dressing her, she obeyed, allowing them to squeeze her into the hateful corset and to powder and perfume the tops of her breasts. A cloud of powder drifted up her nostrils and she tried not to cough. Did Dustan like all this makeup? Maybe when they were bonded, she'd be allowed to leave her rooms without it.

After hours of preparation, Adela led Rose out onto the terrace. A retinue of ladies-in-waiting accompanied them. The sun hid behind an oak tree, spreading shadows over the hedges as their party entered the main garden. A table stood near the fish pond, and sitting at it was . . . Prince Murkel.

Rose's hopes sank.

She reached Murkel and extended her hand. He stood to kiss it with his damp lips. As they sat, Adela and the others turned to go. Avianna wasn't among them, but most of the ladies peeked back at Murkel. Rose turned to Murkel in time to see him wink at them.

He turned to her. His skin had an odd look, as if he had powdered it, and a dank cologne scent drifted off him. He squinted in the sunlight. Rose forced herself to listen to him—he was asking about her.

"I'm well, thank you," she said. "I trust your stay is comfortable?" The drawn-out moaning that she'd heard through the hedges two nights before popped into Rose's mind, and she had to stifle a smile. Murkel answered, something about the beach.

"Tell me more about Merlandia," Rose said, batting her eyelashes, and as Murkel launched into a description of his lands, she helped herself to a cucumber sandwich. Where was Dustan right now? With her father? Rose licked the creamy dill spread from her fingers as she finished the sandwich, then glanced around, but Adela was nowhere in sight to chastise her for her manners. She reached for another sandwich as Murkel talked on. And a third.

"Would you like to learn to swim?" Murkel asked.

Swim? He'd been talking about his extensive fisheries located along the lengthy coastline. Merlandia apparently had not only mountains filled with ores of all types but also fertile farmland and leagues of coastline. Swimming, he'd asked.

"Oh, yes," Rose said. "I would love to be allowed in the water. But I can't imagine learning. I'd sink right to the bottom."

Murkel smirked. "No, you wouldn't, not in the ocean. If you did nothing, you'd still float. Give a few kicks to keep your face up. It takes very little effort."

"You certainly make it sound possible," Rose said.

"I will teach you myself, when we arrive in Merlandia."

Rose's heart skipped. "Have you arranged something with my father?"

Murkel smiled, looking away down the garden. He crossed his legs, one ankle on the other knee, and leaned back, stretching his arms along the back of his seat and thrusting his crotch out. Sprawled out, he resembled the octopus they occasionally served at supper. "I plan to make an offer he'll find hard to resist."

Her father couldn't pick Prince Murkel, he just couldn't. What could she do to stop him?

A squirrel scurried across the path, a nut in its mouth. It paused, then scampered toward Murkel's foot. Murkel kicked at it, and it scurried away.

"Your father does love his shells," Murkel said, "and I have plenty of them."

Rose stared as the squirrel buried its nut under a hedge. Murkel had so much wealth. What could Dustan possibly offer her father that would sway him to choose Dustan instead?

The squirrel turned back to Murkel, and Rose could sense the squirrel's intention, as if she could see into the little creature's mind. Her mouth dropped open as the squirrel dug its claws into the grass and sprang forward. It landed on Murkel's leg and clamped its teeth onto his ankle.

Murkel shrieked and leapt from the seat. He shook his foot but the squirrel held on. More squirrels appeared, a dozen of them, and they swarmed up Murkel's legs, nipping everywhere that showed skin, clawing their way up his sleeves. His arms flailed and he cursed as he tried to shake them off.

Rose simply stared. What was happening? After a moment, she came to her senses. No one else was in sight. Rose stood and backed away, and when Murkel didn't appear to notice, she slipped into the hedges. She headed straight for the herb garden, retracing her steps from the last time. The sounds of Murkel's distress faded in the thick hedges. When Rose came out into the space, there was Dustan, standing in the sunlight.

She went toward him, smiling. He was just as beautiful as she remembered, and he held out his hands to her. They were warm as they curled around her fingers. She stopped herself from leaning in. She'd been about to kiss him. What had come over her?

"I've been longing to see you," Rose said.

"And I you. I think we'll be safe here." Dustan invited Rose to sit with a gesture toward a bench.

"You can't believe what happened," she said as she sat, arranging her skirts to make room for Dustan. "Squirrels attacked Prince Murkel. I've never seen squirrels act like that."

"Don't worry, they're not usually aggressive," Dustan said. "There must be something about Prince Murkel they dislike." He brushed something off his hands—dust—that sparkled as it scattered through the air.

Rose squinted, trying to see it, but it was gone. She turned to study him. His face made her flush with excitement, with his thin lips barely curved in a smile, the spark in his eyes, and that messy dark hair. His warmth radiated toward her arm as he sat beside her. "Were you supposed to visit me, after Prince Murkel?" Rose asked.

"Not exactly," he said. "But it wouldn't be fair if only Murkel had a chance to woo you."

"Woo?" Rose snorted. "Not likely. Besides, it's my father you need to woo, not me."

"I would rather have your favor than his."

"That's not what I mean. I won't be allowed to give it, unless you impress *him*."

Dustan shook his head. "You can give your heart where you like, and the rest will follow."

When he said it, it almost seemed possible. "What's it like in Skye?" she asked. "Is it nearby?"

"I made the journey quickly."

"Are you staying here, though? Do you have a caravan and a tent you sleep in? Prince Murkel said he's staying on the beach.

There's plenty of room in the castle, though, so I don't see why it's necessary."

"It's a way to show off," Dustan said. "The bigger your caravan, the richer you must be. I am staying here. I'm afraid I brought no attendants and only one tent. Does it disappoint you?"

"Only in that it lessens your chances with my father," Rose said.

"Don't worry about that," Dustan said. "I have a plan. My only concern is getting to know you."

His words captivated Rose. He didn't just inspect her and talk about himself. He wanted to know her.

"Are you camped on the beach then?"

"No. In the woods."

The woods! "Aren't you scared?"

"Scared of what?"

"Of the wild animals, and the creatures who dwell there and play tricks on humans."

"It's easy to be safe from the animals, if you know them. Take the bears. They're bigger than a man, with claws and teeth, but they only want to be left alone. They attack when men shoot them or steal their cubs to perform on leashes in your circuses. If you stay back and leave the bear alone, she will not harm you.

"As for other creatures," he continued, "I think that's an invention to scare children into staying away. Has anyone you know ever seen one?"

Rose shook her head. She remembered her father, towering over her in anger. "My mother took me once," she said. "It was like her storybook, the one she taught me to read from. We looked for wildflowers and birds, and there was a white tree where she stopped and ran her fingers over the bark.

"But when we came out on the forest road, the guards were waiting. They pulled my mother onto one horse and me onto another, and took us to my father. He called her foolish for taking me into the forest. I can picture his fingers, cramped into claws and swiping at me, and I remember him growling. My mother tried to take me again, but I was too scared and she gave up."

Dustan watched her but remained silent.

"I wish I could remember more. She died when I was six."

Dustan shook his head slightly, as if coming back from his own memories. "She sounds kind," he said.

"What are the women like in Skye?" Rose asked to end the silence. "Do they dress as we do here, with all this powder and perfume?"

"I'm afraid not," Dustan said. "They go about plain faced, but their faces are anything but plain. And they don't wear such heavy dresses, or jewels, or any of the confining gadgets that are worn in your society. They like to run and climb, so their legs must be unencumbered."

"Run and climb? Do they hunt?"

"Mmm, some of them, in a way. But it's nice just to go up in the trees."

"Up in the trees?" Maybe he was teasing her again. "The royal court, or only the peasants?"

"One is the same in Skye," he replied.

"You mean everyone works?"

"It's not much work when everyone does it."

His answers weren't helping. Could it be that Skye had no king or queen, that he was simply a peasant? If he brought her freedom, she didn't think she'd mind.

Her gaze came to rest on his hands, folded in his lap. She thought of her daydream yesterday, of his hands stroking her shoulders and moving over her, and how good it had felt to imagine. Simply remembering it made the feeling return. Her face heated and she looked up to find Dustan watching her, which made her blush more.

"The farmers," Rose said, struggling to think of words. All she wanted was to touch him. "They have cows?"

He watched her another moment. He lifted a hand to rub his

brow and blinked. "Yes, farmers. Cows. No, they raise chickens and goats."

She forced her thoughts to the conversation. "Do you have a celebration? For the harvest? We do, after the harvest. Of course." Now she was blushing because she sounded like a dolt.

But Dustan simply replied, "We have many celebrations. There's one coming up."

After that, he began to ask her things, things about growing up in the castle, but mostly about her—what she liked, her thoughts, her hopes for the future. Rose tried to focus on answering his questions, and not on thoughts of touching him. He studied her as she replied.

The sky was growing pink at the edges when Rose realized they'd been talking for hours. She snapped to attention.

"You should be getting back?" Dustan said.

"I can't understand how so much time has passed," she said, "without someone coming for me."

He stood and offered his hand.

"Will I see you again?" she asked as he pulled her to stand before him.

"I'm sure you will."

"When?"

"That's up to you." He squeezed her hand.

The late sunlight slanted through the hedges, highlighting his face, his kind eyes, and his perfect lips. Rose wanted more of him. Should she try? She stepped closer and tilted her face up, rising onto her toes to close the distance between them. Dustan dropped her hand and held her from behind. She closed her eyes.

His lips met hers, kissing her softly. She'd never felt anything like it. After a moment she remembered to kiss him back, pressing herself closer, and his arm tightened around her. His other hand rested gently on the back of her neck. She wished it would never end.

He moved to whisper in her ear, "Just wish for me and I'll come." His arms released her.

She opened her eyes.

He stepped back, caressing her cheek with his thumb before he turned and walked away.

Chapter 7

ALL THE NEXT DAY, ROSE hoped for a chance to be alone with her thoughts. She wanted to go over her long conversation with Dustan, to remember every detail. Especially the ending. She yearned to savor the memory of their kiss, to feel again the twist in her heart each time she reimagined the moment.

But after the commotion caused by her disappearance the previous afternoon, no one would let her out of sight. They doubled the guard at her door, and one of the ladies was stationed in her rooms at every hour, even when Adela was with her.

Rose poked at the embroidery, jabbing at another fish, as the long hours passed. She kept the vial of potion in her pocket, although she didn't see how she'd manage to use it, not with two people watching. With all the excitement yesterday, she'd completely forgotten to thank Dustan for it.

"And poor Prince Murkel," Adela said for the hundredth time, as they sat in Rose's sitting room after supper. "With those bites becoming infected."

The newest arrival at court, Corella, sat knitting by the door, her face meekly bowed.

"Your father ordered the gardeners to set traps for the rodents,"

Adela continued. "How embarrassed he was. And you didn't help matters, disappearing like that."

"I don't know why the guards didn't find me," Rose said, also for the hundredth time. "I was sitting in the garden the whole afternoon."

"Hiding, more like."

"I told you Adela, the creatures frightened me. They were swarming everywhere, and I fled. I wasn't thinking."

Adela huffed but didn't continue. Her knitting needles clicked. Rose glanced at the fading twilight from her seat on the divan. Would Adela never tire? Would she never send Corella to bed?

There was quick knock and the door opened. Kate stepped into the room before Adela had time to put down her knitting. In her worn hands she carried a tray with a jug and cups, and beneath the cook's cap that kept her wispy hair in place, a smile beamed from her soft face. Kate was the head cook so she seldom brought a tray herself.

She addressed Rose. "I thought you ladies might like a cup o' warm milk before bedtime," she said, walking to the low table and depositing the tray. "After all the excitement we've been having." She cast a glance back at Corella. "I'm afraid I only brought two cups, dear. I didn't realize the princess had two . . . *attendants* now."

Adela's jaw fell open, and she dropped her knitting by her side. A few stitches slid off each needle. "Well, I didn't—"

"It's no trouble, ma'am," Kate said cheerfully. "I was all done with the day's cooking, and it's always a pleasure to visit the princess." She turned to Rose. "Looking more like your mother every day, love," she said.

Rose beamed.

Adela rose quickly and moved to the tray, wedging her elbow in front of Kate to push her away. "I can serve it," she said, pouring the steaming milk from the jug into the two cups.

Kate winked at Rose. "What you need is a nice breeze. It's

lovely this time of night." And before Adela comprehended, Kate stepped to the window, undid the latch, and pushed the glass out. "Well, if you're all set, I'll be going," she said.

"Please do," Adela muttered. And Kate bustled from the room, leaving the door open and Corella staring out after her.

Adela lowered the jug with a thud, glaring after Kate. She stepped for the door and hesitated, looked back at the window and again at the door.

Corella's head swiveled, wide eyed, watching Adela.

Rose's slid her hand to her robe's pocket, readying the vial of sleeping potion.

Apparently, the open window was more of a threat, because Adela moved that way first, shaking her head. As soon as Adela turned away, Rose stood, making a show of reaching for the cups as she blocked Corella's view. She drew the vial from her pocket, hiding it until Adela passed behind her. She tipped it over one cup of milk. A drop of potion fell. Rose slipped the vial back into her robe and picked up the untainted cup of milk as Adela returned from closing the door. Rose sipped meekly, standing beside the table.

"That woman," Adela muttered. She grabbed the other cup and gulped her milk. Adela emptied her cup and placed it on the tray before slumping toward the floor.

Rose dashed forward and caught Adela with one arm, splashing her with milk. She tugged Adela's body to the nearest divan as Adela began a quieter version of her usual snoring.

"Oh, Adela," Rose said over the snores as she struggled to pull Adela onto the divan. "Did you overdo the wine at supper?" Would Adela open her eyes? She snored on.

Rose put down her cup and looked toward Corella, frozen in her seat, her knitting clutched to her chest. "Corella, is it? Come help a moment."

Corella slowly put aside her knitting and shuffled forward.

"Don't worry," Rose said. "She does this all the time. Help me get her on the divan." Corella moved to grasp Adela's ankles and tugged weakly. Rose pushed Adela's torso all the way onto the divan and finished yanking her legs on.

Rose turned to Corella. "I suppose Adela told you to return to your room?"

"No, m'lady. Just to sit by the door."

"That's fine. You can go now. The guard will lock the door after you. And"—Rose lowered her voice conspiratorially—"Adela won't like it if you tell anyone what you saw. She tries to hide it when she overindulges."

"I won't tell a soul!" Corella said. She practically fled from the room.

Rose watched the door shut and heard the click of the lock. Adela hadn't moved a smidge. A smile crept across Rose's face. The potion had worked again. She was alone for the night.

Energy surged through Rose, from the thrill of using the potion, tricking Corella, and now a whole night to herself. She paced to the window and back across the confined room. If only she could escape the castle. She would find Dustan's camp. It couldn't be far. She threw open the window again, bathing in the night breeze as her robe fell open and the wind rippled her nightgown. The moon was up, almost full, and its light illuminated the treetops below her.

But there was no escape. She could pick the lock, but guards were stationed throughout the castle. Two of them stood at her door, and two more at the steps to her tower. After her disappearance, there was no way she'd convince them to walk her anywhere.

Rose left the window. She took a blanket from the back of the divan and covered Adela. She retrieved her cup and stood at the window, sipping the rest of the rich, sweet milk. The moonlight glinted on the panes of glass.

The milk soothed her, and she yawned. The last time she'd been alone, she'd imagined Dustan with her. It was as close as she could get to him tonight, and she wanted to feel that closeness again. She left her cup on the windowsill, lowered the lamps, and climbed the steps to her bedchamber. She opened the window there as well, slipped off her robe, and crawled between the bed curtains, letting her slippers drop to the rug.

Rose nestled in the pillows, pulled the coverlet around her, and closed her eyes. No one hovered nearby. Adela would sleep through the night. She had Dustan to thank. He'd made her wish come true.

Just wish for me, he'd said. Rose smiled and murmured, "I wish Dustan were here."

She pretended he'd come. She imagined his eyes, his dark hair. A breeze crossed her face, carrying the tang of the forest. What would she do with him, if he were here?

She replayed their kiss in the garden. She'd worn out the memory, but now she imagined the same soft kiss happening in her bed. It would start soft, but then his arms would tighten around her, his lips would press against hers. Just thinking about it made the longing start inside.

"Would he want to do lie with me?" Rose whispered. She came back from her imagining and felt a moment of guilt for having Dustan in bed with her.

"Of course I'd want to," a voice whispered.

Rose gasped and opened her eyes. Dustan sat on the windowsill, his hair flickering in the breeze. Moonlight glinted around him.

"Dustan," she whispered. Heat filled her. But he couldn't know what she'd been imagining, could he? He made no move.

He had come. Impossible, but somehow, he had. He stayed in the window, his gaze never leaving her, and she stared back. How she'd wanted him to hold her, and now here he was. In her bedchamber. And Adela deep asleep. She should be scared, yet she wasn't.

She sat up and reached out a trembling hand to part the bed's curtains.

Dustan slipped off the windowsill. His feet were bare and silent as he came toward her. He wore a loose shirt and britches that hugged his body. She blushed again when he neared and she realized she'd been staring at the tightness of his britches. She dropped her gaze to his feet as he came inside the curtains.

"Where was it you wanted me?" he said. His voice was kind, and her embarrassment faded. His fingers softly stroked her hair. He leaned toward her. "Don't worry," he whispered, "I think I know."

He kissed the top of her head as he slid down beside her. The night air blew through the open curtains, giving her goosebumps, but then he was holding her and his body was warm. She pressed herself against him, and through her thin nightgown she felt his hand on her back, pulling her in. She slid her arm around him.

Rose looked at Dustan's neck. She'd never been this close to anyone. She could smell his skin, and it was good, the way freshly laundered sheets were good to smell, or a sleeping cat's fur. Her mind leapt about. She remembered petting a cat, with her mother talking nearby. She tried to calm herself, to focus on what was happening. Dustan was holding her. In bed.

Dustan didn't speak, just held her, his hand slowly rubbing her back.

When she'd gathered her courage, Rose tilted her face up. The tip of her nose brushed against his smooth chin. She lifted her eyes to his. In the semidarkness, he studied her. She could barely feel his breath on her face.

"What are you thinking?" she whispered.

He didn't respond for a moment. "I'm wondering what you really want."

Wasn't it obvious? She'd have to make it clearer. Her hand was low on his back. She began to explore, sliding it up his torso, feeling the muscles through his shirt. She closed her eyes and leaned in to nuzzle the tip of her nose against his, and slowly he moved closer, his breath mingling with hers. She found his lips, grazing them with hers, then going back for more.

It began soft, but soon they were rolling in her sheets, kissing and touching. It was like her imaginings, only better. Their clothes came off, and they wrapped their bodies together. She'd never known anything could feel so good.

FROM THE PEAK OF THEIR bliss, Rose's mind resumed functioning. Dustan lay with his face against her belly, his weight comforting. Her hand clenched his hair. She loosened her fist, petting his hair before combing it with her fingers.

What had she just done? If anyone caught Dustan here, he'd be killed.

"Dustan," she whispered. "If anyone finds you . . ."

He turned to look at her. "Hmm?"

"They'd kill you for being here."

"They won't find me."

"But what if someone comes? Or Adela wakes?"

"She won't. But if someone comes, I'll leave before they see me." He rested his head against her again.

"How? How did you get in?"

"I climbed the wall."

Rose tugged on his hair, and he looked up.

"I flew," he said.

Rose narrowed her eyes.

Dustan smiled and shimmied up the bed until he was beside her. "I told you, I climbed," he said. He rested his head on her breast and put his arm around her.

"You climbed the wall?" she said. She gently pushed him off and looked in his face.

Dustan sighed, and it ended in a yawn. "I made a ladder," he said. "I'll show you later." He tried to snuggle against her again, and again she pushed him back.

Grinning, he rolled out of bed. He reached to the floor and handed her the bunched cloth of her nightgown. He stretched and pulled on his shirt in one smooth motion.

Rose sat up, aware of her nakedness. After what they'd just

shared, it shouldn't matter, but she'd never been naked with a man before. She fumbled with her nightgown, hurrying both arms into what she thought were the sleeves, only to find herself tangled in the twisted cloth, just as Dustan turned to her. He bit his lip as if he might grin again. But he stepped forward and straightened her gown, pulling it over her head until her arms slipped in properly and the skirt fell straight around her torso. He held out a hand and pulled her up, up and into his arms, where he held her.

"You're so precious," he whispered.

She felt precious and perfect, instead of awkward, as she so often felt in court.

Dustan led Rose to the window. Together they leaned out. The moon had risen higher, and its light illuminated the tops of the forest, and the faint hoot of an owl drifted up through the soughing of the wind. Dustan pointed across her to the tower wall at her right. "Look there."

Rose saw nothing but the smooth rectangular stones in the pale light. He stepped closer, pressing himself against her, and his finger moved out and touched something. A strand like a spider's thread glinted in the pale light. Rose followed the thread up to a metal hook embedded in the tower wall.

She pushed herself up to sit on the sill, leaning tentatively out the window. Dustan's hands moved to hold her. There were two hooks, side by side, a hand's length apart. Another filament glimmered, disappearing as it swayed in the breeze. Rose reached to touch the nearer hook and tried to wiggle it, but it held firm. Her fingers felt the filament tied to the hook. Sliding her fingers down, she found the first rung of a ladder.

"Dustan," she said, barely breathing, "you climbed up the tower wall on that?"

"It's stronger than it looks," he said. "Try to break it."

She reached both hands out the window, and his grip on her hips tightened. She took the ladder in her hands and pulled, working it back and forth, but it wouldn't break. On a sudden impulse, she leaned out, trying to rip the ladder with her teeth.

Dustan pulled her back, laughing. "Why don't you try your embroidery scissors?"

Rose shook her head. "I believe you." She slid off the sill and into his arms.

He smiled. "Would you climb it?"

"Me?" Rose imagined the dizzying height. "I'd be scared."

"You won't have to do it alone," he said, leaning closer and lowering his voice. "We could leave together. There's so much I could show you."

Rose wanted him to show her everything. "I'd do it."

"I'll come for you tomorrow, an hour after the moon rises." He leaned to kiss her lips, wrapping himself around her.

Inside, she stirred again, wanting him closer, but he pulled away.

"Tomorrow," he repeated. He stepped to the window and vaulted himself over the sill so fast Rose jumped. She leaned out. His hands gripped the all-but-invisible ladder. He blew her a kiss and then he descended, far quicker than she'd be able to. She leaned as far as she dared to watch until he disappeared.

Chapter 8

ROSE PACED DOWN THE CORRIDOR behind Adela. Just a few more hours, and Dustan would come.

As they entered the dining hall, she scanned the head table, but only her father and his men sat there tonight. She followed Adela to their usual spot. Adela stepped carefully, as if to hide her unsteadiness. When she'd finally brought Rose's tea that morning, with the tray shaking in her hands, Rose had pretended to be just waking as well. She'd recalled to Adela how the warm milk had put Adela right to sleep. Adela's brow had furrowed, but she hadn't responded.

Rose sat and began to eat the food Adela put on her plate. Where would Dustan take her? Surely not the village, where people might recognize her. And how would she serve the potion to Adela? What if Adela didn't want milk tonight? Should she slip the potion into Adela's drink now? But then Adela would pass out in the dining hall, and that would arouse suspicion.

All through supper Rose ignored the dining hall's clatter, her mind circling the problem. She had to find a way, or Dustan would be caught sneaking into her room.

"Rose, dear," Adela said, back in Rose's sitting room after supper, "I'm afraid I slept poorly last night. Do be a dear and get yourself ready for bed. I'd like to retire."

Rose couldn't believe her luck. How would the old Rose respond—the docile, passive Rose? She could no longer remember, so she simply nodded. Two ladies came to remove her powder and brush out her hair. They braided it into one long braid and helped her out of her supper dress and into her nightgown, before helping her into bed. The ladies left, and Adela moved about in the sitting room. Finally, Adela's pallet creaked.

As soon as Adela's snoring drifted in from the next room, Rose bolted off the bed. She carefully unlatched the window, making no sound, and retrieved the sleeping potion. It still nestled in the man's gloves she'd found on the beach that day—the day she met Dustan.

Those gloves had seemed so important—was it only a few days ago?—when all she'd had were her daydreams. But since meeting Dustan, she had something real. Real kisses, a real body pressed against hers. She no longer needed to hold on to the possibilities she could imagine from the gloves.

Adela slept on her back with her mouth open. Creeping toward her, Rose watched for any sign of waking, but there was none. Rose tipped the vial over Adela's gaping mouth and let a drop of potion fall in. Immediately the snoring quieted. After watching a minute, Rose returned to her bedchamber.

She stood vigil at the open window, inhaling the night air. Every few minutes she leaned out to see if Dustan was on his way up the ladder. Her heartbeat quickened when a golden glow appeared in the sky behind the forest. He would come soon. Where would Dustan take her?

The glow brightened until the moon crested the treetops and beamed down, round and golden in the sky. Rose leaned out again and a feeling of dread seized her. She still wore her nightgown.

Dustan would arrive any moment, and she hadn't dressed.

But what could she wear? Her dresses, with full, heavy skirts, were sewn to fit a corseted body. She could manage a corset by herself, but how would she climb the ladder in one? Rose turned from the window, considering her trunks.

Maybe she had a simple dress from her younger ages. Rose moved to the furthest trunk and pulled out the gowns. The dresses were too small. She tried another trunk and found clinging bodices and tiny waistlines, completely impractical. She was near the bottom when she sensed someone in the room. Rose stopped pulling out the dresses, staring hopelessly at the pile on her lap.

But Dustan's voice was kind. "I see you're still getting ready."

Rose turned. He sat on the windowsill again, his feet bare and his clothing simple.

"It's only that I don't know what to wear," she said. "Usually I'm put in a corset."

"Hard to climb in," he said.

She nodded.

"And you don't know where we're going," he continued, as he slid down and came toward her. "Do you have a scarf?"

Rose dug in the dresses until she found a mossy-green velvet scarf. She tugged it free and held it out. Dustan took both the scarf and her hand and pulled her to her feet. He ran the velvet through his fingers as he bit his lip, considering, and Rose watched his thumb rub the material and wished she could be the scarf.

Dustan reached his arms behind her and her breath caught. She held it, waiting to see what he'd do, but he only positioned the scarf and pulled it tight around her middle. He moved closer, his arms around her again as he tied a knot at her back. He stepped away, adjusting her gown. Every time his fingers brushed against her skin, she felt a jolt shoot through her body. She began to wish they could just spend the night in her room.

He turned her toward the mirror and she saw her form in the uneven glass. Using the scarf as a sash, he'd gathered her nightgown, fastening it up in back so that Rose's legs were free. Next to his simple clothing, the gown looked right. Thank goodness her makeup had been removed. She'd have looked garish in it next to him.

Her dark hair still hung down her back in a thick braid. Dustan took the end of the braid in his hand and gently pulled on the ribbon until it slipped off. She watched in the mirror as he softly combed his fingers through her hair, loosening the braid. Her hair came free.

"A nightgown?" Rose said, trying to ignore the feelings stirred up by the touch of his hand in her hair.

He gathered her hair and moved it to the side, leaning in to kiss her bare neck. "Where we're going, it will suit just fine."

And Rose suddenly knew it would be just the two of them. She couldn't wait to go.

"Are you ready?" he asked, and she nodded. "Put on your slippers," he said. "Your feet aren't as callused as mine."

Maybe they would be someday, she thought, slipping on the shoes. After they were life-mates, she'd go about barefoot, too.

He led her to the window. "I'll go first." He pushed himself up onto the sill and turned and stepped onto the ladder, where he swung for a moment. When the motion stilled, he offered her a hand. Rose pushed herself up after him. She swung her legs out the window and tried not to look at the ground so far below.

Dustan leaned toward her. "Put your arms around my neck," he said. When she let go his hand, he put it on her back. As her arms went around him, gripping tightly, he pulled her toward him. "Put your legs around me, too," he said. The ladder brushed her knee as she moved her legs. She hugged herself tightly against him, and they swung free on the ladder.

"Ready?" he asked. She kept her focus on his face as she clung to him and nodded. His hand moved off her back and he began to descend. He moved more slowly than he had alone, but within a minute, branches appeared around them. The ladder took them down into a cluster of trees against the wall of the castle.

The ladder ended over a large bough. Rose lowered her legs to stand on it, and Dustan's arms went around her again, supporting her as she wobbled. When she grew steady, he helped her sit on the bough, and then she dropped the distance to the ground. Looking up, she saw no sign of the ladder, only branches.

Dustan dropped down beside her.

Something snuffled nearby. A dark horse stood, untethered, under the trees. The horse tossed her head at Dustan, who took Rose's hand and approached the horse.

"Are we going to ride?" Rose whispered. She reached out a hand to pet the horse's nose.

"Unless you'd rather walk."

The horse snorted gently and nuzzled Rose's hand. "No, I want to ride the horse." She petted the horse's forelock.

"Her name is Redbud."

"Hi, Redbud," Rose said, stroking the horse another moment. To Dustan, she said, "Are we going far?"

"Not for me, but it might be for you."

Rose looked down, unsure what to say. He was probably right.

He took her hand. "I'm sorry I said that," he said. "It's not your fault. I know they don't let you out much." He squeezed her hand and held it until she looked up again. He made everything feel right, just by being with her.

Dustan pulled a dark cape off the horse's back and placed it around Rose's shoulders. He lifted the hood over her head. She wrapped the cape tightly to conceal her white gown. He knelt, linking his hands above the ground. Rose stepped into them as she'd seen the young men of court do when mounting a horse.

"Other foot," Dustan said. "Unless you want to ride backward."

Thankfully the darkness hid her blush. She switched feet, and Dustan pushed, lifting her up, and she swung her leg over Redbud's back. There was no saddle, only a blanket. Her nightgown bunched up around her thighs, but the cloak was long enough to hide them.

Redbud wore no bridle or reins. Dustan swung up behind Rose—she missed seeing how he did it, without a stirrup—and without a word Redbud stepped out from the shadow of the trees.

Rose wobbled with the motion of the horse. Dustan pressed against her back, solid and still. "You can hold her mane," he said in Rose's ear. "She won't mind." Rose wrapped her fingers into Redbud's soft, chestnut-brown mane, trying not to pull.

Beyond the trees ran the cart path that connected the castle to the village of Woodglen. Redbud clopped onto the path, heading away from the castle. They passed only one person, a villager who staggered sideways with his gaze focused on the ground at his feet. They passed the turn to the village and continued alongside the forest. Fear nipped at Rose as the branches reached closer and closer.

Redbud turned off the path and entered the forest.

Rose's nerves began to jangle. She halfway turned in her seat. "Dustan—"

"Shh," he said, and his arms wrapped around her. "You're with me. I won't let anything bad happen to you tonight. I promise."

His words soothed her. Enclosed in his arms, she did feel safe, forest or not. She focused on the memory of coming here with her mother, before her father had scared her. After all, nothing bad had happened that time. She turned to look up at Dustan. His face was calm as he balanced on Redbud's back. He looked back at her and smiled.

The earthy forest scent filled the air. Redbud stepped through the trees without guidance. Her gait had changed from that of a clopping workhorse to a graceful stride. She moved around low branches that would knock off her riders and never had to backtrack from a dead end. The forest was old, with towering trees that blocked all light, leaving no undergrowth. When Redbud began climbing a rocky slope, Dustan leaned forward, holding Rose steady.

What was she doing? Riding into the forest at night with a man she'd just met? And wearing only her nightgown! Adela would faint if she knew. Rose remembered the prince of Perland, that first prince she'd met so long ago. At first sight, she'd been taken with him. But she'd quickly realized the appeal was all a dream in her head, that the real prince was nothing like her imaginings. Could she be making such a mistake now?

She thought of her mother the next time she had seen her, a week after their visit to the forest, and remembered the fading bruises on her mother's arms. Her mother had been a prisoner in all but name after that, just as Rose was a prisoner in the castle now. Tonight, she was free. She wasn't turning back.

At last a light appeared ahead, and Redbud entered a clearing. A broad tree stump stood in the center with a linen cloth draped over it, a bouquet of wildflowers in a vase, and several covered dishes sitting among unlit candle stubs. Lights twinkled in the branches overhead, and embers glowed in a circle of stones. Behind the stump, a tent stood in the shadows. It was low with a slanted top. The tents Rose had seen on the plain from her window had been striped in bright colors. This one was plain canvas.

Dustan slid from Redbud's back and turned to lift Rose down. Her legs had already stiffened from the unfamiliar motion of riding.

"Are you all right?" Dustan asked as he helped her out of the cape. She nodded as she stretched her muscles. Dustan turned to hang the cape on a tree branch.

Rose didn't feel any chill, even though the fire was too low to heat the space. Redbud stepped into the shadows, and when Rose turned back to Dustan, candles glowed on the makeshift table. He lifted a cover off a plate of fruit and cheese. The food glinted in the twinkling light.

"Now you see where I've been staying," Dustan said.

"By yourself, you said?" Rose asked.

"Aye. I have no need of attendants." After a pause, he asked, "Are you hungry?"

Her nerves felt jangled, from the climb down the tower, from the journey through the forest. And now, from being here alone with Dustan. She avoided the tent. If she looked at it, he might guess how badly she wanted to go into it with him.

"Maybe in a little while."

"Then I have something to show you," he said.

He took her hand and led her to the thick trunk of an oak tree. He lifted her fingers, kissed them, and brought them toward the bark, where he placed them onto the strands of another invisible ladder. "Are you able to climb?"

Rose reached for the ladder with her other hand and tugged. It held. Her foot searched until she felt a low rung. She stepped on and swung free. Dustan's hand touched her back to steady her. She went up one step, then another. Once she was used to the feel of it, she climbed easily. The tiny filaments were sturdy under her feet.

She climbed into the branches. Lights twinkled around her. The ladder swung as Dustan stepped on beneath her. She kept climbing and the glow of the campsite dimmed. Her eyes adjusted to the darkness. The leaves thinned as she climbed, and silver moonlight fell from above. The trunk split and twisted away, and the ladder ascended into the air. Rose focused on climbing the rungs and didn't look ahead.

At last Rose came to a thick bough and the ladder ended. She pushed herself up through the leaves. The top branches of the tree were strung with thick ropes, crisscrossed to create a tight net that cradled a cushion as large as her bed. She crawled on and it shifted beneath her. Rose kept still, waiting as Dustan appeared, and a moment later he had crawled to her and bundled her in his arms.

"It's safe," he said. "Watch." Still holding her, he bounced up and down, shaking the branches beneath them. The cushion swayed but stayed firm.

Rose relaxed as they reclined side by side. Overhead, the stars were dim in comparison with the bright moon, now silver-white and high in the sky. The treetops spread around them like a strange garden.

"There must be trees where you come from," she said. "You seem at home in them."

"Aye, there are many forests."

"What are the homes like in Skye?" she asked.

"I'm afraid you'd find them simple. There is no castle. Just small dwellings. Like the huts in your village, only made of stone."

"I wouldn't mind a hut, if I were free to come and go," Rose said.

"That you would be. Everyone is free to do as they please, so long as they harm no one."

"It sounds like a paradise," Rose said. She stretched her arms over her head and pretended to touch the stars.

They stared at the sky in silence, but her thoughts ran about. Had anyone at the castle discovered her absence? She turned her face to the right. Over Dustan's shoulder, the castle's silhouette towered pitch black against the night sky. They hadn't traveled far, but the castle was diminished behind the treetops. Her tower, the tallest, was easy to spot. Her window was dark.

What was her father thinking? Had he even considered Dustan as her mate? She was sure he hadn't, unless Dustan had lied to the king about his wealth. Since she'd met Dustan, she'd felt hopeful that her life might change into something wonderful. But her hope was as much a fantasy as her daydreams, like the one about being rescued from the beach by a handsome fisherman in his boat. She would never escape.

Yet here she was, alone again with a man she liked, this time out of the castle. And atop the branches of a tree! She could never have imagined this moment. Maybe there was a future for her, waiting out there, a future she simply couldn't imagine, and all she had to do was walk bravely toward it.

She focused on the gentle breeze, on being in the present moment, on swaying above the treetops. Life in the castle didn't seem real. Did she have to go back? Could they simply leave? She'd tell

Dustan he didn't have to pay her father, that he could have her, and they could leave for Skye that night.

But her father would hunt them. He'd start a war with Skye. It wasn't fair to Dustan, to make him an outlaw and endanger his people.

She turned her face away from the castle. In the opposite direction was nothing but treetops. All was darkness. Except . . .

A strange glow hovered over the trees in one spot. Rose frowned. Could it be a campfire? Guards? It didn't flare as a fire would. In fact, it pulsed like a slow heartbeat.

"Dustan," Rose said. "What do you think that is?"

"What?"

"That glowing light over the treetops."

There was a long pause. "Perhaps a campfire, or a lantern hung in a tree."

"It seems odd, somehow." He didn't respond. She turned to him and placed her hand on his chest. His heart beat quickly. When she leaned in to kiss his cheek, he didn't move.

"Are you all right?" she asked.

He sat up, placing his hand over hers and turning to her.

"Yes, I'm just hungry, that's all."

"Shall we go down?"

"Yes, let's."

Rose sat up, looking again at the glowing light across the trees. It couldn't be that far from them, maybe fifty treetops away. Dustan moved to the ladder and began to descend. She turned to crawl after him. He waited while she found her footing and then continued down. As she emerged from the branches, a fire crackled and danced in the ring of stones. Redbud stood in the flickering shadows, her head drooping with sleep.

Rose followed Dustan to the table of food, where the candles still burned. He snapped up a strawberry and ate it.

Rose copied him, but she could barely swallow. She still sensed that something was bothering him. She felt desperate to bring back his easy smile. She could think of only one way to do it.

Taking his hand, she drew him toward the tent. She had to pull. He stared out at the trees.

"Whatever is bothering you," she said, "put it aside for the night. Be here, with me. I might not get another chance."

He turned to her at last, his eyes liquid in the firelight. What was going through his mind as he gazed at her? He allowed himself to be led to the tent. She pushed aside the door and stooped to enter.

The firelight glowed through the walls as she crawled onto the carpet inside. Some merchants traveled with furniture, she'd heard, even hanging lanterns and beaded curtains. But here there were only carpets and a large nest of pillows and cushions and woven blankets. Rose kicked off her shoes and crawled onto the cushions. When she reached the middle, she stretched out, enveloped in softness. The cushions dipped as Dustan joined her. She rolled over and into his open arms. They settled into the pillows and Dustan pulled a blanket over them. He stroked her hair, but he didn't speak, as if he were still troubled.

"I haven't known you long," Rose whispered. He looked in her eyes and waited. "I haven't known many men, only these princes who've come, and I never liked any of them. But you . . ." Should she go on? What if it turned him away? But she didn't know when she'd see him again. She had to tell him. "I long to be with you every day. I feel joy when I see you and sorrow when I think I might never again. I want to bond with you, not any of the others. I love you, Dustan. If my father doesn't choose you, I would run away to be with you."

He continued stroking her hair and watching her. Had she said too much?

"Sweet girl," he whispered at last. "I was sent on a mission. I did not expect to find someone I could love."

An unfamiliar warmth spread through her body. He loved her.

She leaned forward to kiss him. The first time he didn't respond. She opened her eyes to find him watching her still. She tried again. This time, his fist closed in her hair, and his lips moved against hers.

Her hands sought his skin, pulling at his shirt to untuck it, to pull it off his body. The familiar feeling had begun, down below her belly. This time she wanted more than his lips and hands on her. She wanted all of him.

MUSIC WOKE HER.

Bells. The gentle ringing of tiny bells, and the eerie song of flutes.

The tent was dark. Beside her on the pillows, Dustan slept. There was no sound from the fire.

Rose sat up, wide awake. Her heart beat as if the strange music were seeping inside and beating in time. She looked at Dustan's body, stretched beside her in the dark. She'd made love with him mere hours ago, and he'd been marvelous, holding her and calling her precious. He was still beautiful. But making love with him seemed a distant dream.

She felt about for her gown. The cool material shimmied down her skin as she pulled it over her head. Quietly, she crawled toward the tent door.

Outside, the music was louder. The embers of the fire glowed, and behind it, Redbud stood asleep. The candles on the table and the lights overhead had gone out, but moonlight reached down through the branches. The food glistened in the pale light. Somehow, it hadn't attracted any insects. Rose helped herself to more berries and a hunk of cheese. She listened to the music as she ate. It was nothing like the music she'd heard the castle minstrels play.

She wiped the berry juice off her hand with the edge of the cape she'd worn earlier and stepped out of the clearing into the trees in the direction of the music.

Rose was glad of the full moon as she picked her way between the tree trunks. The music should grow louder, but as she moved, it shifted. Now it came from behind her. Had she gotten turned around? She walked back and recognized a trunk she was sure she'd passed. But now the music came from off to one side.

She thought of the strange glow she'd seen from the treetop earlier. She picked her way back to the clearing with the tent and looked at the tree to orient herself in the direction of the glow. Redbud shifted.

Rose marched into the trees. The roots of the forest floor dug into her bare feet, her shoes forgotten in the tent. But she kept going, compelled and curious. This time she didn't shift when the music did, and eventually it gave up its game. It grew louder and louder, and Rose slowed when a glow appeared between the trees, the same glow she'd seen before. It pulsed in time with the music.

The light brightened as she neared. Figures moved between the trees. Rose trembled, but she couldn't stop moving toward the music. An immense oak stood directly in her path, silhouetted against the light beaming out at its sides. Rose crept forward, heart hammering.

The music seethed out from the tree, an eerie cacophony yet strangely beautiful. Rose drew close enough that someone might see her. She quickened her pace until she'd pressed herself against the rough bark. After taking a moment to compose herself, Rose looked around the trunk.

She gasped.

The light streamed from a large clearing filled with dancing figures. The music swelled, and the shapes danced, but not like the dancing she'd watched at the castle. Castle dancing was orderly, with neat pairs of dancers, one man and one woman. Here the women and men were all mixed up, arms around each other. They leapt wildly, tossing their dark hair—some of the men had long hair, too—and as she watched, some came together as if making love standing up, pressed against each other in the dance. Some of the women wore britches, and some of the men wore gowns, and all of the fabrics flowed like water. The people were willowy and graceful, not stout like the peasants of the village. Their skin shone in the silver moonlight and the light of glowing lanterns that hung in the trees.

When Rose glimpsed the regal woman at the far side, lounging on cushions above the dance, she knew for certain. "Fair folk," she whispered.

They were real. Her mother's book of fairy stories had shown dancing just like this. Rose tried to remember more. The book had shown the fair folk gathering food, talking with the birds, and dancing. And they could alter their appearance and cast small spells. They could harvest the magic of herbs.

But were they dangerous? She should go before they spotted her. But the fairies fascinated her. She had to see more.

Carefully, she stepped back from the tree and made her way around the clearing, keeping in the shadows. At one side, wide wooden boards served as tables, piled with platters of food. Fairy children chased each other and older folk sat on stumps.

Rose neared the woman on cushions, who was elevated on a shelf of rock above the clearing. She must be the fairy queen. Rose crept behind another tree and pressed against it, peeking out to see more of the queen. She was no taller or prettier than the other fairies, but she looked over the crowd with a haughty smile. She seemed oddly familiar. Her gown was fancier than the simple, flowing clothing the others wore, and hers was decorated with jewels that reminded Rose of Prince Murkel and the other visiting princes. Children stood around her, cooling her with feathered fans, and a tiny girl held a goblet. Rose shivered. There was something about these children. Their eyes were dull, and they moved like golems.

Someone touched her arm.

Rose spun to find Dustan there, standing in the shadow of the tree. She couldn't make out his face with the lights of the fairies blotting out her vision.

"Dustan!" she whispered. "There are fairies!"

"We should go," he said. "They can be dangerous."

She didn't move. "You've seen them? They're dancing."

"Aye, I've seen them dancing plenty of times. Please, Rose, we should go."

His voice entreated her, but she couldn't bring herself to leave. But when he held out a hand, something within her shifted. She took his hand. He turned and led her away from the clearing.

"Leaving already?" a high-pitched voice taunted.

Someone swung down from the trees in front of them, a thin fairy with a pinched nose. She dropped to the path. Dustan's grip on Rose's hand tightened.

"We didn't mean any harm," he said. "We heard the music and wondered what it was. We'll leave you in peace."

The fairy made a tsk-ing noise and shook her head as if Dustan were a disobedient child. She turned to Rose and her face lit up with a mockery of delight.

"Oh, *Dus*-tan," she said, smirking. "You've found someone new?"

Rose felt heat rising in her body. She kept ahold of Dustan's hand.

Dustan's voice stayed even. "This is Princess Rose. Her father is seeking her mate. I would like it to be me."

"She's a pretty one," the fairy said. "She'll make a—"

"That's enough," Dustan said, and he clenched Rose's hand and dragged her past the fairy. The fairy's cackling drowned out the music.

They walked in silence as the music faded behind them. Dustan's name, said in the sneering voice of the fairy, played over and over in Rose's mind. Dustan dropped Rose's hand and led the way back through the forest. In a few minutes, Rose entered the clearing with the tent. Dustan stood with his back to her, his head down.

"You knew her?" Rose said. She felt shaken, queasy. Dustan didn't respond. "Who is she?"

"Just a spiteful wench."

"But how do you know her? What have you to do with fair-ies?" The truth rose up before her. The sleeping potion. The strange material of the ladders. The mysterious attack by the squirrels on Prince Murkel just before Rose met Dustan in the gardens.

"You're one of them," Rose whispered.

He didn't deny it, just stood with his head down.

"What do you want with me?" Tears filled her eyes.

"Just to love you."

"But how can I believe that?" How could she believe he wouldn't hurt her, after everything she'd heard about the fairies—about fairy men taking lovers, just as Dustan had taken her, and stealing their babes? He hadn't forced her, but he hadn't needed to. She'd fallen right into his arms. If he was a fairy, could she trust him? Her tears overflowed.

He clicked his tongue and Redbud stepped forward. "I'll take you back," he said.

Rose didn't want to leave, not like this, but what else could she say? Dustan wouldn't look at her. He helped her onto the horse, passed her the cape, and pulled himself on behind her. This time, he didn't press himself against her. Even as Redbud stepped care-fully down the incline, Dustan managed to leave a space between their bodies. Rose wished he'd speak, wished he'd make everything right somehow, but he didn't.

The night was growing old when Redbud stepped out of the forest. The moon had passed its peak and was headed down the western sky. Redbud picked up her pace, as if she, too, wanted to be rid of Rose. No one was out this late to see them, and soon Redbud was flying down the road, but Rose was too anguished to enjoy it. The drunken villager they'd passed on the ride out was lying in the ditch, snoring loudly. Too soon the castle appeared before them. Redbud cantered into the cluster of trees.

Silently Dustan helped Rose down from Redbud's back. She looked up at the vertical climb, now in shadow since the moon had passed over the castle. "You don't have to—"

"I will follow you." He still wouldn't meet her gaze. Had he changed his mind about loving her? Had she changed hers? It was all happening too fast.

Rose got herself onto the tree limb where she could reach the ladder. She fumbled to find it and began to climb. The skirt of her gown flapped around her legs. Once she might have been terrified, looking down below her swaying feet at the ground receding farther and farther away, but any fear of heights was dead. All she feared was losing Dustan, or the dream she'd had of him these past few days, and the joy she'd felt in his presence.

When Rose reached the window, Dustan climbed up behind her, still keeping his distance somehow. His hands touched her sides, ready to catch her should she fall. She pulled herself onto the sill and climbed in.

Her heart ached, and her thoughts leapt about. She'd come to love him. She had to talk to him, to give him a chance to explain why he'd kept his identity a secret, even after they'd been in each other's arms. She turned back to the window. But Dustan had already disappeared, sliding down the ladder into the trees.

Chapter 9

WHEN ROSE WOKE THE NEXT morning, she had a brief respite before the previous night's events crashed in. She pulled the coverlet over her head, wishing the memories would go. Dustan had lied to her about who he was. What if he'd lied about everything? Her nose was clogged and dried tears crusted her cheeks even as new tears threatened to form. She couldn't possibly feel any worse.

Adela yanked the coverlet off. "Rose, get up at once. Your father is coming."

Adela moved away to the sitting room—moving too fast and oblivious to Rose's disheveled state. A feeling of dread crept up in Rose, mounting on top of the crushing weight of confusion and sadness. She sat up and clutched the bedpost, even as footsteps pounded up the tower and Adela rushed to open the door.

Her father strode in, wearing one of his fur-lined robes. "Where is she?" he said.

Adela looked through the doorway and pinned Rose with her stare. The king's gaze followed. He looked at Rose only a moment.

"A decision has been made," he said, looking away. "You will bond with Prince Murkel."

Rose gripped her bedpost and tried not to faint. "When?"

"That's up to him. He would like the rites to occur in Merlandia. You'll be brought to him tonight." Without looking up, her father left the room.

Rose sat motionless, and for once Adela left her alone. How could this have happened so quickly? She had to see Dustan again. But he'd lied to her and turned away when she'd learned the truth. There was no one to help her.

No matter how humble Dustan had seemed, Rose had clung to a hope that he'd be chosen. Now the hope was gone, her heart broken. Her father once again controlled her fate.

Adela bustled around silently, packing Rose's trunks. Guards came and went to carry away her things, and the court ladies came and went, apparently just to get one last look at her before she was handed over to her new owner. Rose refused lunch, knowing she wouldn't be able to keep it down.

Once the shock wore off, dread filled her. The thought of being Prince Murkel's bride, of lying with him as she'd done with Dustan, was too horrific. Part of her wanted to cry, to argue against the injustice of it all. But deeper down was another feeling, something new, the tiniest kernel, but she knew she should grasp onto it.

Anger.

In the afternoon, she submitted to being washed and dressed in a fancy new gown that Adela had, apparently, secretly ordered, awaiting this day. Rose ignored the cooing of the ladies. What did she care if her neckline was sewn with aquamarines? It was another chain binding her to a life she didn't want. The maids didn't bother to put up her hair. At last they let her lie down, and she listened to the ladies gossiping in the sitting room, just loud enough that she could hear.

"Piles of gold coins," one was saying. "And trunks full of jewels, all kinds, some he'd never seen before. Never seen so many shells in all his winters of service."

"Skies! Why is she worth all that?"

"He could have anyone."

Tears rolled from Rose's eyes. She hoped they'd streak the powder on her face.

Guards came for her at sunset. They led her down the tower steps, two in front and two behind, forming a box around her. Their heels echoed on the hard stone. Rose focused on the back of the guards' heads as they exited the castle and crossed the lawn. She didn't look to see if anyone was watching her leave. She had nothing, had no one, to say goodbye to.

They escorted her through the gardens to the beach gate. Rose dimly remembered that Murkel and his attendants were encamped on the beach. As she stepped onto the sandy path, the wind tossed Rose's hair and buffeted her skirts. A guard took her arm to help her walk on the sand. Or, maybe, they'd been warned that she might try to flee. Where would she go? She had no powerful allies in the castle. She knew no one anywhere else.

Except Dustan.

Dustan had said he loved her. But he'd been lying to her about who he was—a fairy. How did she know anything he'd said was true? Still, he was the only person she could think of who might help her. But *would* he help her if she could find her way back to his tent? Rose rejected the thought. Going to him would put him in danger, now that her father had chosen Prince Murkel. And no matter what Dustan had done, Rose didn't want to endanger him.

Grand tents appeared in the twilight as the party rounded the dune and arrived on the beach. Pennants fluttered wildly and the tents snapped in the wind. Rose's trunks stood piled on the sand. Clouds were rapidly filling the sky, which was barely visible now that the sun had set. Rose's hair blew across her face, and her flapping skirts hindered her steps.

Prince Murkel emerged from the nearest tent. The sight of him sickened her. How could she stand being his wife? After knowing Dustan, she would never love Prince Murkel.

Realizing this, the spark of anger kindled within Rose. Anger that her father's greed dictated whom she'd bond with. Anger that Prince Murkel could buy her with gold instead of love. Maybe she had to go with the prince now, since she had nowhere to run. But she would escape. She'd find a way. She'd be braver than she had been all these winters as a prisoner in her father's castle.

Her guards stopped in front of Murkel. "Our ship is on the way," Murkel said. "You may leave her with me."

The guards shifted uneasily, but none would dare contradict the man her father had bargained with. Several cast sideways glances at her, but they all turned and marched back up the beach.

Murkel stood, watching them go, and then turned to her. "Enough of this nonsense."

"What?"

He wrapped his long fingers tightly around her upper arm. "We won't be taking a ship," he said. "Come with me." He marched away from the tent toward the crashing ocean, dragging her with him. Her shoes slipped off in the sand as she tripped after him.

She wrenched and struggled, pulling away from him, but his hand was a vice. "There is no escape, little princess," he said. "Your father has sold you. He won't help you, no matter what you say of me."

"You don't want me," Rose said.

"And why not?"

"Prince Dustan loves me."

Murkel's hand squeezed harder on her arm as he hauled her toward the waves.

"And he's a fairy—he has magic. If you take me—"

"If I take you, what?" Murkel interrupted. He stopped and began shaking her until she nearly collapsed. "He'll what? Come after you?" Murkel smirked. "He won't. A fairy would never brave the ocean. He'll simply find another woman to serve his purposes."

"What do you mean?"

"He's only after you because he needs to produce a servant for his queen. They use half fairies, servants who can see the fairy paths and enter their realm, but who don't have the power to escape. He'd have kept you until you had his baby, then stolen it away and discarded you."

Cold fear shivered through Rose as she remembered the children surrounding the fairy queen in the forest the previous night. Were they stolen children, whose mothers had been discarded? She wouldn't believe it. Dustan had never shown her anything but kindness. Had it all been an act? He hadn't told her he was a fairy, after all. She'd uncovered it herself.

And those children, unsmiling, shining less brightly . . . they were half human. Where else would the queen have gotten them?

Murkel stopped at the water's edge.

"Time to learn to swim," he said, sneering. He clamped a hand on Rose's shoulder, bracing her, and raked his other hand down her front, catching in the ribbons on her dress. He yanked them undone, ripping them open. Rose screamed and struggled, but he kept on until her dress was piled on the sand. She stood shivering in her chemise and corset. The wind whipped the skirt about her legs.

Murkel dragged her into the icy waters that bit at her calves, then her knees. She lost her footing, but he kept walking, tugging her behind him, out into the waves. His motion changed, surging forward, pulling her after him. He released her and she kicked away, but there was no sand under her feet, only her skirt, now heavy with water, swirling around her legs. Her head dipped below the surface and she gulped for one more breath, and she tasted salt. There was nothing but water.

Panicking, Rose tried to remember what Murkel had said earlier. Her body would float. She stopped flailing her arms. Miraculously, her head came near the surface. She kicked herself up and sucked in a breath, then kicked her legs again. Her body rose and fell with the waves.

Her panic began to subside. Prince Murkel was a madman! She turned her head left and right. He was nowhere in sight. Maybe he had drowned. Her eyes swept past the empty beach, two hundred paces away, the waves crashing on the sand. Slowly, Rose pushed a hand through the water, her legs continuously kicking, forcing her skirt to churn around her. She could reach the beach. The waves would help her. She took another stroke.

Something brushed past her leg. Something scaly.

The water broke a few hands' lengths in front of her. His slimy curls emerged first, then his leering face, his sluggish lips twisted in a smile, revealing tiny teeth. His skin looked different, sickly and shadowed. His naked chest appeared, covered with wet curls of hair. He rose up like a phantom, not bobbing on the waves as she did.

"You're going the wrong way, my bride," Murkel said. "Our home is that way." He nodded at the open ocean. "You won't drown," he continued. "I'm a very good swimmer." And with that, his body shot out of the water, curving over her head. A rain of salty drops showered down from a giant tail.

Rose shuddered in horror. Prince Murkel no longer had legs. He wasn't human. He was some kind of monster, taking her to his lair at sea.

Behind her, the water stirred and she heard his panting. His cold, clammy arms slid around her. She shrank away from his touch, but there was no escape.

"I have a place prepared for you in my castle," he murmured in her ear. "A chamber of air where you'll be comfortable, where I can visit you at night. Of course, it's always night in my kingdom." His tongue licked the back of her ear.

Rose forced down the bile that rose in her throat. She stopped struggling, knowing it was hopeless against his powerful arms.

"You won't be lonely," he continued. "My other wives will see to that."

Rose swallowed hard. "Your other wives?"

"It's only fitting for a king of the sea to take many wives. Yes, king. I am King Murkel, not merely a prince, as I told your father. Does that make you desire me more?"

Rose closed her eyes. There had to be a way out.

"Now swim," he ordered, releasing her. Rose struggled to keep her head above the waves. Murkel watched her with amusement. Grabbing a fistful of her hair, he launched himself out to sea. Her hair yanked at her scalp as he towed her behind him. She sucked in the night air, breathing in the briny wind, perhaps the last free air she would ever breathe.

The cliffs receded from her peripheral vision. How far would he take her? If she ever escaped, she'd never make it back to land.

Without warning, she crashed into Murkel's body. His grip slackened. She floundered in the water, tossed in the waves created by Murkel's thrashing tail.

Birds. White terns circled above and dove at the water. The terns attacked Murkel, pecking and darting away. His hands fought them off, missing one after another.

Rose's heart leapt in hope. A boat was sailing toward her.

Murkel thrust himself into the air, scattering the terns, flipped, and disappeared under the surface. Rose tried desperately to swim toward the boat, keeping it in sight with help from the golden moon, rising just below the clouds on the horizon. The terns circled the boat, calling to her. She made out a person in a white shirt and dark vest holding the tiller, her long-dreamed-of fisherman coming to save her.

But it wasn't a fisherman—it was Dustan.

For a moment, it seemed they'd reach each other. The boat careened toward her as she struggled through the water. But the boat rocked violently and flipped sideways, the sail crashing down into the waves. Rose suppressed a scream as Murkel arced out of the water, dripping, and dove back in. Dustan clung to the side of the boat for a heartbeat, and then he vanished into nothing. Had he fallen into the water? Rose would have seen that, even in the darkness. He had simply disappeared. Murkel surfaced, reached toward the boat, and ran his hands along it. The terns resumed their attack, driving him back under.

Something nudged Rose, startling her, tearing her gaze from the place where Dustan had disappeared. A friendly face bobbed on the water beside her, like a fish only bigger, much bigger, with a rounded snout and intelligent eyes. It nudged her again, then dipped below the surface. Its rubbery skin slid under her hands. She wrapped herself around the creature, and it lurched forward in the water. Rose hung on, dragged through the waves, her face barely above water. They circled around the churning water where Murkel had been, and the creature carried Rose away.

Another creature streamed through the waves alongside her. It surfaced, and when Rose looked again, Dustan was there, crouched low on the creature's back. Rose almost lost her grip in her surprise.

"Stay still," Dustan said. "It helps them go faster."

"What are they?"

"Dolphins." Dustan looked back. "He's below the water. I don't know how long they can delay him."

Rose was grateful to whomever was delaying Murkel. She would never eat fish again.

The dolphins streaked toward land, a rocky cliff reaching out into the sea. Behind it on one side was the castle, towering over the tiny beach where she'd stood only minutes ago. The white sand and pale stone of the garden walls stood out in the dark. The cliff loomed closer, and Rose dared to hope.

Her dolphin was yanked to a stop and she lost her grip. It rolled, struggling, and Rose slid down its body before wrapping her arms around it to hang on. Sideways in the water, she looked back. Murkel was at her feet, his teeth clamped into the dolphin's tail.

Rose drew up her knee and kicked Murkel's face as hard as she could. She felt the crunch of his nose, and the sick feeling of his teeth collapsing. The dolphin jolted free. It raced on with Rose hanging off its side. The water washing over her face blinded her, and she inhaled some and coughed.

A minute later, the dolphin slowed. It twisted gently, but Rose clung to it, gasping for breath. Dustan's hands touched her, pulling her free, and her body sank into the shallow waves. She coughed up the last of the seawater. Rolling and crashing on the tiny beach, the waves sloshed over her. The cliff towered up just beyond.

Rose pushed herself up onto her knees, still in the shallow waters. Sharp grains of sand scratched her legs as she flailed away from Dustan and tried to stand, but her knees collapsed and she fell with a splash. He gripped her sides, lifting under her arms, and dragged her toward the dry sand. Her sodden skirt tugged at her, pulling her back.

Dustan looked over his shoulder. "Go, my friends," he said, and Rose heard two squeaks followed by a splash.

The water fell away, and Rose got her feet under her, but her legs tangled in the wet skirts. Dustan practically carried her out of the rolling waves. He held her, hugging her tight as she panted and waited for the strength to return to her legs.

"I know you're exhausted," he said, "but we have to get away from the water."

Rose nodded. With his arm still around her, she tried to take a step, but the skirt tripped her. She sucked in a breath, restricted by her corset. Her wet fingers fumbled with the hooks down her front, but she couldn't manage to undo them. Dustan moved her hands away and did it for her, and the corset dropped to the sand. She gulped, filling her lungs with air. As she pulled her skirt free of her legs, Dustan held up a short dagger.

"Hold still." He gripped the cloth and cut it, keeping it taunt as the bottom of the skirt fell away. When he finished, the dripping edges of the shortened skirt flapped against her knees. He slipped the dagger into a scabbard on his thigh.

"Come." Dustan took Rose's hand and led her to the boulders at the base of the cliff.

Rose watched as he scrambled over the rocks. She followed his path. At the cliff wall, he reached up for a handhold and pulled himself up, one step after another. He turned back to check on her. As she slowly moved up, her fingers clung to the rocks, hanging on as she waited for each next step. She panted as they climbed away from the beach.

When they were halfway up, Dustan looked down past her. Rose held on tighter and turned. Murkel was crawling out of the water, his powerful arms dragging his body. The terns swooped around him but he ignored them. Blood seeped from his nose, staining the sand. The waves washed back, revealing his gigantic tail covered with scales.

"He won't form legs until he dries," Dustan said, turning back to the cliff. "We should get as far as we can. He'll lose his advantage on land, but I'd still rather not fight him. Maybe he'll give up if he can't find us."

"Would he do that? After giving my father all that gold?"

Dustan pulled himself onto a narrow ledge and leaned down to extend a hand, pulling Rose up beside him. "Soon your father will realize the coins were an illusion. They have no gold in Merlandia. Only seaweed and the fish they prey on. Murkel's pride might push him to follow us. But he could easily find another victim to lure into his trap. I don't know that it matters who she is."

Rose felt cold inside, remembering Murkel's words. He'd said the same about Dustan.

Chapter 10

THEY'D BEEN RUNNING FOR HOURS, it felt, before Dustan allowed them to rest. They'd crossed the tilled fields at the top of the cliffs, skirted around the village, and entered the forest as soon as they could, carefully crossing the deserted forest road. Even in the cover of the forest, Dustan hurried for many leagues before his pace slowed, and exhaustion crept upon Rose. As she trudged along after Dustan, deeper into the woods, he picked up branches. Soon he carried a bundle under one arm.

Dustan led them straight, as near as Rose could tell, as if he knew exactly where they headed. Her bare feet ached, and now that she wasn't running, a chill set in. Rose doggedly followed Dustan, trying not to think of her discomfort, and just when she thought she might collapse, he led her into a clearing. After placing the branches on the ground, he reached inside his vest and extracted a pouch. Rose stood shivering as he took a pinch of whatever was in the pouch and sprinkled it onto the wood. The branches burst into flame, startling Rose.

"Sorry," Dustan said. "I should've warned you."

"Don't be sorry for lighting a fire," Rose said, tentatively stepping closer to it. The fire already felt hot, and as the shaking finally subsided, Rose realized how hard she had been shivering. She crept as close to the fire as she could.

Dustan walked in a slow path around her. "I'm setting a shield," he said when he noticed her watching. "To conceal us."

Rose recognized the sparkle of the dust falling from his hand. "You did it in the garden," she said. "That day the squirrels bit Prince Murkel."

"King Murkel. And yes, I did. It hid us all afternoon."

"And the squirrels? Were they your doing?"

"Aye. But they were happy to bite such a foul creature, even without my offering of nuts."

"You talk to them."

He nodded.

"And the dolphins?"

"The sea creatures have always been friends. Murkel would do better befriending them than eating them."

Dustan completed his circle. He tossed the remaining dust into the air and it sparkled, slowing as it fell and then moving up instead of down until it faded from view. "It will trap the heat of the fire," he said.

Rose's shivering had abated. Dustan came to her side. He carefully pinched the front of her damp chemise in his fingers and shook the cloth free where it clung to her body. Nearest the fire, the bottom edges had dried.

"It would dry faster if you took it off," he said, not meeting her gaze. "I must gather more firewood. I'll be gone for a bit."

"Is there no chance that Murkel could come upon us? Or my father's guards?" she asked.

"If they came near, I would know well before they'd see us. Which they wouldn't. They'd see only forest." Dustan turned away from her, unbuttoning his vest. He slipped it off, followed by his damp shirt. The muscles of his back stood out in the glow of firelight. Rose averted her gaze before he saw her looking. He hung his clothing on a branch. "I won't go far," he said without turning. "I'll hear you shout, if you need me."

The air shimmered as Dustan crossed the magical screen he'd created. With a few strides, he disappeared into the trees.

Rose closed her eyes and listened to the crackling of the fire. "I'm safe now," she whispered, trying to believe it. Safe from Murkel, from her father . . . but what about from Dustan? Murkel had accused him of seducing her only to get a child for the fairy queen. And Dustan had deceived her . . . but had he ever really hurt her? She tried to think rationally, to sort out her situation, but feelings kept creeping in, feelings that she loved him, trusted him, and desired him. The feelings of love were so strong, Rose wanted to give in, to simply forget that he had hurt her, to go back to blindly loving him.

Rose forced her thoughts to her most immediate problem— Murkel and her father. She depended on the king for everything, but he'd sold her to a sea monster. Did he know? If she told the king what had happened, would he protect her? He would, once he learned he'd been cheated, of course.

But what then? A new prince would come, possibly just as bad. Now that she was away from the castle, the thought of going back made Rose cringe. She would rather be a pauper than a prisoner.

But the king would start looking for her—as soon as the gold disappeared.

Dustan had rescued her. He was hiding her. But what did he want? And would he keep helping her after he got it? She didn't know if she could trust him, but staying with him seemed her best option.

Rose tugged her chemise up and off and hung it on the branch nearest the fire. She hesitated, then peeled off her damp underclothes and held them over the flames. The circle of magic felt delightfully warm. She exhaled, trying to relax. All around her was silent, dark forest. But if anyone were lurking nearby, Dustan would know. Rose didn't know much about fairy magic, but Dustan had walked through the forest with such confidence, his steps silent, turning at sounds she hadn't even noticed. She believed that no one could sneak up on him.

Firelight danced on her bare skin, and the dampness drifted away. Within a few minutes, her skin was hot and dry, and she was able to slip her underclothes back on. Her chemise was still damp. She took it down and held it close to the flames, until it waved crisply in the rising heat. She pulled it over her head.

A few minutes later, Dustan appeared from the trees. He had moved soundlessly through the forest. He hesitated, holding a bundle of branches. Rose lifted her hand in a wave, and Dustan came forward.

He knelt by the fire to add the additional wood. Strangely, the fire didn't react, but kept crackling as it had been. "Are you warm enough?" he asked.

"Yes. Are you?"

He smiled. "I'm fine."

"You . . . you can dry your britches." Rose flushed as she said it. "I won't look." His gaze embarrassed her more.

"Thank you."

She stared at the fire as he stood and struggled out of his damp britches. Was he naked? Don't look, she told herself. Don't look, don't look. He came beside her. For a moment, they stood in silence by the fire.

"You could go back," he said. "Once your father finds out that Murkel cheated him, you'll be safe."

"Safe from Murkel. But who would come next?"

"The castle was your home."

"It was my prison."

"So you don't want to go back?"

"No."

"He'll want to try again, your father. You'll have to hide."

Rose didn't answer.

"Would you like me to help you?" Dustan asked.

A lump formed in Rose's throat. "You don't have to."

Dustan's fingers gently touched her arm. "I want to, Rose. Let me help you. It will help me make amends for deceiving you."

"Okay," she whispered.

Dustan stepped away. She stole a glance as he walked to the edge of the space and hung his britches alongside his shirt. He wore his undergarments. Rose sighed.

A fallen tree rested under the ferns, and as he bent to roll the old log into the clearing, his muscles tightened and the firelight glimmered on his skin. Rose shivered in spite of the fire. He rolled the log close to the fire, his muscles tensing with the effort. Dustan scraped the bark off one side with a stick. He straightened, brushed the dust from his hands, and sat. "It's a bit scratchy," he said.

Rose tentatively sat beside him.

It was quiet save for the crackling of the branches. Overhead, the trees moved in the stiff breeze, but among their trunks the forest was sheltered, even without Dustan's magic.

"The fairies in the woods last night," Rose said. "Would they shelter us? They must live nearby."

Dustan shifted on his seat and ran his hand through his hair, which had dried in its usual spikes. "They are near, but I'm afraid we can't enter their land." When Rose didn't respond, he continued. "Humans cannot see the way into the realm of the fair folk."

Rose's chest tightened. If she couldn't enter fairy lands, he'd never planned to bring her to Skye. What had he planned to do with her? Had Murkel been right? That was the past, she told herself. But still, they'd eventually have to part, unless he intended to abandon his people.

Rose tried to sound calm. "Then where are we headed?" she asked lightly.

Dustan paused before answering. "There's a cabin deep in the forest. My brothers use it for . . . hunting. We'll be safe there until I can figure out what to do."

Some force urged Rose to leave it at that, but part of her mind rebelled. "If you can't take me to your home," she said slowly, "why did you come to meet my father? What if he had chosen you?"

Dustan leaned forward, resting his elbows on his knees, his head down. "Does it matter, if I love you now?"

Rose's thoughts flew from her head. He still loved her. When he said that, nothing else seemed to matter. She let go of her fear, let the feelings of trust and desire wash over her and carry the worries away. She moved closer to Dustan on the log, resting her fingers lightly on his leg.

But Dustan stood, letting her hand fall. "Let's try to sleep," he said. He surveyed the ground and offered his hand to pull her up. "It's not quite as soft as last night."

Rose blushed, remembering the last time they'd been together. It seemed like a dozen moons ago. Was Dustan thinking of what they'd shared? He was looking overhead, scanning the trees.

"It's plenty warm," Rose said, just to say something. Her skin felt tight with the fire's heat. Even her hair had dried, tangled and curling, stiff from the residue of ocean salt.

Dustan turned to her. "Stay here a moment."

He picked his clothing off the branch and hopped for a moment as he donned the britches. Rose watched for the ripple of air as he passed through the boundary. Dustan approached a pine tree with low branches. He reached for a branch and lithely pulled himself up, and within a heartbeat, he had scaled the trunk and disappeared. How patient he'd been the previous night, waiting for her to climb the ladder up the oak tree. He didn't even need a ladder.

A few minutes passed. What could he be doing, Rose wondered, up in a tree? The tree's branches shook, as if an eagle had taken off. She peered up into the darkness. But still nothing happened. The branches continued to shake, while the nearby trees only swayed slowly in the wind. Rose kept watch, praying he wouldn't fall. The tree stilled.

Dustan emerged from the branches, swinging himself down with one hand as he clutched his bulging shirt against him. He dropped to the ground. Rose ran toward him. A few steps beyond the fire, the air squeezed at her as she left the protected circle, moving into the frigid night.

"Get back where it's warm," Dustan said.

Rose turned, but she could no longer see the fire, only a faint glow where she knew it should be. Dustan's arm came around her, and he ushered her back into the circle, and the warm air enveloped her.

By the side of the fire, he used his feet to build up a pile of dried leaves from the forest floor. When he released his shirt's hem, a cascade of feathers tumbled out, spreading as the air caught them and they drifted down.

Rose stared. "Where did you get those? You wouldn't harm a bird."

"No, it's a few feathers from many birds. I simply asked them."

The feathers floated through the air. Soft and tickling, they landed on the leaves and around Rose's ankles. Dustan shook the last few from his shirt and rolled it into a bundle, and dropped it on the feathers. "I hope it will do," he said.

Rose was still staring in wonder.

"Lie down," he said gently. He touched her hand, and as she gave it to him, he sat, pulling her after him. He moved to sit close beside her, and her head came to rest on the bundled shirt.

"Would you like me to stay by you?"

Rose looked up at him. The soft feathers made her drowsy, suddenly, as did Dustan's soothing voice. "Always," she murmured. He squeezed her hand. The fire dimmed without losing its warmth. Rose yawned. Her eyelids drooped.

When her eyes closed, the crashing of the sea returned, as did the feeling of being dragged through the waves. She again felt Murkel's clammy body pressed against her, and she shuddered.

Dustan's hand smoothed back her hair. "You're safe now," he said quietly, stroking her hair until she fell asleep.

Chapter 11

ᴢ

ALL THE NEXT DAY, WALKING through the forest, Dustan followed no path that Rose could see, but he walked in a straight line through the trees. He repeatedly looked up, so that Rose wondered if he was steering by the sun. They reached the cabin late in the day. As they entered the clearing with the cabin at one side, a tiny sparrow fluttered down to land on Dustan's shoulder.

"Thank you," Dustan murmured to the bird, who hopped across to the cabin's porch and waited. Dustan climbed the steps, glanced back at Rose, and opened the door.

Rose scanned the clearing. The cabin walls were made of long, roughly hewn logs, the gaps filled with mud. A stump with an axe wedged in it stood near the center of the clearing, and flowers nodded around the cabin porch. Rose ate her last hickory nut as Dustan reappeared, crouching to spread seeds on the porch. The sparrow hopped over, chirped once, and began to peck at the seeds.

He feeds the birds as well as me, Rose thought. Dustan had been cracking the hickory nuts with his bare hands as they'd walked, passing her the insides to eat. She'd wondered if he'd gathered them as she slept, or asked a squirrel to do it.

"Will you come in?" Dustan asked her.

Rose moved toward him. She was tired from the long day of walking, stiff from sleeping on the ground, and hungry in spite of the nuts. But she felt peaceful. Her chemise, crusted with salt, scraped about her knees. She'd never walked outside in so little clothing, and while she wouldn't want anyone but Dustan to see her, she'd enjoyed the freedom. Walking through the forest, she'd felt more free than she'd ever been in her life. A strange feeling had filled her. A lightness, like she might float off the ground.

When she'd mentioned it to Dustan, he had stopped walking to address her. "I think you're simply happy," he had said.

Had she never felt happy before?

Rose climbed the porch steps. The sparrow looked up at her, then resumed its pecking. Rose stepped over it to enter.

Outside, the cabin was much like her father's hunting cabins. Not that she'd ever seen one. There were paintings of them in the game room in the castle, along with the deer heads and animal skins that covered the walls.

But as she crossed the threshold, she saw that this was no human hunting cabin. A tree filled the space inside, growing up through the ceiling to the sunlight. How had she not noticed it from the outside? A hammock stretched between two limbs. Behind the tree, an oak settee stretched the length of the wall, with cushions on the seat, and more cushions were strewn on the floor. Fantastic artwork covered the walls, from metal forged into delicate leaves to glass ornaments sparkling in the light from the windows. Closer to the door, clay jars filled the shelves, and a neat stack of wood rested on a tall stone hearth. But in lieu of the usual cast iron pot hanging from a hook, a copper vessel stood on a tripod over the ashes.

Dustan came to take her hands.

"It's amazing," she said, looking again at the tree. "How did I not see it when I was outside?"

"A spell," Dustan said. "A human looking in the window

would see only an ordinary cabin, with dead animals and traps and firearms mounted on the walls. But you're with me."

"You can climb right out into the forest."

"Aye, but there's a spell to keep out the rain. Would you like to wash?" Dustan asked.

"I'd rather have a nap."

"Of course."

She thought he'd join her, but he dropped her hands, went to the pantry, and began peering into the jars.

Rose crossed the room. The hammock fascinated her, but she didn't know if she could manage to get into it. Instead she sat on the settee. Its cushions were stiff and a little dusty, but Rose was tired enough to sleep on the floor. She stretched out her stiff muscles and sighed as she settled on the cushions. Her feet ached from walking—when Dustan had asked, she'd insisted she was fine, for fear that he might try to carry her, or summon a deer to do it. Now the soles of her feet were cracked with raw blisters. Despite the pain, she fell asleep.

Something sizzled. Rose opened her eyes. Across the room and behind the tree, Dustan knelt on the hearth, which was ablaze with firelight. He scraped something from a pan into the copper pot. Overhead, the tree disappeared in darkness, and the cabin windows were dark.

A smell wafted through the air, something savory, making Rose's mouth water. She pushed herself up and stretched, feeling a thousand times better. As she crossed the floor to the hearth, she hobbled to avoid the blisters. Dustan glanced at her as she climbed beside him, before turning his attention back to the pot.

She looked over his shoulder. Hunks of potato were the only thing she recognized.

"What is it?"

"Stew."

"Yes, but what's in it?"

"Wild onions. Old potatoes. Dried mushrooms, resurrected

with water. Beans, likewise resurrected, and barley. And spices, of course. Flour to thicken it."

"It smells wonderful."

"Let's hope it tastes it."

He ladled the stew into bowls. Rose sat beside him on the edge of the hearth and he handed her a steaming bowl. She inhaled the mouth-watering scent.

The first swallow was delicious. It warmed her insides. She spooned another bite into her mouth, and she remembered Adela chastising her for eating too fast. Her father hoarded the wealth of the kingdom, yet she'd never had enough to eat, save the few times she sat at the head table. Rose again sensed her new freedom—a wideness filled with hope of happiness.

When she looked up from the empty bowl, licking the last bits off her spoon, Dustan's bowl was empty as well. He sipped water from a cup and handed it to her.

"Good?"

"It was delicious. Thank you."

"So this is the cabin," Dustan said.

"I've never seen anything like it."

"I would hope not. We're safe here, but I'll have to think of something else. I don't fancy being here if my brothers come."

"Are they trouble?"

"Trouble. Yes, that's one way to say it." Dustan patted her knee. "Wait here a moment." He went to the pantry and rummaged about, looking behind pots and jars until he found something. He returned with a small glass vessel. Rose thought of the sleeping potion. Was it still outside her tower window in the castle, wrapped in the pair of gloves she'd found on the beach? She'd never learned where the gloves came from. Not that she'd tried. Once Dustan had appeared, she'd had someone real to daydream about.

Dustan sat by her side and gently lifted one of her legs, swiveling it until her foot rested over his lap. He poured a few drops from the vessel into his hand. When he touched her foot, she winced, but the pain evaporated. He rubbed the salve over her sole. When he returned her foot to the ground, the blisters no longer hurt, and they looked less raw.

"Other one," he said, and repeated the treatment with her other foot.

As he finished, she rubbed her foot against him. "So, what's there to do around here?" she asked, her toes pressing against his body just below his belly. He smiled, but he shook his head.

"Not tonight." He squeezed her ankle. "I need to rest." He lifted her leg off his lap, stood, and pulled her to her feet. "Will you be able to sleep again so soon?"

"I will lie with you, whether I sleep or not."

"You want to try the hammock, don't you?"

"Yes."

He pointed to a knob on the tree trunk. "Put your foot there, and pull the hammock toward you, and get your seat on it. Then let go and swing back."

Rose stood tentatively, but there was no pain. She approached the tree and climbed onto its thick roots, and pulled herself onto a low branch. With her foot on the knob, she reached for the hammock. She sat, let go, and swung free.

"Now turn and lie down," Dustan said from below. As she relaxed, he followed her up. "Hang on."

Dustan pulled the hammock toward himself, and the world tilted. She dipped as he sat, nudging her over, and then they swung again.

Overhead, faint silver light illuminated the still branches. Rose could no longer see the ceiling, only stars, as if the roof of the cabin had vanished. But neither the wind nor any night animals made a sound. Occasional pops crackled from the dying fire. Rose rested her chin on Dustan's arm, breathing in his scent. The hammock slowed until it hung still. Soon Dustan's breathing changed, quieting into the gentle rhythm of sleep. Still awake, Rose watched him. She would never get tired of this.

THE DAYS PASSED. DUSTAN SHOWED Rose all kinds of things—the spring down in the trees where clear and clean water flowed, the stems of the wild onions that grew in sunny patches in the forest, the berries that were safe to eat. He taught her how to light a fire with sticks and hay, and how to handle the axe to chop firewood and kindling. She marveled at the blister that formed on her hand, but Dustan rubbed more of his salve into her skin and the blister hardened.

Their second night, he rolled out a giant tub and filled it with several buckets of water he had heated over the fire, and Rose enjoyed her first ever bath with no one watching. Dustan ignored her, making an inventory of the jars and vessels in the pantry, and calling out their contents—desiccated mushrooms, salt, acorn flour, balms for wounds, and soap for cleaning. The bath water never seemed to cool.

But he wouldn't make love to her. She hinted, reaching for him, pulling him with her onto the cushions of the settee, but he resisted. He said he was tired, or busy, or once he simply replied, "Not yet." And then he'd pull her in and kiss her forehead and hold her until she stopped worrying. But she didn't understand what he was waiting for.

On the fourth day, Rose ate her breakfast of hot barley sweetened with honey, along with the fairy tea Dustan made her every morning. Dustan came to sit beside her.

"I have a plan," he said.

Rose stopped eating.

"I could pass as a forester," he said. "In a small town. I could find work. If we left Sylvania, traveled far enough, you wouldn't be recognized."

Rose gasped. He would leave his home to be with her? She hadn't dared imagine how they could end up together, but now he was offering to give up everything for her. And they'd leave Sylvania. They'd be free of her father.

What would it be like to live in a cottage, to tend a garden, weave baskets, clean laundry? She didn't care, as long as she was with Dustan. But he hadn't mentioned bonding rites. Maybe he didn't intend to form a life-bond with her. Or maybe the customs were different for fairies.

"You don't like the idea."

"I do. It's just a lot. You'd leave—"

Something scratched at the door.

Dustan leapt to his feet, surveying the windows. Rose saw only the forest.

"Get back," he said, pointing, and she scrambled to the wall. Dustan approached the door and opened it.

"Well, hello," he said, and in walked the dog from that day on the beach, tail wagging as he sniffed Dustan's ankles.

Rose moved from the shadows. "I know this dog. He belongs to one of the guards."

Dustan focused on the dog. "He's warning us. Stay out of sight." Dustan led the dog outside and shut the door.

Rose peeked out the corner of a window, hesitant despite the cabin's spell. When she had peered in from outside, she'd seen both a hunting cabin with its animal heads and muskets, *and* the faint outline of the tree. Plus, she wasn't sure if the fairy spell would hide *her*.

Dustan walked to the stump where they split firewood and pulled out the axe. He picked up a log and chopped the axe into it. An animal howled. Three hunting dogs loped into the clearing, circling each other and panting. One howled again. The beach dog stayed near Dustan.

A moment later, six guards rode into the clearing, their clothes askew. A scratch ran down one horse's flank, and briars clung to the guards' legs. Dustan stood still, holding the axe.

"State your name," said the forward guard.

"I am Prince Dustan of Skye, a recent guest of your king."

"A prince? Chopping wood? Why are you still in the king-dom?"

"I have leave to stay in my friend's cabin. I wanted to be alone with my broken heart, now that Princess Rose has been given to another. Lucky man."

"He won't be lucky when we find him," the guard said, and he dismounted. Walking over to Dustan, he continued, "He took the princess and disappeared. After we delivered her, the king discov-ered he'd been tricked. Shells, my ass! Trunks full of pebbles. Well, we hadn't seen no ship leave so we hurried to the beach. Left all his tents, the whole company gone. And the princess. All we found were her shoes on the sand, and her dress stuck in the rocks, all in pieces. When we find him, he'll suffer."

Dustan's face looked horrified. "You don't think she's drowned?"

"She better not. If the king don't get her back, we'll all be in for it." The guard reached into his breast pocket. "We found these in the princess's room," he said as he withdrew the gloves. "The dogs led us here. We hoped to find her with Murkel, but we find you. Explain yourself."

"I gave the princess my gloves as a token of love. She asked for something to remember me by."

Rose held her breath. If the guards realized the gloves actually led to her, they would pack her onto a horse back to her father. And they'd kill Dustan.

"And this?" The guard held up the vial of potion. "We tried it on a peasant. We know it's a sleeping potion, a real powerful one. She had it wrapped in your gloves. Any idea why?"

"Maybe she hoped to use it to escape Prince Murkel."

"How would the princess buy a potion like this?"

Dustan lowered the axe and held out a hand for the vial. He examined it. "I'd ask her ladies-in-waiting. One of them should know."

The guard flung the gloves to the ground and cursed. Dustan slipped the vial into his pocket.

The guard's horse abruptly stepped forward, nudging him and snorting. The guard turned, swatted the horse away, and turned back to Dustan. Dustan held out the vial of potion. Rose shouldn't have taken her eyes off him. She had missed something.

Dustan put a hand on the forward guard's shoulder. "I will rally my people and return to join your search. If there's any hope of recovering the princess, I will continue looking. Maybe her father would look more favorably on me."

The guard didn't reply, just glanced at Dustan's clothing and nodded. The guard remounted and the group turned their horses to go. The pack of dogs lit out into the forest, all but the beach dog, which stayed at Dustan's feet. One guard whistled, and Rose recognized Aidan, but the dog didn't budge. Aidan whistled again. After the other guards had filed out of the clearing, Aidan turned and followed them.

Dustan reached down and picked up the gloves from the dirt. He scanned the cabin windows until his gaze stopped on Rose. He nodded. When she came outside, Aidan's dog leapt at her, licking her face as she bent to pet him.

"Your gloves, m'lady?" Dustan said, holding them out.

Rose stood and smiled. "I found them on the beach, before I met you," she said. "I imagined they might belong to a prince. I kept them secret, so I could daydream about him."

"But they do belong to a prince." The spine-chilling voice echoed through the clearing.

Rose cried out, stumbling back, and Aidan's dog growled. Dustan's hand tightened on the handle of the axe.

King Murkel emerged from the trees.

His face looked broken, his nose crooked. His skin had a strange greenish hue. He wore ill-fitting peasant clothes. The trousers hung not quite over his knees, and the shirt struggled to close over his hairy chest.

"What do you want?" Dustan said.

"I wanted to see who the king's men were tracking, so I followed them. And I find you."

"The king knows you're a swindler. There's a price on your head."

"*I'm* a swindler?" Murkel said. "The princess deserves the truth, Dustan. I'm not the only swindler here."

Rose's heart pounded.

Dustan stood silently as Murkel continued. "You've brought her to your family's hunting cabin. Isn't that sweet. But fairies don't hunt, do they? Foolish plant eaters, they won't even kill a fish or steal a bird's eggs. Why don't you tell the princess what your brothers really use the cabin for?"

A river of fear coursed through Rose. Dustan's hand was white where it gripped the axe.

"And why don't you try on the mysterious gloves the dear girl found on the beach? I believe they'll fit you, won't they? Because you were on the beach that day. I watched you from beneath the waves as you put a spell on her. Can't get a woman to love you without magic, can you?"

Murkel turned to Rose. "What you feel for him, it's an illusion. If you'd—"

Dustan swung the axe, knocking the blunt side into Murkel's head. Murkel slumped to the ground.

Rose trembled, her breathing short and labored. It couldn't be true. But when Dustan turned to her, pain filled his eyes. Pain and guilt.

"Dustan, why?" Her voice was a whimper. "I would've loved you. Why did you do this?"

His hand released the axe and it clattered to the ground. He took a step toward her, and she resisted the urge to step away. But he didn't reach for her.

"I needed a tribute for the queen," he said. "I needed a mate. I used the spell to ensure success. But things changed. I'd thought humans heartless and foolish—until I met you. You changed me, Rose. And I pitied you, sold into a sham life-bond. I wanted to free you. And then in my tent, I knew I loved you. But you found out I'd lied to you. I didn't know if you'd forgive me. Then I heard you'd been sold to Murkel. I knew what he was, how dangerous he was. I climbed to your window, thinking I could overcome your womenfolk and help you escape, but you'd already been taken. So I found a fishing boat at the dock and called on the ocean creatures for help."

He'd rescued her. Gratitude and love swelled inside her. But were they real? Were any of her feelings real, or were they all just fairy magic? Of course she'd be grateful for the rescue, but would she love him without the spell? Would she lie with him the way she had?

"But I'm still under a spell," she said. "You say you love me, that you want to free me, but you've kept me enchanted. I'm your prisoner, instead of the king's."

"I was scared of losing you. The spell will wear off, it's probably already begun to—"

"But it wasn't real. My feelings weren't real."

Dustan's eyes closed, and his head bowed. "I'm sorry. Do you want me to remove the spell?"

"Yes," Rose whispered. Part of her wanted to go on loving him, however blindly. But removing the spell was the only way she'd ever know if her feelings were real.

She didn't have time to change her mind. Dustan moved quickly toward her, placing a hand on her head. His lips moved, mumbling words she didn't recognize, and tears formed in his eyes as she stared into them. Her eyelids fluttered and she crumpled to the ground.

PART 2
THE PEASANT

Chapter 12

ø

SOMETHING LICKED ROSE'S FACE. SHE opened her eyes.

It was a dog, a mutt, one ear up and one down, with a matted brown coat. The dog sat back on his haunches, watching her.

She was in a cabin, a hunting lodge, she guessed, based on the animal heads decorating the walls. A spiral staircase rose up the middle to a loft overhead. For a moment, the stair looked like a tree. When she looked at the dog, she saw branches in her peripheral vision. But when she looked back, it was simply a staircase. She squeezed her eyes tight. Her head felt fuzzy.

How had she gotten here?

She'd been at the beach, a beautiful windy day. She'd fallen asleep under her canopy, with all the usual attendants nearby. But then her memory went blank. The guards would never have let anyone take her. But here she was, alone in a strange cabin, wearing only her chemise.

She struggled to remember. There had been more princes, a dinner. Something bad had happened. She could feel the dread. But a fisherman rescued her . . . well, that was just her daydream again. But it felt real now, like it had actually happened. But what would a fisherman have to rescue her from?

Rose sat up on the settee, again looking around the cabin. She was sure she'd never been here before. Her groggy head refused to wake. She tried to stand but her knees wobbled, so she lowered herself to the floor and crawled to the window. The dog followed, tail wagging with encouragement.

Outside, the cabin was surrounded by forest, trees in every direction. Rose's heart began to hammer. She couldn't see any sign of the village—any village. She was in the middle of the forest. How would she get out, without being eaten by the bears or killed by one of the other hideous creatures that roamed through the woods?

She gripped the windowsill and pulled herself up. The cabin was in a clearing.

And a body was lying on the ground outside.

Rose clung to the sill as a shudder ran through her. The body didn't move. Pressing a hand to the wall to steady herself, she edged her way to the door. She opened it a crack and peeked out.

The body was facedown on the ground, as if dead. It was large—a man—and his hands and feet were bound with impossible-looking knots. Around the clearing, the trees were still.

Rose slipped out, glad the dog was following, and sat on the top step of the porch. Sunlight filtered through the leaves, but the forest was eerie and quiet; its earthy scent filled the air. She slid herself down until her bare feet were on the earth. Her knees wobbled as she stood, from fear or from something else, she wasn't sure. She waited till she could balance and stepped toward the man.

The dog walked ahead to sniff him and growled, then scuttled around him, sniffing madly as Rose crept closer. The man's face was mushed sideways on the dirt and his mouth drooling—his skin was a strange shade. Green. Had he been poisoned? But his body moved with breath. He was hideous, and familiar. He couldn't be one of the princes, not in the ill-fitting rags he wore. But how else would she know him? The princes were the only men she was allowed to meet.

Had her father given her to this man, and had he brought her here? What had he done to take her memory? Something rested on the ground near his head, an empty glass vial.

She had to get away from this spot. No matter how dangerous the forest was, she'd have to risk it. This man would wake eventually and try to get loose and hurt her. Or someone would come for him and find her there. Was that why he'd been left bound? Had guards been called? If her father's men came, they'd force her to honor her life-bond, if there'd been one. Or they'd bring her back to the castle so her father could sell her off as he'd planned. A terrible feeling reared up when Rose thought of the castle, a feeling worse than that of the miserable winters of living imprisoned there, without friends or hope. Something had happened. She didn't know what, but she couldn't go back.

And she was free. She didn't know how, but some miracle had set her free. Hope, excitement, and joy pushed through her fear of the forest. She barely recognized the feelings as they were so rare in her life, but now they swelled inside her. She would stay free, she decided, even if it meant walking into the forest alone.

A breeze blew through the clearing and Rose shivered in her thin chemise. It was ripped across the bottom so that it hung only to her knees. The sun was partway down the sky, its light blocked by the trees.

Rose returned to the cabin and rested against the doorframe. Now that she was moving, her legs lost their wobbliness. On the hearth, dried apples and nuts sat on a kerchief, and a small blanket was folded beside them. She hated to steal, but she would need food. She wrapped the sides of the kerchief up to make a bundle. She used the blanket around her shoulders like a shawl. She didn't see anything she could use as shoes.

She looked at her reflection in the glass of a window. Her face was smudged with dirt and streaked with tears. But her hair still looked like a princess's, a bit tangled, but glossy and long. She hunted through the shelves until she found a knife. It was plenty sharp, and when she sawed at the thick bunch of hair, the knife sliced right through. She cut the front extra short, so that bangs hid her eyes. She took the cuttings outside and scattered them, letting the wind blow away her old life. Should she take the knife? If she did encounter a bear, or something worse, she'd have no idea how to fight. A knife wouldn't help.

Rose called to the dog, and after he ran outside, she pulled the door shut.

"I don't know your name," she said to the dog. He sat and tilted his head to look up at her. "I will call you Aid, because you seem to be guarding me, and Aidan was my favorite of the castle guards." She climbed down the porch steps and faced the woods, avoiding the body on the ground. Her legs were steady now, though the fog hadn't cleared from her mind. At least she had daylight.

"Where's the nearest village?" she asked Aid. "Do you know which way to go?"

Aid turned his nose to the woods and set off, and Rose had only one choice—to follow.

Aid trotted through the trees and she picked her way after him, pulling her chemise free from the brambles that reached out to catch it. Once she and Aid left the clearing, birdsong echoed from the trees overhead, and the afternoon drone of insects surrounded them. Each time Aid got too far ahead, just before Rose called to him, he'd stop to sniff the ground, allowing her to catch up. He never acted alarmed, even when something rustled in the leaves or shook the branches inside a thick bush. The dog's calm spread to Rose. Surely if a dangerous creature were near, Aid would react. Rose saw only squirrels and once a deer who stood motionless as they passed.

The sun had been past midday when they'd left the cabin, and it was sinking quickly, but Rose didn't want to stop in the woods. She didn't think she could sleep on the ground under the trees, even with Aid for company. The dog kept on, and as all glimpses of the sun disappeared behind the trees, they at last came to a road through the forest. Aid turned left.

Rose didn't recognize their location. Not that she'd ever been on the forest road, save that one time when her mother had taken her into the woods. But she didn't see the castle spires through the trees, or hear the sound of horses. As they walked, she kept finding herself searching the treetops for any sign of the castle, relief coming each time she did not see it. With the sunset on her left side, they must be moving northward.

They walked on the packed surface of the road, but her feet didn't hurt. The forest floor had been remarkably soft, but now the hard road felt soft as well. As the light faded from the sky, the trees thinned. Night insects began to trill all around her. The road emerged into a pasture, and Rose breathed in the sweet smell of hay and sighed in relief. She was out of the woods, and this wasn't Woodglen. Overhead, the stars winked. The land looked different somehow, and she couldn't hear the crash of the ocean. Wooly sheep huddled behind a fence, and a curl of smoke rose up from the fire of the shepherd.

Rose kept walking until at last a village appeared around a bend. The moon had not yet risen. Starlight glittered in the night sky. Walking had warmed her, but as Rose entered the village, the chill spring air nipped at her thin dress, and she pulled her shawl tightly around her.

The streets were mostly empty as Rose followed Aid between the dwellings. After passing several cottages, they came into a cobblestone square. A shopkeeper locked his door and turned away from her. Laughter rang out at a pub. The two villagers who passed didn't seem to notice her.

Rose hesitated. She was no longer a princess. She couldn't ask for help and promise her father would reward her helper. And she couldn't give her real name.

The tower of the local grange hall rose up against the night sky. The sight of it reminded Rose of her mother. Before her mother had died, she had frequently taken Rose into Woodglen, and they would stop to chat with that village's grange leader, and then her mother would visit the homes of those who were sick or unable to get out, or where someone had a newborn baby. There had been a basket on her mother's arm, and she'd remove all kinds of wonderful things from it—jars of jam from the castle kitchens, fresh biscuits, vials of medicine. And they would share tea with the villagers, and sometimes there would be other children, although they always seemed as scared of Rose as she was of them.

Rose blinked and found herself back in the dark village square. She'd call herself Grace, she decided, like her mother.

A stone wall surrounded the village garden beside the grange hall. Rose approached the iron gate. The cold metal bit her fingers, and the hinges creaked terribly as she swung it open. She glanced behind her, but the square was deserted. She entered the garden.

Even hours past sunset, a faint warmth radiated from the stones of the wall. The late-day sun must have shone on it. Rose untied her shawl and spread it on the ground, lay down, and wrapped the shawl around her body. She scooched back until she pressed against the stone. Aid walked in a circle and sank down against her other side.

Rose was still. She watched the dark silhouettes of the spring flowers blooming near her as they waved in the starlight, and she heard the whisper of the leaves of the willow tree on the far side of the garden. Faint voices reached her from the pub, but as the hours passed, they quieted. She couldn't fall asleep, in spite of her fatigue. But she must've slept because now the sky lightened. She kept still, watching the sky brighten as birds sang and a rooster crowed.

Her situation was hopeless. She had no food, no coins, no friends. The grange might help her, but they'd want to know where she'd come from. If her father were looking for her, if he'd made an announcement, they might guess her identity. Of course, she could still go back, find the nearest guard, and turn herself in. She'd be warm and well fed by lunchtime. That's what she *should* do—stay safe, follow the rules.

But she'd vowed to stay free. She couldn't stop looking at the wide sky; at the pale, waning moon high above; at the first birds, flitting across the space. They managed to find food and shelter, and to avoid danger. Surely she could, too. It was worth the risks, not to live in a cage.

Chapter 13

ROSE WANTED TO STAY BY the garden wall all day, hidden from the village. The thought of being seen triggered an uncomfortable gnawing in her chest. But her stomach grumbled, and she'd eaten all of her apples and nuts. If she was to stay free, she would have to figure out what to do. Besides, better to be about early, before any guards appeared.

Aid stretched beside her, and when she looked at him, he thumped his tail.

Rose sat up and wrapped the blanket around her shoulders, covering her thin chemise. Aid scrambled to his feet, stretched again, and began sniffing around the flower beds. Rose ran her fingers through her hair. Now that it was short, it was easy to work out the knots. She peeked over the wall. In the square, people moved about, some pushing carts, others carrying baskets. A shout of laughter rang out. Since her mother had died, Rose had not been around people. She'd barely spoken with her own ladies-in-waiting. She had no idea how to talk to commoners.

But she didn't have a choice. With Aid alongside, she walked out into the square, hoping to find someone who might help her.

But as she walked slowly along the cobblestones, the villagers who cast glances her way quickly hurried on.

A small boy with a ball stopped near her, his eyes on Aid. Aid wiggled his rear, his tail waving frantically, and the boy came closer. In a flash, Aid snatched the boy's ball, ran five paces, and dropped it, asking to play. The boy ran to the ball and tossed it, and squealed when Aid caught it midair and brought it right back.

"Shamus!" Near Rose, a woman exited a shop with a parcel. "Away from that dog! He's a stray."

"He's my dog," Rose said, adding an awkward "ma'am" and a small curtsy. She wasn't sure of the villagers' language.

The mother's expression softened. "You never know, some-times they're practically wolves," she said. "But yours seems well behaved."

Aid pushed his head between the boy's legs and paraded about like a pony with the boy clinging on his back.

"What is your name, dear? Have you come far?"

"Yes," Rose said. "My name's Grace. I lived, er, south, on the other side of the forest." Once she'd begun, a story tumbled out. "My mother died, and my father sold me, but the man was a beast. He tried to kill me, and a neighbor helped me escape. I cannot go back to my father, and I won't return to that husband. I've walked through the forest, hoping to get away, to hide. But I don't know where to go. I don't even know where I am."

The woman's brow wrinkled. "You're in Woods Rest."

Woods Rest was north from Woodglen through the forest. She was lucky Aid had headed north on the forest road.

The woman pointed to the hall. "Past the hall there's a house, all stone. Just keep walking and you'll come to it. The grange keeps it for the poor, and several widows live there. They sew and raise chickens and do any number of things, but they live respectably. They may take you in."

"Thank you, ma'am."

The woman nodded, called to her son, and left.

Filled with new hope, Rose called Aid. She retraced her steps toward the hall. More villagers crossed the square now, and she was glad to leave, given her ragged clothing. The public house was quiet in the morning light. As Rose passed, a horrible face sketched on a poster plastered on the wall caught her attention.

It was the man from the woods.

Rose approached and tried to read the poster. She didn't know all of the words. She worked out the name in bold letters at the top. Murkel. Prince Murkel of Merlandia. So he was a prince. And the king was offering a reward for him, ten coins of gold. The king wanted Murkel for "crimes against the kingdom of Sylvania." That could be anything—killing a stag in the forest or not paying the annual crop taxes.

Rose studied the face, with its protruding lips and hooklike nose, and a quiver of fear shot through her. She'd have sworn that Murkel was one of the princes at the supper she'd attended, the same day she had been on the beach, the same evening her memories ended. What had he done?

Ten coins of gold, she thought as she turned away. Rose imagined her father's trunks of gold coins—the goblets and plates and chains—and snorted. How stingy. Still, ten gold coins could do much to help her now.

She passed the village garden and continued down the lane. Aid darted left and right, sniffing tufts of grass at the edge of the road. There was a smithy and a cooperage, both made of stone, but Rose knew the widows' stone house when she saw it, with chickens pecking in the yard and linens swaying in the breeze from several lines strung between the trees.

As she neared, the laundry parted to reveal two women rocking in chairs on the front porch. Rose had expected elderly women, as they were widows, but these looked to be thirty or so, older than any of her ladies-in-waiting, but younger than Adela. One had the darker skin and curly hair of a Norlian. Rose had never seen anyone from the sunny northern country, other than in paintings. The woman held a half-woven basket on her lap, and her hands stilled. They watched her approach, unsmiling.

Rose turned up the front path, her anxiety blooming. She curtsied when she reached the steps. "Good day," Rose said, looking from one to the other.

"Good day." The paler woman spoke. She was thin, with her straight hair pulled back tightly. Her hands held knitting, which she lowered into her lap. Still, neither of them smiled. "Can we help you?"

"A woman in the village said so." Rose hesitated, then gave her name and repeated her story, and the women listened without interrupting. They stood when she finished.

"Come in, Grace," said the paler one. "I am Kitty, and this is Ladi. There are five of us here, and room for another."

Relief washed over Rose. She didn't know who these women were, but at least for now, she had somewhere to stay.

She climbed the porch steps. She had not been in a house since before her mother had died. Paint peeled on the porch chairs, all of which were missing one or two spindles, and a worn rag rug covered the floor just inside the doorway. But the house looked tidy. At the end of a hallway, they entered a kitchen where two women chopped vegetables at a wooden table amid a profusion of glass jars. A large pot steamed on an iron stove. They looked up and put down their knives.

"This is Liza and Jane," Kitty said. "Grace."

Jane stepped forward, wiping her delicate hands on her apron, and reached for Rose. She smiled as she took Rose's hand and squeezed it. She was about Rose's age, her long hair pulled back in a loose braid. Liza watched with big eyes, but when Rose looked her way, her gaze fell back to the table, and blush splotches appeared on her cheeks.

Someone meowed. Aid sniffed at a tabby cat on the rug by the stove. The cat reached a lazy paw to pat Aid's nose. Aid walked in his circle and collapsed beside the cat.

Rose began to apologize, but Jane spoke first. "He's made friends with Mouser," she said, her eyes bright. She added, "Maryanne's coming with more water."

"Perfect, we'll have tea," Kitty said.

"Oh, I'll make us something to eat," Jane said, clapping her hands. "Are you hungry?" she asked Rose.

Rose nodded.

"Come," Kitty said, "I'll show you the house while we wait." She turned back into the hallway. A sitting room had a battered dulcimer resting on one of many worn chairs and a spinning wheel in the corner with a clump of white fleece still attached. Opposite was a dining room, with a sewing project laid on the table, as well as numerous half-woven baskets and jars filled with pickles and jam. Kitty folded the fabric, moving it onto a smaller side table, along with the baskets and jars. "We'll eat in here, so you can use the table. We're not very formal."

"I don't mind," Rose said.

"Upstairs are two large bedrooms, like dormitories really," Kitty continued, walking back to the kitchen. "With several beds," she added, when Rose didn't reply. Kitty pointed to the steps behind the stove. "Or, if you'd like a little privacy, there's a cubby back here." She walked around the table, where the abandoned potatoes and green beans waited half chopped. Jane was slicing bread, and Liza and Ladi had disappeared. Kitty stepped over Aid and Mouser and pulled open the curtain that hung from the steps. Behind it were large wooden crates with a thin mattress on top.

The space was small, but it looked so secret and private. "That would be wonderful," Rose said, and finally Kitty smiled.

"It's yours. We'll get you some blankets."

The back door flew open, and a fifth woman banged in, heaving a bucket of water onto the table. Liza came after her and shut the door. "Grace!" the new woman said, holding out a hand to shake. She had ruddy cheeks, dark hair in a messy bun, and a strong grip. "I'm Maryanne. You'll need a hot bath." She reached for a clay pitcher and began pouring the water into another kettle on the stove.

"I must be a sight," Rose said, remembering her face in the glass at the cabin, and that was before she'd slept a night on the ground.

"We've all been a sight at one time or another." Maryanne returned the pitcher to a hook on the wall and moved the kettle onto a different spot on the stove, feeling with her fingers for heat. She rolled out a washtub and poured the rest of the water in. "I'll fetch you some more," she said, and clomped back out the door. Outside the window, she headed across the yard between the rows of a garden, with the bucket in a wheelbarrow.

Jane had a plate ready, so they ushered Rose into the dining room and encouraged her to eat. The table had long benches on both sides. Jane and Liza sat opposite her. The bread was soft and yeasty, and the cheese practically oozed off, held in place by a leaf of lettuce. "It's the best meal I've ever eaten," Rose said, and she meant it. Jane beamed.

Rose had been hungry, of course, but also, the food tasted of freedom. She was sure one of the women had made the bread, another the cheese, and someone, probably Maryanne, had tended the lettuce in the garden.

Kitty came in with the tea, served in dainty but chipped cups on a wooden tray. "We only use the tea set on special occasions," she explained. "Someone donated it to the hall, and Kemp—he's the grange leader—he sent it to us. Said he had no use for it."

"Does he not have a wife?" Rose asked.

"No, she passed a few winters ago. And they were childless."

A silence followed.

From down the hall, the kitchen door banged again, and Rose took another bite. Kitty poured the tea and passed the cups before sitting in the chair at the table's head. A moment later, Maryanne entered and flopped onto the bench beside Rose.

"Your bath water's heating," she said, reaching for a piece of bread. "Is this for me?" she asked.

Jane nodded.

"Thank you," Rose said to Maryanne.

Maryanne nodded, her mouth already full.

Ladi entered, carrying a folded towel and dress. "Try this after your bath," she said quietly to Rose, placing the bundle on the bench. "Might be a bit loose, but 'tis patched and clean. We can make you something better."

Rose rubbed her fingers over the rough cloth. The blue dye had faded. She remembered the dresses she used to wear, brocade with embroidered flowers and jewels sewn in. The tight corsets and layers of petticoats. She smiled. "This is perfect."

After Rose had finished eating, Maryanne accompanied her to the kitchen, where she poured the steaming water from the pots on the stove into the washtub. She tested it with a finger. "Get in there quick before it cools," she said before she left, drawing a curtain across the doorway.

Rose had never had a bath by herself. Or had she? Something flickered in her mind, like a candle that went out before she caught it, and she could only see the smoke, until that, too, was gone. She shook her head. She'd always had ladies' maids hovering over her bath, whether she'd wanted them or not.

She undid her shawl, pulled the chemise over her head, and peeled off her underclothes. She stepped into the hot water and sat, her whole body relaxing, melting into the water, and she took a moment to enjoy it.

Rose hesitated as she picked up the cake of soap and the loofah sponge from the tray on the floor. Someone might recognize her if she looked less ragtag. As she washed the grit from her body, she remembered the powder that had been applied at the castle, the paint on her lips, and the combs in her hair. Even her father might not recognize her without her dresses and makeup.

She scrubbed her face clean, and worked her way down to her

tired feet, which somehow had survived the hours of walking bare-foot without blistering. Her short hair was easy to wash and dried quickly, light and fluffy, in the heat of the stove. Maryanne had left a pail on the stove for rinsing, and it was a good thing because the bathwater was cloudy with grime when Rose stepped out.

Under the folded dress was a pair of knitted wool socks. Rose would need shoes, and she had no way to pay for them. Maybe helping with the chores could be traded for the things she needed. Or . . . Maybe she could get those ten gold coins for turning in the man in the forest. But if she did that, it might draw the attention of the guards. She couldn't risk it.

When Rose had dried herself and donned the coarse blue dress and the thick socks, she didn't know what to do. It would be po-lite to go sit with the others. Their voices drifted in from the front porch. No doubt they had questions for her. They'd want to know if she could be useful, but she knew so little about household chores. She'd never made bread or cheese. At least she could use a needle—maybe she could learn to mend things.

But she resisted. The whole of yesterday afternoon she'd been on her feet, walking through the woods in a daze, trying and fail-ing to remember how she'd gotten there. And the truth was sinking in, more and more, that she was truly free from the castle, from her father and the life she had dreaded for so long. If he couldn't find her, maybe he'd give up, and she'd live out her life in peace.

She'd pushed her feelings down to focus on her situation. Now she was safe, with kind people, and everything she'd been sup-pressing was rising to the surface. She wanted to sit quietly and let it all out. In the castle she'd had to tolerate Adela's presence, hour after hour. Somehow, she didn't think her new friends would mind if she sat alone for a while.

Rose opened the back door. A vegetable garden stretched away from the house. At the far end, Maryanne knelt in a row. The gar-den reminded Rose of someone, a gardener, but she couldn't think who. It was another blank spot in her memory where she was sure something should go.

Maryanne looked up, waved, and continued her work. Rose followed a path of flat stones to the wall that bordered the yard under the trees. Beyond the trees, wide pastures spread in the sunlight. Farther down the wall, stile steps climbed over. She walked to the stile and perched on the top step.

Rose stopped trying to remember what had happened to her after that day on the beach. She listened to the leaves stirring overhead and the drone of bees in the garden. And memories came to her. She saw Prince Murkel at the castle, at a supper and later in the garden. There'd been three princes that night—Murkel; a goofy, drunk young man; and a third. She remembered nothing about the third. Her father had picked Murkel, she felt sure of it. And now he was a wanted criminal. What had he done? Her father wouldn't care if Murkel had beaten her, and she didn't have bruises.

He hadn't paid for her.

The thought came, clear as a lark song at dawn. Of course. Murkel had cheated her father. Nothing else would matter to the king. Which meant that her father would want her back to try again. Murkel wasn't the threat. Her father's guards were.

Somehow, Prince Murkel had ended up being her salvation.

Chapter 14

ROSE AND MARYANNE WERE WEEDING when Ladi called them for midday dinner. Maryanne gave a report on the tomatoes, peppers, and beans. Kitty spoke to Jane about items they needed from the market. She mentioned shoes and fabric for Rose, and Rose wondered what they might be sacrificing to pay for her items.

How could she ever pay them back? Weeding in the garden would never cover the cost of her room and board, much less the clothing. But turning in Prince Murkel would. Ten coins of gold! But if she did it, she'd bring the king's guards to the village. They might want to question the person who'd found him. And once they saw her eyes, they'd recognize her. She'd never met anyone else with the defect that tinted them such a bright green. Or had she? Once again, she sensed she was forgetting something.

She pondered Prince Murkel all through the meal. If she did nothing, said nothing, she'd avoid the risk of capture, but she'd be living in fear. Was that how she wanted to start her new life? She could outsmart the guards. She just had to be careful.

After they'd eaten, Rose pulled Kitty aside in the kitchen.

"There's something I forgot," Rose said. "The man on the

wanted poster, on the wall of the pub. I saw him in the woods. He was passed out drunk, and his hands and feet were bound."

"That prince?" Kitty asked.

Rose nodded. She hoped Kitty wouldn't ask too many questions.

"Skies, passed out and tied in the woods. What on earth . . . ?"

"I was so focused on escape, I kept going. But the poster reminded me. The reward. I . . . I thought it might help out, if we could get it." She avoided Kitty's gaze. Her story sounded deceitful. But truly, she had no idea how she or Murkel had gotten to that cabin. "Besides, if no one else retrieves him, he'll—"

"Could you find him again?"

"Aid could." Aid's ears perked up. He'd spent the morning sleeping with Mouser.

"I'll get Kemp," Kitty said. "He'll find some men to go." She left the kitchen.

"That one's got an awful face," Jane said as she wiped crumbs from the table. "That wanted man. I had a nightmare about him." At the washtub, Liza looked up and grinned.

"May I help?" Rose asked.

"Just rest," Jane said. "To hear Maryanne tell it, you labored all morning in the garden."

"It was nothing," Rose said, but her fingers went to the callus on her hand. Had it formed just this morning? It would still be a blister if it had.

"You can help soon enough."

"He makes me think of a fish," Liza said suddenly, "with those thick lips."

Rose nearly choked.

"A fish!" Jane replied. "You're exactly right. In my dream, he was a dragon, and he was marching through the village, incinerating all the girls who wouldn't lie with him." She and Liza burst into giggles as Rose slipped out.

Rose stood in the hallway, her heart racing. A fish . . . She felt Murkel's clammy body pressed against hers, on the beach. She remembered now. Murkel dragging her into the sea, planning to keep her prisoner in an undersea dungeon. He'd been mad. And he'd had a giant tail.

Whatever had addled her memory was making her thoughts nonsensical.

But even if she *had* been on the beach with Prince Murkel, how had she gotten from the seaside to the cabin in the forest? She let the dark memory in. Murkel shredding her dress, dragging her into the ocean, the cold waves washing over her. His arms wrapping around her like tentacles, his breath in her ear. Through the darkness she saw the fisherman who had rescued her. Was it just her daydream again? She couldn't remember his face or his name.

Rose took a deep breath to collect herself and walked out to the porch. Aid followed, and a moment later, Mouser pawed at the door to be let out. He wound around Rose's ankles as she stared up the road, her hand gripping the post that supported the roof. After a few minutes, Kitty appeared down the lane, walking with a man.

"Miss Grace," the grange leader said as they neared. He was shorter than Kitty, balding, and had eyes that Rose was sure would twinkle if he smiled. "I hear you've found ten gold shells."

"This is Kemp," Kitty said. "He's got Robert the cooper and Wells from the smithy to go."

"And me?" Rose asked.

"Let's see what your dog can do," Kemp said. "Besides, you'd need a pair of shoes."

Rose gave directions and sent Aid off. After they left, she sat on the porch, the chair rocking gently. Mouser settled on her lap. Kitty and Ladi worked quietly beside her. The anticipation of Murkel's capture didn't seem to faze them. Nothing did. Who were they? Five young widows, all in one town? Something was strange about it, but Rose didn't dare ask. How could she, when the stories were sure to bring sadness? But the way they'd taken her in . . . it was like they'd known what had happened to her, expected it even. How could they know her story, if she didn't?

The sun was setting when Kemp reappeared. Aid broke into a gallop down the lane.

"That's a smart dog you have," Kemp said when he reached the porch. He jingled something in his hand, held it out to Kitty, and dropped it into her fingers. She opened her hand to show Rose the gold coins.

Jane came out the door and asked, "Did you get him?"

Liza followed her out.

"We did. Or rather, Aid did," Kemp said.

Aid's tail thumped at the sound of his name.

"What will happen to him?" Jane asked.

"They sent word to the castle. Guards will come for him tomorrow. After that, who knows?"

As Rose rested on her pallet that night, Kemp's words echoed in her head. Her father's guards were coming. Did Murkel know she was alive? That she'd been at the cabin just yesterday? Regardless, he'd probably tell them she was alive. If she were dead, his sentence would certainly be death. If he revealed that he'd seen her at the cabin, they'd begin searching. And here she was, in the nearest village. Should she leave tomorrow? Hide in the woods? What would she tell her housemates? She barely fell asleep before it was dawn.

ALL THE NEXT DAY, WITH a knot of fear in her stomach, Rose waited for news of the guards' arrival. Several times she tried to speak to Kitty or Ladi, but faltered. Would they keep her secret if they knew? She couldn't see them turning her in, but she'd only known them a day.

But she couldn't bring herself to leave. She could hardly survive on her own, hiding in the woods. So she kept waiting to see what would happen, even as a noose seemed to be closing around her neck. She stayed on the porch, where she could see if anyone approached the house.

"The town's buzzing with gossip," Jane reported when she returned from the market. "The 'weeping widows' found the wanted man."

"I wish they wouldn't call us that," Kitty said. "Mind you don't say it around Maryanne."

"I'd never," Jane said, but her voice had dropped, and she hurried into the house.

The weeping widows? Rose looked at Kitty, but Kitty appeared focused on her knitting. Ladi stared up the road at the town. Who were these women who'd taken her in?

A cloud of dust rose over the trees near the village. A moment later, the banging of metal on cobblestones rang in the air.

"Looks like the visitors are here," Kitty said.

Rose watched in silence, filling with dread. When a horse and rider emerged from the trees, heading down the lane toward them, she stood.

"I must go inside," she said. "Aid, come." Her gaze met Ladi's, and Ladi stared back at her, her brow wrinkling. Rose broke away and entered the house.

Inside, the kitchen was empty. She sat in her cubby with Aid pulled halfway on her lap, the curtain drawn, and prayed that whoever was coming would leave without seeing her. What if he asked how the women had found Murkel, or if they'd seen a young woman with an unusual green tint in her eyes?

The harsh tone of a guard's voice came from out front. The front door opened.

Rose stood, considered the staircase, and then dashed to the back door with Aid on her heels, as the guard's voice boomed from the hallway. Outside, Maryanne looked up from her gardening.

"Please," Rose said, looking about. "Don't tell them I'm here."

Maryanne's lips tightened. Rose ran to the wall and scrambled over the stile, and sank onto the ground on the far side, pressed against the stones. Aid came after her.

The door creaked open and banged shut. Kitty's voice drifted over. "Grace?" Rose squeezed her eyes tight and kept perfectly still.

Maryanne's voice boomed out. "Here I am. I'm Grace."

Rose rested her head back against the stones as the guard began asking questions. The voices stopped speaking, and the door banged once more. Still Rose didn't move. She heard only quiet steps.

Ladi said, "He's gone."

Rose looked up. Ladi sat on the wall and reached a hand down to help Rose up.

"Are you the princess?" Ladi asked as Rose settled beside her.

Rose pushed her bangs away from her face. "My name is Rose. Were they looking for someone with my eyes?"

"Yes."

"Not many have them. I've never met anyone else."

Ladi smoothed Rose's hair back into place. "I had them myself once," she said.

"You did? But your eyes are brown."

"The green came and then it faded."

"Not mine. I was born with the defect. Although my mother said they were beautiful, not a defect but a blessing."

Ladi's hand had stopped. "You were born with those eyes?"

"Yes."

"That changes things." Before Rose could ask what things, Ladi asked, "Who is Dustan?"

Rose started. "Dustan? I don't know. Why do you ask?"

"Guard said Prince Murkel was raving on about a Dustan, said he kidnapped Princess Rose and put a spell on her, and took her off to do no good with her. Made the king's men frantic. Seems they just encountered this Dustan, and he feigned innocence, and now he's disappeared. They're asking all through the village."

"I didn't mean to bring trouble," Rose said.

"Always trouble, child, whether you bring it or not." They were still a moment.

"What did you mean," Rose asked, "that your eyes were this color? They changed?"

"'Tis no defect," Ladi said, and sighed. "Fakei have eyes like emeralds—the fairies, that is. You know there are fairies, yes?"

Fairies? Like in the storybooks? Rose simply nodded.

"Well, those under a fakei spell sometimes get the eyes. All of us in this house arrived with them, and with the same story." Ladi's voice sounded strained. "We all met a man, fell in love. Just like that. No courtship, no shy meetings, no idea who he was. Just a sultry, handsome stranger promising our every wish." Wishes. A tingle crept up Rose's spine.

"Was a spell, of course," Ladi continued. "We were willing to do anything to be with him. Leave our family, our village. If we dreamed of sharing a life-bond someday, our dreams no longer mattered. All we wanted was to be with him, bonded or not. We went to live with him, away from our village, in the woods. It was bliss. He doted on us, did all the chores, and loved us every night. And of course, we stopped taking our herbs."

"Herbs?"

"Didn't they give you the bitter herbs at the castle?" Ladi asked, surprised.

"The tea," Rose said. "There was bitter tea every morning. Adela said it was for my health."

"The bitter herbs stop the body from forming a child. That's why they served it to you."

"But I was never even in a room with a man!"

"Guess they were taking precautions. In case you met someone. You find a way to be with someone you love."

Ladi's words sent another tingle up Rose's back.

Ladi let out a sigh. "My papa oversaw the Norlian trading outpost at Nor Bay. I loved my papa, but once that spell was on me? I knew I'd hurt him, but I couldn't seem to stop myself. I followed that man, that lying fakei, right away from my home. I thought I was in paradise. Never questioned why I couldn't go back to my papa, share my new family with him, was just a haze of bliss. And then I woke and he was gone. And my child."

Rose listened in horror. Nothing she could say would help.

After a moment, Ladi continued. "Our families wouldn't take us, or we were too ashamed to go. I came here 'bout ten winters ago, went to the grange. Kemp lived here with his wife, and they took me in. When I looked in the mirror, I saw my eyes but didn't understand. They'd always been brown like now, but they were tinted green. Was only later I learned what it meant, from Old Synne."

Rose ached for Ladi. How awful, to be seduced, to think you'd found true love, only to be tricked. Had that happened to her? Surely she'd remember. She couldn't possibly have had a child. It was still springtime. She couldn't have lost a whole nine moons of memories. Could she?

And who was Dustan?

"Then Kitty arrived," Ladi continued, "and a few winters later, Liza, and Jane, and just last autumn Maryanne. Kemp's wife passed, so he left us the house and moved to a room at the hall.

"The spell wore off, the green faded, but not the memories. Each of us longs for her child, and maybe for the man, too, or the man he seemed to be. We don't talk about it. The villagers think we're widows. The men try to court us, but we're not interested. That's why they call us the weeping widows."

Rose nodded in response.

"But you say your eyes have always been this color. That's different. No fairy spell could last that long. Only explanation is, one of your parents was a fairy."

Chapter 15

ROSE FELT STUNNED. ONE OF her parents was a fairy? It certainly wasn't her father. Had her mother been a fairy?

"That doesn't make sense," Rose said. "I lived in the castle. Both my parents were human, unless I've forgotten everything about my mother."

"May have been another," Ladi said slowly. "Another man who loved your mother, or put her under a spell. But she kept you. Maybe he loved her for real. He let her keep you."

"Did my father know?" Rose said. "The king, I mean."

"That I don't know."

If the king was not her father, or if he'd suspected he was not, it would explain why he'd never been warm to her, why he'd called her eyes defective, why he planned to sell her to the highest bidder.

That night, Rose couldn't sleep, going over and over it all. Fairies! Yet it didn't surprise her as much as it should. She had always suspected they still existed. She pictured them dancing in a forest clearing. Her mother had shown her a drawing in a book. In the pictures they looked lighthearted and joyous. Yet now she knew the truth. They were cruel.

And she was half fairy.

Fairies could create illusions to hide themselves. Could she? Now that she'd tasted freedom, she couldn't let it go, but the king would never stop hunting her. She didn't want to spend her life hiding in the house. Maybe she could learn to hide herself in other ways.

Ladi had suggested that Rose visit Old Synne, across the village. Synne, the village herbalist, had helped Ladi and the others when they'd arrived in Woods Rest. She claimed to be familiar with fairy magic because she'd spent seasons in the forest—she had even encountered fairies when she was young. Perhaps Synne could explain what had happened to her and help her fill the gaps in her memory.

EARLY THE NEXT MORNING, ROSE mounted the steps to Synne's porch. When she'd awoken and joined her housemates for breakfast, no one had said a word to her about the guard's visit, just as Ladi had promised. They all had secrets, Ladi had said, and no one would pry into hers.

Rose rapped her knuckles on the thin wooden doorframe at Synne's. The door bounced on its hinges with each knock.

A stooped woman appeared. She took one look at Rose's face and nodded, opening the door wider to admit her.

"Ladi sent you?" she asked in a cracked voice.

"Yes, and this bread for you, and this." Rose handed Synne the knitted shawl Ladi had sent.

"Your name, child?"

"Ro—Grace. It's Rose, but they are calling me Grace, so that my . . . my father won't find me."

"Let me make some tea, and you can tell me more," Synne said. She motioned Rose into a chair by the hearth and hobbled to the stove to pour water into the kettle.

Dried flowers and herbs hung over Rose's head, and their mixed scents filled the room. Clay pots and glass jars filled the shelves that lined the walls. A rough wooden table in the center of the room had tools and twine on it. A fat orange cat slept on the blankets on a pallet in the corner, partly hidden by a curtain.

"Now tell me how you've come to be here," Synne said, joining Rose and bringing two steaming mugs.

Rose thought a moment before beginning. "I lived at the castle," she said. "I thought I was the king's oldest daughter. My mother came across the Sar Sea to bond with him. Their bond secured a peace with Sarland."

"Sarland? Was she a lord's daughter?" asked Synne.

"Yes, I think so. After her death, no one spoke of her, except sometimes Kate. She ran the kitchen in the castle. She used to tell me things."

"How old were you when she died?"

"Six. I don't remember it, although I've heard I was there. She fell from a horse while riding. After that, they never let me out. Mother used to take me places, but after she died I was trapped. One time I tried to visit the village . . . ." Rose shuddered, remembering. "They caught me and locked me in the dungeon for hours.

"Then my father—the king, I mean—began inviting princes to meet me. Everyone said he was waiting for a good price." Rose paused as a mix of shame and anger washed over her.

Synne sat quietly.

"Something happened," Rose continued. "I awoke in the woods, in a cabin. Ladi told me what happened to her, but my story is different. I cannot remember anything, I just see a few pieces of a picture with blank spots. And something else—my eyes have always been this color. Ladi says it means I am half fairy."

Synne put her mug onto the table. "Being half fairy explains your eyes, but there could still be a spell. These blank spots, it could be a spell to hide the memories. Or if a spell were removed abruptly, it might hide the things that happened while it existed."

"Hide?"

"Yes. The memories could not be taken, but they could be obscured."

"Could they be recovered?"

Synne winked. She pushed herself up from her chair and shuffled to the shelves. She took down several jars and put the kettle back onto the stove.

"I can brew you a tea to help you remember."

"How is that possible?"

"Herbs and roots are powerful. Rosemary, sage, ginseng . . . all have power over the memory. Rosemary and sage you know, I'm sure. Ginseng is less common, but I traded with a merchant for some. And you being half fairy will bring the memories back more easily." Synne paused. "Are you sure you want to remember? It may be painful to know what you've lost."

"I would rather know," Rose said. "How can I hide from the king if I'm missing part of the story?"

"You want to hide?" Synne began measuring herbs into a mug.

"The castle was a prison, I know that now. The king was not my father. He planned to sell me. I think he chose someone. That prince on the posters in the square, the one they caught yesterday. I've seen him before. I can't remember it, but I think something bad happened. I don't want any more of that life."

After a moment of silence, Synne began to crush the herbs.

"How do you know about fairies?" Rose asked.

"I spent a lot of time in the woods. Even as a youth, I was interested in plants and herbs. One day I saw them, just a few of them, dancing and laughing. I hid to watch, but they spotted me. They're hard to sneak up on.

"They didn't run. They came closer, curious. They were girls my age. I told them my name, and that I was looking for bloodroot, and they helped me find some. I remember when I saw their eyes how surprised I was." Synne came to sit by Rose.

"At first, they told me they lived near the forest, like me. They knew so much about the plants. They would meet me and help me find things. They told me their names were Thistle, Trillium, and Woodbine. I thought they were teasing me, with names like that, and wished I could have such a name. I learned so much from them. They wanted to hear all about my life—the cabin where we lived, my brother and sisters, the animals we raised. One day we spied on my family from the edge of the woods. When my brother came out to chop firewood, how they giggled.

"We spent a whole summer together, and toward the end they told me they were fairies. I didn't believe them at first, but they showed me their magic. They called to the birds, and Thistle tried to make herself invisible, but it only half worked. They were still learning.

"They wanted to take me home, but no matter how I tried, I simply couldn't see the way in. Only fairies can. And sometimes, half fairies."

The water was boiling, and Synne rose to make the tea. "I added some honey," she said, handing the cup to Rose. "It might taste a little odd."

"What will happen?" Rose asked.

"Nothing at first. The memories will come back slowly. Some might come all at once, if you recognize something, a place or a person, or a food or smell. It will help if you don't try too hard. Try to let go, to focus on now, and they'll return more easily."

Rose sipped the tea. It did taste strange, but she kept drinking.

The cat uncurled itself, stretched, and dropped off the pallet to saunter over.

"That's Sebastian," Synne said as Rose scratched his ears. "He used to be a fearsome hunter, terrorizing my poor birds, but he quieted down. Maybe he realized I'll always have a scrap for him." She reached out and Sebastian hurried over, looking for a treat and then rubbing his head on her hand.

Rose stayed another hour, petting Sebastian and telling Synne about her life at the castle. Synne was fascinated by Murkel, and Rose's memories of Murkel forming a tail. She didn't think it nonsense. She'd heard of creatures from the sea that could form legs to walk on land. They speculated about where Murkel would be taken. Could a creature like him survive in the king's dungeon? And how had Rose escaped him? Rose shared her vague memories of the fisherman. As Rose left, she promised to visit again.

The sun was high as Rose made her way back toward the village. As she neared the square, she glimpsed a horse ahead, draped with the royal colors. Her hands shook, but she straightened her shoulders and continued forward, smoothing the screen of hair across her eyes.

She turned into the next lane and froze. Guards dotted the road, pounding on doors and peering into the windows of the homes. One of them looked her way. She forced herself forward, trying to look brave. But a villager entered the lane, hunched over and scurrying past the guards. Rose was a peasant now. She had to act like a peasant. She lowered her gaze and moved to the opposite side of the lane. The guard watching her turned to enter a home.

Rose turned as soon as she could, this time into an empty alleyway between the backs of the cottages. She made her way down the alleyway, and another, trying to head back to the stone house. The guards must have been moving through the town in a pack, because she didn't encounter any more. The dense housing of the village center diminished as she reached the outskirts, the cottages surrounded by vegetable gardens and chickens squawking in pens, and occasionally a goat nibbling on grass. One goat looked up and watched her pass.

Fairies communicated with animals.

The thought appeared from nowhere. Fairies were friends with the creatures of the woods and with the animals raised by humans. Her housemates had not served her any meat. Perhaps they had lost the taste for it after living with a fairy for a season.

Rose cut through a field, aiming toward where she guessed the house to be. She slowed when she spotted the stone wall that bordered Maryanne's garden. Would the guards come again today? Maybe she should stay out back just in case.

As she wandered across the pasture, she probed the blank spots in her head, hoping more memories might return. She couldn't help trying, although Synne had told her not to. She thought again of the cabin where she'd awoken. The man who'd brought her there, the fisherman who had rescued her from Murkel . . . it seemed like she'd known him before the rescue.

Maybe he was the Dustan whom Ladi had asked about, who'd supposedly kidnapped her to "do no good." Her face flushed when she thought of it, and she had to admit, she rather liked the sound of that. It reminded her of the daydreams she'd indulged in during the long hours of needlework at the castle.

In her nook that night, she fought to remember anything that had happened with him, whether good or bad. Was he a fairy who'd cast a spell on her? As she drifted to sleep, all that came to her was a feeling of being safe.

Chapter 16

ROSE WOKE IN THE NIGHT. Someone was crying.

She crept from her bed and followed the noise to the window. Pressing her nose to the glass, she scanned the dark garden. A sob closer to the house revealed Jane on the bench by the door, wearing only her nightgown and hugging herself. Jane's sobs were punctuated by puffs of breath in the chill air.

Rose hesitated. Did Jane want to be alone? Maybe, but Rose couldn't just stand there. She wrapped herself in a shawl, took another from the rack, and went out. Jane didn't move as Rose approached.

Rose wrapped the extra shawl around Jane's shoulders. Jane looked up, tears glistening on her cheeks in the faint light of the stars.

"I heard you," was all Rose could think to say.

"I'm sorry to wake you," Jane said. "I forgot you were downstairs."

"Is it . . . anything I can do?"

"No. This is where I come when I get overwhelmed by it."

"How long has it been?" Rose asked as she sat by Jane's side.

"Almost three winters. I should get over it, but I can't. I never got to know her, but I miss her every day. And him, though I shouldn't. I come up with these stories. Maybe he didn't want to leave me, maybe someone forced him. I make excuses, hoping there's some explanation, that he'll fix it and bring her back. I can't seem to stop hoping."

Rose couldn't imagine how Jane must hurt. Would she feel as bad when her memories returned? "Would you like me to stay?"

Jane wiped the tears from her cheeks with a corner of the shawl. "I've been out here a while. I'll go in."

Back on her pallet, Rose couldn't sleep. She had remembered something else—children in the woods. She'd seen fairies in the woods, and there had been children waiting on them. Children who looked sad and tired. Children who had been half human, she felt sure of it.

What if those children belonged here?

It seemed impossible, the chance too slim, but the thought went over and over in Rose's mind. And even if those children weren't the ones her friends had lost, they didn't belong to the fairies. Regardless of who their mothers were, those children deserved something better.

All her life, Rose had been dictated to, moved like a chess piece, kept under control. Her mother had tried to fight it by taking her out of the castle and showing her what little of the world she could. But after that trip to the forest, the king had watched more closely. And then her mother had died. That had been the start of Rose's imprisonment.

She'd been twelve winters at the time she'd decided to pack a basket and visit the villagers, as she'd done with her mother. Her skill at picking locks had already been discovered, and guards had been stationed in her tower, so she sneaked away from Adela as the ladies left the breakfast parlor one morning. She used the servants' passageways to reach the kitchens, where she found a basket and some jars of jam.

She made it to the garden wall before she was spotted. Climbing the hedge was difficult, so she was only a few steps up when the guards came. When the first guard pulled her down, the basket fell, and the jars of jam smashed against the ground.

"Look what you did," they told her.

Ashamed, she stood before her father, who yelled about the dangers outside the castle walls. He sent her to a cell in the dungeon, making sure she had nothing to use to pick the lock. The iron door of her cell had banged shut, and her terrified mind thought this was the end, that she'd committed a crime so bad they had locked her up for eternity. She had sat on the stone bed, trying not to shiver as tears leaked from her eyes. In the cell across from her, a man in rags sat listlessly against the wall. In the next cell down, the prisoner sat up and stared as if she were a ray of sunshine in that dank place. The guards returned to let her out a few hours later.

After that, she gave up, she now realized. Her attempts to escape had petered out. She'd accepted that her life was not hers to live and submitted to the rigid schedule, to the illogical rules, and eventually to the plan to be sold off. Her plans of escape had turned into nothing more than daydreams.

Now she was free for the first time. Part of her wanted to hide, to stay free at all costs. But after talking with Jane, a thought badgered her, returning each time she willed sleep to come. Those half-fairy children were imprisoned just as she had been. They had no hope of escape. Someone had helped Rose gain her freedom. What if no one helped those children? She alone might be able to find the way into the fairy realm. Synne had never been able to do it, even with help. But Rose was half fairy.

She would rescue them.

THE NEXT MORNING AFTER BREAKFAST, Rose walked back to Synne's. She went straight through the village square, alert for guards, but it was early and none were about.

"You said the fairies tried to teach you to see the way in to their land," Rose said as Synne made tea. "Could you teach me?"

"Why do you want to go?" Synne asked slowly as she watched Rose.

"I remembered something last night. I remembered seeing fairies in the woods, dancing, and there were children. They were . . . fanning this one fairy, who sat above all the others."

Synne became very still.

Rose continued, "What if those children belong to my friends? If I could find a way to get them? And even if they don't, they're still prisoners."

"I want to believe you could rescue them," Synne said. "But the fairies are no longer as they were many winters ago. Something has changed. It's not just the seductions and kidnapping. The very woods feel different."

"I know it's a risk," Rose said, "and I've only a vague idea how to find them. But I could try. With the guards swarming the village, I'd be safer in the woods anyway. I might as well go and use the time to search for a way in."

"And once you're in?" Synne asked. "It would not be safe. This fairy you saw, with the children, was she female?"

"Yes."

"The fairies have a queen. The last time I saw Thistle, she spoke with trepidation of a new queen, and I never met Thistle in the woods again. I don't like the sound of children being used to fan the queen."

"There will be danger, but I could find the children, and if I succeeded, it would bring such joy."

Synne studied her face. "Have you remembered any more about your fisherman?"

Rose hesitated. "I think he was more than my rescuer. He might've been a fairy."

"Might you be hoping to see him again, by going to his home?"

Rose looked down. She hadn't admitted it to herself. Now that she'd remembered something about him, and the feeling of him, she did hope to find out more. Maybe she *had* been hoping to see him again, and that she might find him in the fairy realm.

"I might. But that is not the reason for going. It's the children."

"Very well," Synne said.

She served their tea, and after they drank it, she donned a sunhat and led Rose outside.

"I can share what they shared with me, but I was never able to see anything, and doubtless there is little of fairy origin to see in my garden," she said. "They told me that the entrance would shimmer. That's caused by the spell keeping it invisible to humans. They told me to look at a tree"—she pointed and Rose looked at the oak in her yard—"but to try to see the space around the tree. Look for traces of fairy spells in the sides of your vision."

Rose stared at the tree, trying to see the space around it—the other trees farther back, a stone birdbath, laundry flapping on the line. Her gaze moved off to the side. She tried again, and this time something glowed. She turned to it, but it was gone.

Synne studied her. "You saw something."

Rose only nodded and tried again. This time, she caught the glowing object in the side of her vision. It was an ornament hanging in the tree. Once she'd identified it, she slowly looked toward it, and it continued to glow.

"This," she said, walking toward it. "This has fairy magic. I can see it."

"That?" Synne stood still for a moment, then joined Rose, staring at the ornament. "I hung that up many winters before you were even born. A wood turner gave it to me."

Rose touched it, almost expecting a spark, or the shimmering of the surface to disappear, but it didn't. She felt the magic on it as she touched it. "It keeps the birds safe from Sebastian," she said.

Synne stared, and then laughed. "A fairy spell hanging in my tree all this time?"

"Maybe they are not as far away as you think."

Chapter 17

ROSE DIDN'T TELL KITTY AND the others her plan. She didn't want to raise their hopes, when the chances of failure were so great. Instead, she told them Synne had shown her a hiding place in the woods, and that she wanted to keep them safe until the royal guards stopped searching the village. They insisted they'd risk hiding her. But she'd given them a story to believe. In the hours before dawn, she sneaked away.

She'd taken some biscuits and dried fruit in a sack and a gourd filled with water. She also had a charm around her neck, a twist of metal that gleamed like the moon, which Synne had lent to her. It had been a gift from Thistle and was made by the fairies, although Synne didn't think it had any magical powers. The curve of it, tapering down into a point, brought Rose a memory. Somewhere she'd seen the same metal, curved into fantastical shapes and hanging as decoration. She tucked the charm beneath her dress.

She and Aid passed through the dark town square and walked up the south road through the pastures. As the hour passed, a slim crescent moon rose in the eastern sky. Rose stopped to rest when they reached the edge of the woods. As Aid sniffed among the trees, she sat on a rock and sipped her water, inhaling the forest scent in the cool morning air. The horizon brightened. The thin moon turned golden and the sky, pink. Before she continued into the woods, the moon had disappeared in the encroaching rays of the sun, which, thankfully, rose as they followed the road into the trees. Though she hadn't seen anything to fear in the woods, a lifetime spent believing them dangerous was hard to overcome.

Sunlight glinted through the trees as they neared the place where their path veered off to the cabin. If Rose hadn't recognized it, she would've known by Aid's reaction, sniffing wildly and dashing off the road, barking for her to follow.

She walked all morning, stepping over rocks and around tree trunks, pushing aside branches to follow the line Aid made. In places, broken branches littered the path, caused, she assumed, by the men who'd retrieved the prince. The new shoes rubbed her feet, but they did not become sore. And the smell of the forest—the leaves scattered on the ground and the wildness all around her—all felt familiar somehow.

She recognized a hickory nut on the ground and stopped to gather a few. She couldn't break them with her hands, so she placed one on a rock and stepped on it, cracking the shell into tiny pieces. She picked out the nut meat as she walked, and when she popped the first piece into her mouth, the taste of it made her mind flash—an image of walking through a forest just like this. She pulled at the memory. Had she walked here before? And how had she known what kind of nut it was? She'd certainly never gathered or shelled nuts in the castle. She couldn't grasp the memory any further, and it slipped away.

They reached the cabin by noon.

Aid scuffled about, sniffing at the bushes and bounding onto the porch and off again. He circled several times over the spot where Prince Murkel had lain, but no visible trace of the prince remained. Rose scanned the clearing. A path led into the trees. It went to a spring, she remembered. And the stump—had she chopped firewood on it? She thought she had, but surely she had never held an axe at the castle. She rubbed the callus on her hand. She reached for the axe and wrapped her fingers around the handle, and it pressed against her hand in the exact spot where the callus had formed. She quickly let go.

She turned and stood before the cabin and looked at the chimney and the sloped roof, and she tried to see at the sides of her vision as Synne had taught her. A tree shimmered into view. She caught it and looked. The tree grew right through the roof of the cabin. No human had made this.

Rose looked to Aid, hoping he might know in which direction to continue, but he had flopped down in front of the door and begun licking himself. She climbed the porch steps after him. When she tried the latch, it stuck but then it came loose and the door swung open.

Inside the cabin, she practiced looking again, past the hearth, past the deer heads on the wall, and past the spiral staircase leading up to the loft. She focused on the staircase—branches seemed to radiate from its sides. So she focused instead on a deer head, and the staircase turned into a shimmering tree. As she turned to it, the walls of the room faded. There were no deer heads or muskets. Silvery-gold metal like that of Synne's charm decorated the walls. It twisted into vines and leaves, with flowers of glass and polished wood attached. Cushions still covered the floor around the settee where she had woken, but overhead, a hammock swung in the branches of the tree.

Her gaze stuck on the hammock. Something was coming back to her. She'd lain in the hammock with someone snuggled warm against her back. Rose dropped her sack and climbed to the hammock, which held a rumpled blanket. She gathered the blanket and climbed down. She buried her nose in the blanket and inhaled. Warmth filled her, and warm arms surrounded her. Rose willed the memory to return, but it eluded her. She'd have to follow Synne's advice and stop trying so hard.

Aid had entered the cabin and sat watching her. The dog had led Kemp to the cabin. If the man from Rose's memories, Dustan, had been a fairy, and if he'd been here, maybe he had returned to their land. Could the dog track Dustan? Rose lowered the blanket and held it out to Aid, who came forward, tail wagging. He sniffed it for several moments, and his tail wagged harder.

"Could you find him?" she asked the dog. "Follow him?"

Rose clutched the blanket and went back outside, and Aid scampered out. The dog circled the clearing but returned to her, looking up and tail still wagging. She held out the blanket again, and again the dog sniffed it. This time, he put his nose to the ground, sniffing in all directions. He kept returning to one spot, and after three times, he stopped moving and looked at her.

"That's our course?" Rose asked. Aid didn't move.

Rose sighed. It was only noon, with a long afternoon stretching ahead. But she was tired from her early start, and being inside the cabin felt safe. Besides, if Aid was about to lead her into the wilds to starve to death, she didn't want to know it yet. At least until tomorrow, she could pretend her mission hadn't failed. "Let's rest," she said, and the dog followed her inside.

She saved her biscuits and instead ate some of the dried foods she found on shelves by the hearth. She went out to refill her gourd at the spring. As soon as the sun got low, she made a bed on the settee, with Aid nearby. She was asleep before the pink light of sunset had faded from the windows.

AID GROWLED IN THE DARK. Rose opened her eyes and scanned the cabin, but nothing moved. Someone shouted outside. Rose leapt off the settee and darted to the window. A pale sunrise tinted the sky through the spring branches, and in the dim forest light, guards on foot entered the clearing. They headed straight for the cabin door, and one of them held an axe.

Rose grabbed her sack with the blanket tucked inside and dashed to the far side of the cabin, her heart pounding. She undid the window latch and pushed the sash open. The guards swung the axe into the door with a *thunk*. Why didn't they simply open it? Rose lifted Aid to the window, struggling under his weight. When his paws reached the window sill, he pushed himself up and through. Rose scrambled after him, dropping to the ground outside. She pushed the window closed. As it banged shut, the latch inside dropped into place. Rose couldn't believe her luck.

Trees pressed against the back of the cabin. The thuds of the axe and the guards' voices carried in the damp morning air. Rose and Aid hurried into the shelter of the trees. When the cabin was out of sight, Rose stopped. She dug the blanket out of her sack and again held it to Aid. After a cursory sniff, the dog put his nose to the ground and moved off, making a wide circle around the cabin. Rose tucked the blanket away and followed as quickly as she could. After a few minutes, Aid's tail wagged and he changed course, leading them away from the cabin into the trees. They left the noise of the guards behind.

They walked for hours, and all the forest looked the same to Rose, an endless maze of tree trunks and fallen branches and underbrush. She never saw a road, but once heard the clatter of horses' hooves. She froze, then lowered herself to the ground. The guards passed about two hundred paces off, their uniforms bright between the trees. Thank the skies for her faded dress and shawl.

Seeing the guards made it clear that she and Aid were near the forest road and headed toward the castle. They could walk on the road more easily, but since guards could appear at any moment, Rose thought fighting her way through the brambles after Aid was the better choice. The thought of being near to the castle almost made her turn back. "I'm safe now," she whispered to herself as she walked. "I can hide in the woods." But as she remembered where she was headed, she laughed at herself. Safe? If Rose had indeed seen the fairy queen, surrounded by her half-fairy servants,

safe was the last thing she'd be when she entered the fairies' land.
If she could even find the way in.

It was nearing sunset when Aid led Rose into the clearing with
the tent. She saw it and her spine tingled. Why? Why did she feel
nervous? It was only a small rectangle of plain canvas, nothing
fancy like the tents the merchants set up outside the village. Was
someone inside?

Aid trotted over and nosed his way in. There was no response.
Broken branches littered the ground, and leaves had gathered in
the folds of the tent and in the center of a ring of stones, covering
the charred remains of a campfire.

She approached the tent, lifted open the door flap, and crawled
in. She felt relief to be off her feet. The tent had a mat on the floor
and a pile of cushions, which Aid was inspecting. She set down her
supplies and her shawl by the door and crawled over to the cushions. She pulled a blanket over herself. After walking all day, this
was luxurious.

She thought back to life in the castle, to the luxury she'd
known—fine foods, a soft bed, rich clothing. Her life had followed
a routine, but had lacked this uncertainty she now faced, her uncertainty of knowing what her next step would be. Even the uncertainty of her bonding hadn't been like this, because though she
had dreaded it, it had been beyond her control. Here in the woods,
there might be guards to hide from or even wild creatures, though
she was beginning to suspect they weren't as dangerous as her father—or rather, the king—had led her to believe. Out here, she'd
go hungry if she didn't find her own food. She tried to imagine
herself back at the castle, but the thought of it made her feel like
she was suffocating, like she was being strangled. She could never
go back. In that life, she'd had no future of her own, no reason to
live. Out here, she was alive.

Rose pulled the blanket up to her nose. It smelled like the spring
wind coming over the forest to her tower window. No, it smelled

like Dustan again. Had he been here, too? It made sense, since Aid had led them here. Maybe they were getting close.

She snuggled under the blanket. The scent made her feel safe, and loved. And lying there stirred her memory. Rose glanced to Aid, who'd settled by the tent door. He would know if anyone came near. Having him there helped Rose relax. She closed her eyes, not trying to chase the memory, just letting it come.

She was in her tower room, lying in her bed, the same as every night of her life, but a man stood by her. Dustan, the fisherman who'd rescued her—they merged in her mind. The fisherman was Dustan, of course. And he'd only been out on the ocean that awful night to save her. And they'd met before. In her tower room.

It couldn't be true. How would he have gotten past the guards, or gotten in without waking Adela?

But she could see him standing over her, as clear as she'd seen Aid lying by the door. She could feel his fingers softly stroking her hair. And she could feel herself reacting, as he'd gently pushed her back and climbed onto the bed beside her.

Chapter 18

☙

THEY'D BARELY LEFT THE TENT the next morning when Aid slowed, sniffing the ground, then scampering to and from the bushes. When Rose caught up to him, he led her through the branches into a large clearing. The early sun beamed through the trees, which cast long shadows across the space. Bare patches showed where the grass had been trampled.

Rose stood still and focused on a nearby tree and tried to see into the sides of her vision. Nothing came at first. But then something moved, swinging. Slowly, she turned her gaze to it. It was a lantern, hanging in the next tree over and swaying in the breeze. When she blinked, it disappeared.

She focused again until the lantern was in her sight. She took in the details, the spirals of decorative flowers on the sides, the unearthly shimmer it gave off even in the daylight.

Rose let go of the lantern and focused on a tree across the clearing. Now in the sides of her vision, many lanterns encircled the space.

Suddenly she saw a whole scene, not because it was before her but because the memory had returned. She saw fairies dancing in the clearing. Their haughty queen. The dull-eyed children who waited on her. She'd heard music in the night and followed it here.

And Dustan had been with her.

He'd come to find her, to pull her away. He'd said the fairies were dangerous, though he was one of them. He had been trying to help her.

What had she done? Had she gone off into the woods alone at night with a man—worse, with a fairy? She'd been under a spell, Synne had thought. Had Dustan been the one to cast it?

"I'm not bewitched now," Rose said into the morning air. She turned her mind back to the clearing and her task. Now that Rose remembered the fairy queen's face, cruel and dangerous, her dread of going into their land only grew. Aid had begun moving again, sniffing his way across the clearing. He looked up at her and trotted into the trees on the other side.

Rose hurried across the exposed clearing and under the branches. Aid sniffed at a thicket under the trees. He growled, lowered his head, and walked forward. Rose started when he walked right through the brambles and disappeared. She reached out her fingers and touched a branch. It felt real, solid, with thorns that could prick her fingers. She stepped back and stared at the tree to her right, and, after a moment, the thicket vanished.

Where the thicket had been, a tunnel now emerged, filled with sunlight. Apparently, if her mind believed the illusion was real, it would feel real as well. Rose stepped through and entered a large clearing with rows of tilled earth. Tiny green eggplants and tomatoes hung from tall bushes, and leafy vines spread across the dirt. The garden stretched the whole length of the space. Trees and a thicket like the one she'd just passed through enclosed it all the way around.

Aid trotted between the garden plants, following the furrows to the other side. He led Rose into the shade of a gnarled tree. Small apples hung from the boughs. It was an orchard, not only apples but green persimmons and pecans and more. Aid stopped by a boulder at the edge of the field. He looked up at Rose and wagged his tail. Rose stared at the boulder, but nothing around her changed or shimmered in any way. But when she moved away, Aid whined and stood his ground.

After ten minutes of trying to see any traces of the fairies, Rose sighed. She reached down to scratch Aid's ears and lowered herself to sit, leaning her back against the rock. The sun had warmed it, and the searing heat felt good on her muscles. Her head tilted back, and when it rested against the boulder, Rose knew. The boulder was the entrance.

She scrambled to her feet and stepped back. This time she looked at the closest tree, and in the side of her vision, the boulder shimmered and disappeared. In its place, a crack appeared in the ground, and stone steps led down into the earth. Rose stared, try-ing to stay calm. She had found it, a way to enter the fairy realm. Until now, she hadn't really believed she would.

She'd found the way in, but what next? How would she ever get those children away from the queen? How would she get them back to Woods Rest, if they did escape?

She didn't know, but she couldn't turn back. She'd been scared long enough, had been blindly submitting to her fate, afraid of what might happen if she rebelled. This was her chance to prove she could be a new person, a brave person who took charge and shaped her own world. There was only one thing to do. She stepped into the opening.

Aid barked. When Rose's eyes met his, he let out a pathetic whine, pawing the ground and backing away.

"I have to go," Rose said. Aid moved to come with her. "No, you can't come. I don't know what's down there." He whined again, taking another step forward.

"Sit!" Rose said, and the dog sat. She softened her voice. "If I don't come back, you go. Don't sit here and starve." She gave the dog a final glance and turned into the opening.

Rose descended the steps. Cool air chilled her as she left the sunlight, and a damp scent of dirt and roots filled her nose. At the bottom, a tunnel led into darkness. Dim lanterns lit the walls every twenty paces. Her throat tightened but she pushed away the fear. She thought of Dustan, who had helped her before. Maybe he was here. Maybe he had loved her and would help her again.

Or maybe he'd left her and wanted nothing more to do with her. If he'd cast a spell on her, he'd controlled her just as much as the king had. How could she ever trust him?

A lantern glimmered ahead, and as Rose neared it, two figures jumped to attention. They didn't look so different from humans. Had she expected them to wear flowers and have wings? They wore simple clothes of woven fabric with emblems on the shoulders like the castle guards. Their faces were distinct, but in the semidarkness, Rose couldn't tell what it was about them that differed from humans. Each held a dagger. Rose stopped ten paces away. Behind the guards, the tunnel ended with a rock wall. But Rose knew better now.

"What brings you here?" the shorter guard asked. The female voice surprised Rose. All of the castle guards were men.

"I'm here to see the queen," Rose replied.

The guards glanced at each other, and the taller guard shrugged. "What harm can it do?" he said. "She'll be tossed out soon enough. And it's not against the law, for a half fairy."

"You take her then. I'll stay here."

The taller guard turned to Rose. "Follow me." He faced the dead end and stepped forward, and the rock wall shimmered as he passed through. Rose walked forward and reached out a hand. Her fingertips brushed against solid rock. The remaining guard smirked. Rose focused, ignoring the guard, and this time the wall disappeared while she looked at it. Her sight was improving.

The taller guard waited farther down the passage, and when she moved forward, he turned. He descended into the cave, leading Rose down.

At first there was just one deserted tunnel. It widened to the

size of a village lane, and they passed openings into other passageways. They passed fairies who looked curiously at Rose. The passage opened into a bright square filled with fairy folk. The tunnel
rocks rose higher, with light shining down. Strange forms twisted
up from the ground. Rose stared upward. They were trees, growing here beneath the ground.

Rose clutched her sack and scanned over the faces. Her glance
locked with that of a young man sitting on a low branch. His lips
curved into a smile, and he winked. She snatched her gaze away,
her face flushing. She'd been looking for Dustan, she realized, hoping to recognize him in the crowd. But what if she saw him and
didn't know it? Would he know her?

Halfway across the square, Rose calmed enough to study her
surroundings. The place was like a human village square, with
buildings around an open space. But the buildings were carved into
the rock. Warm fires burned in metal baskets set on stakes, and so
many lights twinkled overhead that their radiance was as bright as
daytime above ground. Trees twisted up into the light, somehow
growing without the sun.

How had the fairies made this place? Carving all that rock
would take more winters than she could imagine. She had a flash
of memory of a powder that made fire. She had seen Dustan use
it to light a fire that never needed tending. Maybe they also had a
powder that exploded.

"This way," the guard said.

Rose spotted him and moved to catch up, starting to relax.
The fairies didn't seem that different than the villagers in Woods
Rest. "Do you like living down here?" she asked the guard as they
continued through a passage and came out into another chamber.

The guard looked at her. His eyes were a brilliant green. He
looked away and shook his head. "I have no choice, so what does
it matter?"

"Could you not live above ground? I saw your garden."

The guard frowned. "We are not allowed above ground, save

special occasions, or . . . missions for the queen. Only a few tend the garden or gather herbs."

"But you used to go above," Rose said. "I know someone. Thistle, Trillium, and Woodbine were her friends. She met them in the forest."

The guard seemed startled by the names. "We've not been allowed for twenty winters," he said. "It's too dangerous now. The humans want our magic. They'll hunt us. They'll torture us to get it."

Rose began to deny it, but stopped herself. She'd been sequestered in the castle. What if the guard spoke the truth? Rose could imagine the king wanting the power that would come with fairy magic.

They approached a doorway. Rose glanced back. A small crowd had gathered behind them, watching and whispering. The fairies' skin seemed almost to glow, and their features were more delicate than those of the villagers. When she passed close enough, she could see the green flash of their eyes, brighter even than hers. At least her eyes helped her look like she belonged here.

Through the doorway, she entered another chamber, smaller than the first two. The crowd grew denser, although it parted to let them pass. Rose lowered her head as she passed close to the fairies. The more they gathered, the greater the chance of Dustan being among them, and the greater the chance of him watching her cross the caverns. She trembled to think of him.

The crowd broke, revealing the far end of the room, and Rose's fear escalated. Sprawled on a cushion-covered throne sat the queen. She was surrounded by children, who were still and pale. Rose counted six as they neared. Fairies wearing the guard emblems stood at attention around the base of the throne's dais.

The queen didn't turn at their approach, staring overhead while a small child fanned her with a woven fan. Rose studied the queen. How could she not notice the hushed murmurs of the crowd? The queen must know they were approaching and only pretended indifference. Rose drew herself up straighter, feeling stronger. The guard stopped before the queen. Behind them, the crowd closed in.

The queen ignored them a few heartbeats longer, then slowly turned, her eyes contemptuous. Rose caught her breath when she saw the queen's face. A memory of Dustan came back to her—his face, the spikes of his hair, his eyes gazing at her. Not with contempt as the queen did now, but with—what? Interest? Pity? Passion?

The queen was Dustan's mother. Nothing else could explain the resemblance.

"Who's this?" the queen said, spitting out the words.

"She came in the east gate," the guard said with a tremor in his voice. "Asked to see you, your majesty."

"Did she," the queen said, and turned on Rose.

Rose swallowed at the cold voice.

"You must be half fairy. Is that why you are here? You want to claim a place in our realm?"

The room was silent.

Stay calm, Rose told herself. She lifted her chin.

"No. I've come for the children." Rose nodded toward the little girl holding the queen's goblet. She raised her voice over the murmurs in the crowd. "Their mothers miss them. Children should not be servants. They do not belong here."

The queen's nostrils flared, and her lips opened but she remained silent. Behind Rose, the murmuring grew, repeating the words Rose had spoken. She wouldn't have much time.

Rose dropped her sack and stepped forward between two of the guards. She pushed herself up onto the queen's dais. As she did, the crowd gasped. The goblet holder stared in awe as her gaze met Rose's for a mere breath. Rose turned to the crowd, blocking the queen.

"Some of you are mothers," she called over the buzz of talk. "Take pity on their mothers. Let their children go home."

All the sounds overlapped then—the rumble of the crowd, which intensified into a roar, the queen's shout of "Guards!," and the clatter of feet rushing the dais. Innumerable hands pulled Rose down and held her on all sides. The crowd hushed.

"What is your name?" the queen asked.

"Rose."

The crowd murmured again.

The queen's eyes narrowed. "Send Rose to the dungeon," she said.

The hands pulled Rose in two different directions.

"I'll take her." A large fairy pushed his way past the guard and gripped her arm. "I know just where to put her."

Chapter 19

ℒ

THE FAIRY PULLED ROSE AGAINST him and stepped back. He pushed through the crowd, clearing a path and steering her to an exit. A wall of faces watched her go. But they weren't angry. Some of the fairies stared, and some looked down as she passed. Maybe her words had reached them.

The large fairy, the queen had called him Larch, shoved her forward into a tunnel. As the noise of the hall dimmed, his grip softened, and he walked more slowly. They were some distance from the throne chamber before he spoke. "Are you Dustan's Rose?" he asked quietly.

Dustan's Rose? Had Dustan spoken of her? He must have been here, then. And Larch's low voice, now that it lacked aggression, brought another memory of Dustan back to her. She turned to him and saw a resemblance.

"Yes," she said. "I think so. I don't remember much."

"I am his brother. And that"—he tilted his head back the way they'd come—"is our mother."

Dustan's Rose. Why had Larch called her that?

"You spoke of the mothers whose children were taken," Larch said.

Rose's attention snapped back to him. "Yes. I've come from them."

"You know where they are?"

"Yes."

"Is Jane with them?"

Rose started. "Jane?"

"I knew her," Larch said. "She knew me as Cedric."

Rose couldn't speak as she realized what he meant. "You . . . ?"

"Aye."

"You have Jane's child."

"The one with the goblet. She's but three winters."

Rose struggled to keep the anger from her voice. "How could you? Don't you know how she suffers?"

Larch pulled her to a stop and faced her. "I thought the child would be better off here than with the humans. We were taught that humans don't love, that they have no feelings. But it never felt quite right. Our minds were poisoned. When Dustan returned and said he would not bring a tribute, I thought . . . . Well, by then it was too late to do differently. Jane had disappeared."

"Where is Dustan?"

"Just where we're going. The dungeon." Larch began walking again.

"She imprisoned him? Her own son?"

"Aye. She requires many kinds of tributes, for many things. To visit the garden, to have a child of one's own, sometimes to perform the rites for a life-bond. Her mind is fickle. She couldn't let Dustan go free. It would set a precedent."

"So it's her law, the enslavement of the children?"

"What else would it be?"

"I thought it was a fairy law."

"You must think us barbarians." He paused. "We thought the same of you. Shooting the animals, cutting the trees. Humans are brutish and dangerous. No one thought there was harm in getting a baby, because your women are shallow and careless. They won't notice one baby, they'll just make another.

"But Jane never seemed so. And when Dustan returned, he was telling everyone that the human world is not as we've been told, and he talked about your kindness. If she hadn't condemned him for failing to bring a tribute, she'd have locked him away for that. She's told everyone that he's mad, that his encounter with the humans made him lose his mind."

They reached the end of the tunnel. A wooden door with a large keyhole blocked their way. Larch dropped Rose's arm to sort through a set of keys, until he picked one.

"No fairy magic to lock the dungeon?" Rose asked, studying the key he selected.

"This is not the fairy dungeon. There, the magic knows who needs to be kept or not. My mother built this dungeon so she could contain fairies according to her own whims. It uses human cages and locks."

Larch fitted the key into the lock and turned it with a click, and the door creaked open. Rose swallowed. She was about to see Dustan. His shadowy figure had haunted her since Ladi had said his name, but now she would meet him in person. Would he match the vague memories she'd regained? She could not remember any of the words he'd said to her. What would he say now?

The door opened into a cavern lined with iron bars. A central corridor ran between two rows of cells. Fires burned in sconces along the corridor. Rose shivered. It mirrored the dungeon in the king's castle where they'd locked her for hours. But as Rose followed Larch down the row, she looked into the empty cells. Here at least, the cells had stone beds with blankets and small tables with chairs. And it was warm and not too dark, and smelled like herbs instead of unwashed bodies and mold.

"Who else is down here?" she asked. Her voice echoed in the chamber.

"No one at the moment, now that everyone submits to the

queen. It is rare for fairies to turn on each other. Mostly it's just those who've drunk too much elderberry wine and need to sleep it off. And then this one." He slowed as he approached the next cell.

"Who is it you've brought to see me, Larch? Some good company I hope." The low voice rang out, echoing off the empty stone.

Rose's heart nearly stopped.

"A lady, so watch your manners, brother," Larch called back.

"I don't want a lady," came the reply.

"This one you might," Larch said, and grinned.

They arrived at the only occupied cell, and Rose saw Dustan. He was lying on his back on a flat stone that extended from the wall with a blanket underneath him. His knees were up, and one arm rested over his face. He was wearing trousers like the peasants in the village, and a loose shirt, and he was barefoot. She had seen that in her memories, too.

His arm slid away and his head turned. His eyes met Rose's.

He was beautiful. She stared back at him as memories flooded her thoughts. Meeting him in the herb garden. How excited she'd been after talking to him. Learning he was a prince who might be chosen for her. How he spoke of a sleeping potion to help her escape the castle, and one appeared. All the thrill of it came back to her.

But had any of it been real? Why had she been so taken with him? Was it only a spell he'd cast on her? He'd been lying to her the whole time. Looking at him now, she felt only confused.

Dustan's eyes flashed in anger. He pushed himself off the stone bed and faced them. "What is she doing here?"

Rose's heart, already fluttering, sank to the pit of her stomach.

"She came on her own. Found her way in, Ash says, and asked to see the queen. She seeks to rescue the half ones, to return them to their mothers."

"But how did she get here?"

"Why don't you ask her?" Larch said, searching through the keys again. He moved to the next cell down. Rose looked away from Dustan, overcome by awkwardness. He didn't sound happy to see her.

Dustan moved forward, put his hands on the iron bars, but then removed them. His lips were pressed tight as he glared at Larch. Larch unlocked the door of the next cell and stood aside, looking to Rose. She entered the cell and the door clanged shut behind her. "I'll return with supper," Larch said, and his steps padded away.

Dustan didn't want her there. Disappointment flooded over her. She stole glances at him as she stood in her cell, but his head was bowed and she couldn't see his face. When he finally looked up, his eyes shone in the dim lighting. "Do you remember me?" he said in a low voice, not quite meeting her gaze.

"Yes," she said, but her dry voice cracked, inaudible. She swallowed. "Yes. It's coming back to me. It's confusing."

"Do you hate me?" he said.

"I . . ." She didn't know what to say. She didn't feel hatred, but should she? Would she later, when more memories returned? "I don't know."

He looked away again. Rose didn't know what else to say, or what to do. She moved to sit down.

"Do you want to remember?" he said at last. "I could tell you."

Rose panicked. After days of trying to grasp every memory, she could have them all. The possibility terrified her. "Not yet."

After a moment, Dustan sat also. They were silent. He kept his face to the ground.

Rose peeked at him and studied his profile. Had she kissed this man—had she lain with him? She imagined his lips on hers, the thin, perfect curve of them pressing into hers, and an unexpected sensation blazed through her. She'd have to be careful. It would be easy to imagine herself in love.

Dustan cleared his throat. "Larch said you came for the half ones."

"Yes."

"Did you think you'd just take them and leave?"

"I don't know. I had no idea what it would be like here. I had to try."

"How did it happen?" he asked. "How did you know about them?"

"I remembered seeing them in the forest. You were there, pro—protecting me."

Dustan shifted as she said it. "You just remembered?"

"No." Rose wasn't sure where to begin. "I woke up at a cabin in the woods. I didn't know how I got there." Dustan winced. "I walked . . . . There was a dog and he led me out of the woods and into Woods Rest. I had no coins or food, barely any clothes, but there was a house where some women lived. They took me in.

"One of them recognized the signs. She knew I'd been . . . taken by a fairy. They all had. And they'd each had a child who'd been taken." Now she could know for sure how much time had passed since she'd left the castle. "Did I—?"

"No," Dustan said. "You did not have a child."

"How long has it been since my memories stop?"

"Less than one moon."

Rose exhaled. It hadn't been that long. How could so much have happened?

"These women," Dustan said, when she didn't resume her story, "they think of the children they've lost?"

"Yes, all the time. They are sad all the time. Even the ones who've been there many winters, they're stuck, never forgetting."

There was a pause. Dustan said, "While I was in your castle, I heard the woman in the kitchen—the large one with the fancy aprons—"

"That's Kate," Rose said.

"Her son had been ordered into the guards, sent away. She missed him."

As Dustan said it, Rose remembered Maybeth telling her about it. "Yes, he was a shy boy, about my age. He used to hide behind Kate's skirts when my mother took me to visit the kitchen. Kate tried to keep him out of the guards, using him around the kitchen to carry the water. He wouldn't last in a fight, she said. It must've broken her heart when they made him go."

"I didn't know," Dustan said. "I didn't think humans cared like that."

"Some of them do. Most of them. It's just a few who are twisted, like the king."

Silence fell between them. Dustan hadn't said anything about missing her or loving her. He hadn't even seemed glad to see her. Not that her own feelings were clear. Each time she glanced through the bars at him, her stomach turned over in a not-unpleasant way, but she immediately chastised herself. How could she feel attracted to him when she knew she couldn't trust him? She'd have to hear the whole story, or at least his version of it.

In the meantime, she could figure out how to get out of there. If the queen was as unstable as Larch implied, there was no telling what she might do to her. The cell door would be no problem. The lock was the simplest she'd ever seen, and she'd gotten a good look at the key before Larch used it. And the dungeon door didn't look much worse. She didn't have a hairpin or a corset bone she could use to open the lock. She had Synne's charm, though, with its tapered end. Hopefully Synne would forgive her if she scratched it.

The trouble was the children—finding them, getting them away from the queen, and finding her way out of the caverns. And once they were out, how would she get them to Woods Rest? Two of the children had been small enough that they'd barely be walking. She couldn't take them through the woods for two days. How would she feed them all?

And what should she do about Dustan? She wanted answers, but it might take time, time she didn't want to spend locked in a cell by a malevolent fairy queen. Leaving Dustan locked away as she escaped didn't feel right.

First things first. Rose cleared her throat. "I counted six children with your queen. The half ones. Are there but six?"

"Seven," Dustan replied. "Her newest is a babe."

Rose's anger flared at the thought, but she swallowed it down. "And they are always with the queen? Or does she leave them at times? Do the caverns have a nursery for them?" She looked at the floor but felt him studying her.

"Why are you asking?"

"Because I plan to rescue them."

After a moment, he said, "They live in her apartments. When she's not with them, Snowdrop takes care of them."

"Snowdrop?"

"My sister."

"You have quite a family," was all Rose could think to say.

Dustan leaned forward, resting his arms on his knees. "You haven't even met my older brothers." He ran his hand through his hair. "Hopefully, you never do."

Rose shuddered. If they were anything like their mother, she hoped she never did either.

Chapter 20

☙

LARCH BROUGHT THEM BREAD AND cheese and pickled vegeta-bles for a midday meal and sat at the table in Dustan's cell, telling him bits of news. He insisted their mother had said nothing about Rose. When Dustan begged him to take Rose out of the caverns, he refused.

Rose stayed quiet, nibbling her bread and hoping she might hear something useful. Larch kept shooting her looks, as if waiting for her to speak. Did he hope to learn something from her? Well if he did, Rose thought, he could be an adult and simply ask her.

After they'd finished eating, Larch took their plates and left.

Dustan moved from the table to his stone bed. "The afternoons are the worst time here," he said. "They drag on. I usually lie here and stare at the shadows in the rocks overhead." He sat back so Rose could no longer see his face.

Rose copied him, lying back on the hard bed. They were silent. She waited long enough that Dustan might have fallen asleep before gathering the courage to whisper, "Dustan?"

"Yes?"

"Tell me what happened between us."

At first he was silent, but then he began to speak. "There was a spell that made you love me. I put the guards and your ladies to sleep and cast it when you were on the beach. Later, at the castle, I presented myself as a prince."

"Didn't they know you were a fairy?"

"I cast an illusion on myself to hide it. You might've seen through it, though, because of the spell. The spell makes a human have a bit of fairy about them."

"What was your plan if my father didn't choose you?" Rose asked. "You must've known he'd only pick someone with loads of gold."

"I had gold. Or rather, piles of acorns and pinecones that I planned to turn into fairy gold at the right time. It doesn't last that long once you make it. But then I met you in the garden, and we talked, and . . . ." He paused. "When you told me you wished you could be alone, I wanted to help you. I grew distracted by it, and I forgot about your father. And before I realized it, he had chosen King Murkel as your groom."

"*King* Murkel?"

"He's not a prince, but the ruler of Merlandia. It's a kingdom under the sea. I believe he has several wives already, but all of his own kind."

"What is he? I remember a horrible tail."

"He's a merman."

"Are they all . . . ?"

"They're not all monsters—the fairies used to trade with them, ages ago."

"What did he do to me? Do you know?"

"I arrived as he was dragging you out to sea. I don't think he could have done much. I'd gotten a boat, but I'm not much of a swimmer. Thankfully, I had friends to help."

"The birds," Rose said, remembering. "And those fish we swam with."

"Dolphins."

"I thought a fisherman rescued me. I used to daydream that,

when I sat on the beach, and when you appeared, it was just like my daydream. But afterward, I just remembered a fisherman. I thought it was he who brought me to that cabin. But it was you."

"Yes."

"Why did you leave me there?"

"It wasn't fair. I loved you, I swear it. But you only loved me because of the spell. You found out about the spell, and you asked me to remove it. So I did. You wouldn't love me when you woke. You wouldn't remember anything about me, or the time when you were under the spell. And you'd gotten what you wanted—you were free of the castle. But something must have happened, because you remember me now."

"A woman helped me," Rose said. "She'd seen fairies in the woods as a child, and they'd shown her things. They were her friends until they disappeared. This woman, Synne, helped Jane and the others. Synne gave me herbs to restore my memories, because I wanted to remember. It was like . . . like you were haunting me. I could feel the memory of you, but there was only a blank spot."

"I'm sorry, Rose," Dustan said, leaning up on an elbow and looking at her. "You shouldn't have remembered anything. I thought you'd be happy to find yourself free of the castle, without any memory of me. I don't know why it didn't work."

Neither of them spoke for a moment.

Finally, Rose continued. "Synne insisted that the fairies have not always been this way, seducing women and taking their babies. She didn't understand what changed. But now I think I might."

"My mother," Dustan said. "She didn't dare make fairies wait on her, so she came up with this idea of half fairies to serve her. She stirred up antagonism toward the humans, pointing out the worst of them—their hunting, the damage they do in the forest. The younger fairies are convinced that humans are dangerous and heartless.

"I was a baby when it began, but older ones shared their stories, and now I have seen her lies. Not that I fought it. I was privileged and never had a quarrel with the queen. Until I met you."

His words sang in Rose's ears. Until he'd met her.

He didn't continue. She hadn't asked about the memories that haunted her. Like the memory of lying in the hammock with someone pressed against her back. Or the memory of gazing up at him in her tower room at the castle, as he stroked her hair and slipped into the sheets beside her. Or the memory of being alone with him, in the woods, in the middle of the night. But he remained silent, and she had enough on her mind. She closed her eyes, remembering the things he'd said.

He had loved her. Maybe he didn't now, but he had.

LARCH RETURNED AT SUPPER. THIS time he left the plates and said he'd return in the morning. Soon after they'd finished the meal, the fairy lights hanging overhead began to dim.

"That's how we know when the day is ending," Dustan said when she glanced up.

"Have your people always lived down here?"

"We've always had this place, but it used to be only for winter. There were dwellings in the trees above ground for the warmer days. But since my mother's been in charge, that has changed. She's poisoned everyone with fear of the world above, or barred those who would go anyway."

Rose went through the motions of unbuckling her shoes and left them on the floor, so that Dustan wouldn't suspect anything. Not that he could stop her escaping—if he'd even want to. He seemed to want her gone. Should she help him escape? She pulled the blankets over herself. The lights were even dimmer. "How dark will it get?" she asked.

"Not completely," Dustan said.

Rose counted, the way she used to count to make sure Adela was fast asleep before opening her tower window. Ten minutes passed. Then twenty. Dustan's breathing was steady, as if he were asleep. The lights were pinpricks overhead, illuminating the cell just enough to see the shape of the table. Thirty minutes.

Slowly, Rose sat up, slipped on her shoes, and moved around the table to the door. She pulled Synne's charm from her dress and over her head. She held it tightly as she reached through the bars, feeling for the lock and inserting the charm. It took only two pushes before the lock clicked open. She froze, listening for movement from Dustan, but he was silent.

She would open his lock and go. He could free himself if he chose to. The silence continued, so Rose stood and pushed on the bars.

"Rose?"

She flinched.

"What are you doing?" A moment later, he was at the bars of his cell beside her. "How did you open the lock?"

Rose moved out of her cell and leaned close to see the keyhole on Dustan's cell door. "Human magic," she said as she sprang his lock.

"Are you leaving?" he asked, stepping out of his cell.

Rose straightened. "Not without those children."

"You'll never manage it, not against the queen and her guards."

"I can't leave them here, Dustan."

"I know. Let me help you."

"You should escape. If they catch you, you'll be back in that cell."

"Let me help you," he repeated. "I can at least show you where they are. And Snowdrop will listen to me."

Rose had given him a chance to walk away, and he hadn't taken it. A warmth curled around her heart. And relief that she wouldn't have to find the children alone. "Okay."

Together they moved past the cells to the dungeon door. Rose knelt at the lock, listening as she moved the thin metal of the charm inside it, until she found the place to press. The lock slid open.

"You never told me you had this skill," Dustan said as they stepped out of the dungeon.

"Would it have helped you?" Rose asked. The vague memory of being out of the castle with him returned.

"I had my own tricks," Dustan said, watching her. "But now I know why you had so many guards."

Rose couldn't meet his gaze, and her face flushed in reaction to the way he looked at her.

Dustan turned to the deserted passage, and Rose followed. He took one corridor after another, and miraculously, they didn't encounter anyone, or maybe Dustan was leading them through the corridors no one used. Finally, they reached an intersection where he waved her back. He looked out before moving into the open, hurrying to the first door in the passage. He opened it and ushered her inside.

It was clearly an apartment for living, with a mat for sleeping on one side, but the sparse furnishings included only a table with some rolls of parchment, and shelves with jars and pots like the ones Rose had seen at the cabin. Dustan lifted a pack off the floor, rummaging through the contents and tucking a cape inside. "Have you thought of how to overcome my mother?" Dustan asked.

"I thought I might just kick her hard and grab the children," Rose said.

Dustan was shaking his head. "Don't forget her magic, Rose. She won't hesitate to harm you."

"Then I'll need to subdue her. Don't you have a sleeping potion?"

"That one only works on humans. Moonflower would help, but we'd have to get her to inhale it."

"What about alcohol?"

"You mean like your father's wine?"

"Yes, but stronger."

"Stronger than wine? Your father's wine was deadly."

"Much stronger."

"That would be perfect, but we won't find any here. My mother only allows elderberry wine, and she punishes drunkenness so no one dares."

"How about a medicine?"

"We don't need human medicines."

"How about an extract, like Norlian vanilla—would anyone have any?"

Dustan's face lit up. "They should." He pulled out a pouch and beckoned her forward. "We'll have to travel on the road with the children. I can't hide you from the fairies, but I can hide you from the king's men."

Was he planning to go with her? Rose didn't want to question it. She was much more likely to succeed with his help. And she didn't want to part from him, not until she'd learned the whole story about their time together.

He looked up from his pack and fumbled as his gaze met hers. He was only a few hands away, and Rose stared into his eyes, the brilliant emerald color the same as hers, and remembered how it had felt to be his—his prisoner, maybe, but his—and part of her wanted to be with him again.

He reached forward but stopped short of touching her. "Your eyes," he said. "The spell is gone, but—"

"They've always been this color. I was born with them. Ladi told me what it means."

Dustan's eyes were shining. "That's how you found your way in," he said. "That's why you didn't forget everything when I removed the spell."

Rose waited. He was standing so close, she could smell his skin.

"Was it your mother?" Dustan said.

"She was a human."

"And certainly the king is no fairy. It must've been someone your mother loved."

"Do fairy women not carry human babies?"

"Aye. But none would touch a man as revolting as the king. How many winters are you?"

"Nineteen," she said.

"It's been over twenty winters since my mother became queen. Your father might have been one of the first required to bring a tribute. But I've never heard that any failed."

"Must he have been working for the queen? Don't fairies—doesn't it happen anyway?"

"There's been less . . . interaction with humans since my mother's rule."

"Do you think he's still here?" Rose asked.

"I don't know. I can find out."

"It's been twenty winters, you said. But there are only seven children, all young."

"I'm afraid they don't live long, down here. Humans need true sunlight."

An ache formed in Rose's chest. They were silent for a moment.

Dustan reached out as if he would touch the ends of her hair, hanging near her face, but again stopped himself short. "You cut it."

"I wanted to hide. The king is looking for me. His guards took King Murkel, who told them I was with you. They will be hunting us."

"Let me hide you." Dustan waited, and Rose nodded. He took a pinch of dry leaves from the pouch and faced her, considering. "We'll make your hair curled, and your eyes brown, and cover you with freckles, and larger teeth. I'll have to touch you."

Rose nodded again.

He muttered a few words and crushed the leaves, sprinkling them over her. He gently touched his fingers to her face and spoke more words in a language she didn't know. Rose felt warm, but nothing else changed.

Dustan squinted as he looked at her, as if trying to see beyond his own sight if his illusion had worked. "It will hide you from the king's men, for sure."

Rose felt her hair as Dustan turned to lift another cape off a hook on the wall and placed it around her shoulders.

"It feels the same," Rose said.

"That's because you can't see it. You're expecting to feel it as it was. I haven't really changed you, but whatever you believe is there is what your mind will show you. Here, look."

Dustan pulled a glass jar off the shelves. A dark liquid swirled inside. He held it up so she could see her faint reflection. At first glance, she had a cloud of frizzy hair surrounding her head. She reached out to touch it again, watching her reflection, and this time her fingers brushed against the frizz.

"That's why the wall at the entrance was solid when I reached out to touch it, until I believed it was not there."

"You see and feel what you believe, but it doesn't change what's real." Dustan stilled, and as Rose watched, his hair brightened and curled, and his face shimmered and changed, with freckles appearing across his nose.

"You don't need the spell?" she asked. "And the herbs?"

"Not to change myself." He shouldered the pack. "We'll have to hurry now. Ready?"

She nodded.

They left the room and stole down the tunnel, running. After a few turns, they entered a large kitchen. The lights were dim, the pots clean, and the fires burning low. Dustan hunted along a shelf. As Rose watched him, she practiced seeing through his illusion until she could see the real Dustan at a glance. He picked out a small bottle of vanilla, just like the one they'd had in the castle. When Rose was little, Kate used to let her open it to sniff the marvelous scent, all the way from Norland.

Dustan pocketed the bottle and moved to a doorway. They exited the kitchen and hurried along another corridor until they reached a door in an alcove. Dustan pulled Rose in beside him and knocked quietly.

The door opened slowly to reveal a young woman. Her dark hair was cut short, like Dustan's. She held a baby asleep in her arms. "What are you doing here?" she hissed. Her eyes shifted to Rose and back to Dustan. "Are you mad?"

"Snowdrop," Dustan said, reaching out to touch her arm.

"She'll let you live in the dungeon," Snowdrop said, a whine entering her voice. "You'll make her angry. She'll—"

Dustan put his hands gently on Snowdrop's elbows and pulled her closer, the baby sleeping between them. "I have to get Rose out of here. And we're taking the children."

Snowdrop's mouth opened but no words came out.

"Is she asleep?"

Snowdrop's face fell, and she sighed. "She's got Bluebell fanning her and Cedar playing. How'll you get them away without her seeing?" She glanced over her shoulder and stepped back, admitting them into a sitting room with seats and small tables.

The furnishings were grander than those in Dustan's apartment. On a shelf of trinkets Rose saw a decorative metal box that looked human made. Through a doorway came the faint sound of a stringed instrument. Snowdrop lowered the baby into a basket.

Dustan led Rose behind a screen that hid a hearth where a small fire glowed, its smoke curling up the chimney. He pushed open a door that led into a pantry. Snowdrop came after them. Dustan reached for a short knife from the rack on the wall and slid it into a pocket in the side of his trousers. He pulled a bottle of wine from the pantry.

"Get her to drink this," Dustan said, pouring the wine into a fancy glass tumbler. He pulled out the vanilla and tipped it over the wine.

"It won't kill her, will it?" Snowdrop asked.

"No. Have a sip to show her. It's only the vanilla extract made by humans, but it's made with alcohol—like wine only much stronger. If she has enough, it will dull her senses."

"And then what?"

"I'll overpower you, and we'll take the children and go." He smiled. "Just screech like you usually do, she'll never know you helped us."

"I don't screech." Snowdrop punched Dustan's arm.

"I'll give you moonflower, too. I'll do yours first."

"I don't want you to go," Snowdrop said.

"It's not forever, Snowdrop. She can't live forever."

"And who's next? Beech? Syc? They're as bad as she is."

"They're not bonded yet. You know the fairies need a queen. And they might not be chosen. The fairies might choose you."

Snowdrop snorted. "They won't choose me."

The music paused.

"There's one other thing," Dustan said, lowering his voice further. "Rose's father may be here."

Snowdrop finally looked at Rose, once again speechless.

"It would've been nineteen winters ago," Dustan said.

"I'll try to find out."

"Now go," Dustan said, handing her the tumbler as he leaned in and kissed her cheek.

Snowdrop huffed but took the wine and stepped out from the screen.

Rose stood motionless, listening for the voices from the bedchamber. Dustan had his eyes closed, as if he, too, were focused on listening. He shook his head, stepped out from the screen, and padded silently to the doorway. Rose followed.

"You'll have to test it, dear," said the queen's cold voice. "You know many wish to harm me."

Rose couldn't believe it. What kind of mother would use her own daughter to test for poison?

"Of course, Mother," Snowdrop said. "The fairies love you.

But it's best to be safe." There was a pause. "It's a new vintage. It has a real zing to it. Here, try it."

There was silence. A minute passed. "You think they love me?"

"Yes."

"How do you know?"

"I hear them talking."

"I don't think they love me."

"Mother, it's the elderberry. Give me the glass. Let it take you to sleep."

"I need Bluebell."

"I can fan you. The child is sleepy."

"No. Bluebell can sleep later."

"Very well."

Dustan's fingers slid between Rose's and squeezed. He dropped her hand and entered the queen's bedchamber. Rose peeked in after him. The queen reclined on a chaise, her eyes closed, with the small child who'd held the goblet beside her—Larch had said she was his and Jane's child, Bluebell. Dustan grabbed Snowdrop and pinned her against him. A puff of dust sparkled from his hand. He clamped his hand over her mouth. Snowdrop inhaled the moonflower. She struggled, held fast in his arms, and completely forgot to scream.

Bluebell held a fan, but she stood frozen and stared at Dustan and Snowdrop. The other children slept on pillows in the corner.

"Why have you stopped?" The queen's eyes opened in slits. "Wretched thing, keep—" The queen's gaze landed on Dustan, who was lowering a limp Snowdrop to the ground. The queen swiped clumsily at Bluebell, who stumbled into her. The queen reached into her robe.

Rose dashed across the room. The queen took a desiccated flower from her robe. Rose swept the child into her arms and kicked at the queen's hands. The queen cried out.

Dustan brushed past Rose and squeezed his mother's wrist until she dropped the flower. "None of that, Mother," he said. "You've done enough harm."

Rose stepped back, hugging Bluebell tightly. Snowdrop was sprawled on the floor, smiling upward with her eyes glazed.

Dustan knelt on the queen's sofa, holding her down as she tried to rise. "They would love you more if you were less cruel," he said. He quickly held up one hand and blew something at the queen before pinning her down again. She twisted her face away. "You can't hold your breath forever," he said. The queen shook her head, but a moment later, she gasped in a breath. She relaxed and sagged onto her chaise.

"Well that was impressive," said a voice from the doorway, and Larch strode into the room.

Chapter 21

LARCH FOLDED HIS ARMS ACROSS his chest, blocking the door-way.

"Don't make me fight you," Dustan said.

"I think I can take my little brother."

"But you haven't seen Rose fight," Dustan said, and Rose turned so fast she almost dropped Bluebell. She hitched the child up on her hip, staring at Dustan.

Larch smirked. "Her? With the child in her arms?"

Rose stepped forward. "Your child, you mean."

The smile faded from Larch's face.

Rose took another step. "This child belongs with Jane, and you're going to help us get her there."

"Mother will flay me alive," Larch said, looking away across the room.

Rose hoped he was exaggerating.

"She won't know you helped," Dustan said.

"She'll think I let you out of the dungeon," Larch said. "How did you manage that?"

He was weakening, Rose sensed.

"Apparently the humans have magic to open their locks. Serves Mother right, building such a place down here."

Rose turned to the pillows where the children were lying. A few of them had awoken and were watching her. She bent down and touched them, urging them to get up. She reached for the smallest and stood her up, wondering who her mother might be. The other four were older and stood at Rose's command. Rose grieved to see their sickly skin and dull eyes. Dustan came and lifted the smallest into his arms. He moved toward Larch with the other children straggling behind him.

Larch watched them, his face emotionless, before stepping aside. "Ash is at the northern gate," Larch said. "He's alone."

Dustan nodded and left the room, trailed by the children. Rose clutched Bluebell and followed. Dustan murmured to the oldest boy, who reached for the baby before they moved into the passage. Rose felt Larch watching them go.

Rose strained her eyes, peering down the darkened corridor ahead and glancing back into the dim space as they urged the children on. Dustan made a few turns, and each passage looked the same to Rose. She never would have found her way out alone. At last a light appeared ahead. One guard stood by, watching them approach.

As they neared, something knocked the guard back. A blaze of fur raced toward them.

"Aid!" Rose said as the dog leapt at her, pawing her skirt. He danced around her feet.

"He's been sniffing around every gate," the guard said as they arrived. He was the one who'd led her into the caverns. "He's been making the rounds, trying to find a way in." After licking Rose's outstretched fingers, Aid turned briefly to Dustan, who scratched his ears. Aid circled the children, sniffing them and nuzzling against their small fingers.

"Ash," Dustan said, and they clasped hands.

"So you got out," Ash said.

"Assuming you don't stop us."

"Just make it look like I fought you," Ash said, and before Rose comprehended, Dustan drew back his fist and punched Ash in the face.

"Stars, Dustan, you couldn't give me some moonflower first?" Ash asked, leaning forward with his hand on his cheekbone.

"Sorry. I've got a lot on my mind."

"I'll bet."

Shifting the child on his hip, Dustan took out the pouch of moonflower. He opened the top, held it toward Ash, and blew lightly. Faint dust puffed out, and Ash inhaled deeply. After a moment, Ash chuckled and slumped against the wall. His cheek was red and starting to swell.

They continued up the passage, and when Rose looked back, a wall of rock stood where Ash had been.

As they ascended, she inhaled the freshness of leaves and grass. The night air was full of the smell of the forest. Rose longed to run to it, to be free of the cavern. They came at last into the night, the stars overhead bright in the moonless sky. Rose looked at Bluebell, whose head tilted back in wonder. One of the older children tentatively stroked a hand down Aid's fur, and Aid turned to lick the child's face.

Dustan led them through the trees to a stable with a cart parked beside it. Horses snuffled from inside.

"Wait here," Dustan said, lowering the child he carried to the ground. He entered the stable and returned with a horse, who stamped her hooves as he hitched her to the cart with a strange halter. The back of the cart had a cloth hung over it. Rose lifted it and motioned to the older children. She helped them climb in and tucked the little ones into the space. If only she had a blanket to cover them. Her cape, that would do. She untied it and spread it across the small bodies. Aid leapt in to join them, climbing over them until he found a place to settle, with three sets of hands petting him. Rose put up the backboard and latched it in place.

Dustan was having a word with the horse, an old mare named Jo, whose stamping hooves had calmed. He turned to Rose. "Ready?"

"Yes." She climbed up onto the seat. The reins were tied at the front of the cart, but when Dustan climbed up beside her, he merely clicked his tongue, and the horse lurched into motion. He reached up to a lantern hung on a pole at the corner of the cart. Before Rose realized he'd touched it, the lantern burst into life.

"Where is Redbud?" Rose asked, as the name came to her.

"My mother claimed her. I think she's alive, but I know not where."

The lantern illuminated the branches ahead, and after a moment, they emerged onto a cart track. Dustan turned the horse onto it.

"You know your way," Rose said.

He nodded.

The light reached ahead twenty paces or so. Rose watched the road as it appeared before her, one bit at a time. There was no sense trying to peer into the darkness of the forest. They rode in silence. But she was alert and restless, with the excitement of escape still coursing through her body. She remembered the queen's face as they'd left her. What would she do when she recovered? And when they arrived in Woods Rest, and her friends saw the children, what would they do? Rose's nerves jangled each time she thought of it.

The motion of the cart began to soothe her thoughts. The children were deathly silent. Rose twisted back and peered under the cover. She couldn't see the motion of their breathing, but Aid met her gaze and wagged his tail. She turned back to the road.

Her eyelids began to droop. She forced herself awake, only to nod off again a minute later. This time, Dustan's arm came around her, gently pulling her against him. She rested her head on his arm, allowing sleep to come.

When consciousness returned, her arms were cold. Rose

pulled the cover over her tighter, trying to stay warm in the chill. She snuggled against the warm body beside her. Where was she? And who—? Rose bolted upright. Beside her on the seat, Dustan sat as if he hadn't moved a smidge all night. He glanced at her long enough to smile and turned back to the road. The lantern was out, but a faint light revealed his silhouette. The cart's wheels creaked as they rolled down the dirt track. The sky showed gray through the dwindling branches, and the scent of the damp forest floor filled the morning air. Rose hugged the cape tighter and turned to check on the children, who slept beneath a cape—hers. Rose looked again at the cover over her—Dustan must have put his cape around her last night.

As the sun rose, they rolled out of the forest and Rose recognized the pasture outside of Woods Rest. The sheep huddled on the grass. A soft thud caught her attention, and Aid trotted up alongside the cart, looking at her before dashing into the fields.

The early rising villagers were about as Dustan reached for the reins and drove toward the town square. Thankfully, the children slept on, hidden under the cloth. In the square, half a dozen horses with royal colors stood tethered at the pub. Murkel's eyes gazed out from a shredded poster on the pub wall. Rose flinched. Farther on a new poster was plastered, with two faces sketched on it, hers and Dustan's. "REWARD" it read across the top.

She glanced at Dustan, who regarded the poster as well.

His gaze flicked to her face and he smiled. "Don't worry," he said. "They can't see us."

Rose touched the frizz of hair that surrounded her face, both there and not there, thanks to Dustan's magic.

Aid reappeared and led the way past the hall. The widows' stone house came into sight, a sunbeam striking the front porch, where Ladi rocked gently in a chair. Rose waved, and Ladi's rocking halted. She stood and came down the steps. Dustan pulled the horse to a stop.

Rose slid from the seat and moved to embrace Ladi, but Ladi drew back.

"Ladi," Rose said. "I'm Rose."

Ladi squinted. "You're not . . . but you sound like Rose."

"It's an illusion," she said. "It was Dustan's doing, to hide us from the king." She looked up to where Dustan sat on the cart's bench, and Ladi did the same.

"Dustan?"

"He used magic."

Ladi nodded. She understood.

"Ladi, I'm sorry I left, but I had to," Rose said. "I didn't tell you in case I failed."

Ladi looked away from Dustan, her face scrunched in confusion.

"I brought something." Rose reached for Ladi's hand and led her to the back of the cart.

Rose lowered the backboard and Aid jumped in, nuzzling aside the cape.

Ladi caught her breath. "Child, what did you do?"

"I went to the fairies."

"Are these—"

Rose nodded.

"Do you know whose?"

Rose lifted the cape's edge, and Bluebell's large eyes looked out. "This one is Jane's," Rose said. "But Ladi, they are all younger than ten winters."

Tears welled in Ladi's eyes.

"Could I go back for her?"

"You won't find her. They don't grow past eight winters," Rose said gently. "There's no sunlight there."

Tears rolled down Ladi's cheeks, and she bit her lip.

"But could there be other places, other—"

Rose rested her hand on Ladi's arm. "Not all fairies steal children," she said. She glanced up at Dustan, and he nodded. "Only the one queen we came from." Rose fell silent. Nothing she could say would fix this. She hated to have brought a new grief to Ladi. She glanced again at Dustan, but he stared at the ground in front of the cart.

Ladi sighed. "I didn't ever expect to find her. It's better to know." She took in the faces, all now turned on her, and her voice grew gentle. "Hello," she said, and the older children shifted, looking down. "Poor babes," Ladi whispered. She turned to the house. "Let me get the others."

Rose watched her friend walk back to the house. Dustan came down beside her.

When the women appeared on the porch, Rose knew Ladi had told them what she'd done. Jane and Liza clutched each other, as if scared to move. It was Ladi who came forward. Gently, she took Bluebell from the cart and brought her up the walk to Jane. Jane's arms shook as she let go of Liza to take her child, and Ladi supported her, holding on until Jane had Bluebell safely against her chest, her chin resting on the small head.

Kitty and Ladi began helping the children out. Maryanne took the baby from Ladi's arms and stood with it pressed to her. Liza looked like she might faint, standing motionless on the walk. Kitty must have realized that the children were too young for any to be her own, but she hid her feelings, instead ushering everyone into the house. The children tolerated the fuss and the hugs without resistance, only looking wide eyed at the trees and sky, with Aid nudging them from behind.

Dustan followed the group into the house. Before she went in, Rose looked back to make sure the horse was secure. A figure stood beyond the road at the edge of the trees. It was Larch. Their eyes met, and he slipped into the morning shadows.

Inside, Kitty and Ladi's voices came from the kitchen, along with the banging of pots. "They may need help," Rose said, but Dustan stopped her with a hand on her arm.

"I'll go help. You stay here." He nodded toward the dining

room, where the children sat on the benches at the table. Maryanne held her baby as she spoke to the oldest child.

"Could it be John?" she asked gently. He shook his head a tiny
bit.

"Fairies name children after nature," Dustan said quietly.
"Flowers, plants, trees. It might be best to choose a new name."

Maryanne looked up and considered Dustan, her eyes sharp.
She turned back to the boy and softened. "What name would you
like, then?" she asked, reaching across the baby on her lap to tap
the boy's nose with her finger. He twitched his nose like a bunny
and a smile almost crept across his face. "How about Amare, like
the noble king across the water?" The boy looked down, shifting
on his seat.

Dustan walked down the hall and disappeared into the kitchen.

"Who is that on your lap, Maryanne?" Rose asked.

"This is my Jacob," she said, rocking the baby. "And Liza has
found her daughter."

"Aislinn," Liza said from the other end of the table, where she
held her little girl beside Jane. She tilted her head. "Is that really
you, Grace?"

Grace? Rose looked behind her, then remembered. "It is. Dustan cast a spell. He's a . . . ." Rose hated to mention the fairies
after they'd caused so much harm. "He helped us escape. But my
father is looking for us."

Maryanne looked up. "Your father? Not your husband?"

Rose couldn't remember her story. "There was no husband,"
she said. "Well there was, but I escaped him. With Dustan. I made
up a story."

"Dustan is the prince," Liza said. "The one the king's looking
for."

"Yes." Rose said. "My name isn't Grace. It's Rose."

Maryanne's eyebrows lifted. "You're Princess Rose?"

"Not anymore."

Kitty and Ladi bustled in with bowls of hot cereal, a pitcher of cream, and a dish of blueberries, and Maryanne turned back to the children. Ladi passed a bowl to Rose. The blueberries had been arranged in the shape of a heart.

Rose looked around. Across the hall, Dustan sat on the edge of a chair in the sitting room. She went to sit beside him. She took a bite of the porridge, avoiding the berries. She passed the bowl to Dustan. "What was your name . . . your other name?" she said.

He picked off a blueberry, leaving a hole in the heart. "Broad-leaf."

"And Larch is Cedric?"

Dustan nodded. "My mother forbid us to use human names."

"Does your mother have a name?"

"Of course. It is Oleander." He passed the bowl back. "Do you wish to stay here?"

Rose swallowed hard to get the bite she'd just taken past the lump that formed in her throat. She had thought she would, but the way Dustan asked made her think he'd be leaving. The thought left her feeling desperate—she did not want to part from him.

She watched the scene across the hall, the mothers and children. They didn't need her here, especially not if she might draw guards upon them. "I want to keep everyone here safe," she said at last. "I'm hidden now, but will the spell last on its own?"

"A few days."

Rose stared at the broken ring of blueberries. "Where are you headed?"

"Rose."

She didn't move.

"Rose," he said more softly. "Look at me."

Rose looked at him, into his brilliant green eyes beneath his dark unruly hair. The feeling overcame her again, of wanting to be his. Was it a spell?

He must have seen the panic in her eyes.

"You're free of your father," he said. "And of my mother, and King Murkel. And you're free of me. But I won't leave you unless you want me to."

"I don't," she whispered.

PART 3
THE FAIRY

Chapter 22

THE ROAD NORTH FROM WOODS Rest meandered across open fields. Rose and Dustan had taken only the old mare named Jo. Aid had stayed behind. Rose's friends had not wanted her to go, and she'd struggled to explain why she must. She could barely explain it to herself, but she needed to uncover everything that had happened to her in the past moon, and she needed Dustan to do it.

"It's about two days to Knotty Knob," Dustan said over his shoulder. Rose shifted her focus from balancing on Jo to listening to Dustan. She rode sidesaddle to avoid drawing attention and was quickly deciding it was a silly custom as she wobbled on Jo's rump.

"Are you still feeling nervous about the guards?" he asked. They'd seen more guards than ever in the village square, and they had passed some companies on the road.

"Ladi said she couldn't tell it was me at all."

"It's a good thing I'm able to hide us. I doubt we could outrun anyone on this nag." He patted the side of Jo's neck and she snorted, turning her massive head to look at Dustan. "I'm just kidding," he said to her.

"You've traveled this way before?" Rose asked. She kept thinking of him as a stranger in the kingdom where she'd grown up, but he knew it better than she did. In spite of the fairy queen's rules, he'd seen many places.

"Different plants grow in different forests and in the mountains and along the shore. We've always traveled to gather them."

Jo stumbled and without thinking, Rose clutched Dustan. Her fingers felt his warmth through the fabric of his shirt. She blushed, glad he couldn't see her face, and made herself let go. It would be a lot easier to balance if she could simply put her arms around him.

"Will the road pass into forest soon?" she asked.

"Yes."

"I'm excited to sleep outside." She knew Dustan had some coins, but not how much. And Ladi had packed blankets and bedrolls in the saddlebags.

Dustan didn't speak again, and Rose resumed her balancing game. Trees appeared ahead, and as the sun rose higher, they entered the shady forest. It no longer scared Rose to be among the trees.

Before they'd entered the forest, Jo had lumbered past cottages and barns, and once, past a farmer trundling down the road pushing a handcart of vegetables. But now that they were in the woods, they passed no one. Rose had only a vague idea of the whereabouts of the manors of the king's underlings, but none were in the forest that covered the center of Sylvania. Along with a few outposts, only the villages of Woods Rest and Knotty Knob were in the forest, connected by the forest road and surrounded by the fields the villagers had cleared to farm.

Rose replayed the happy scenes she'd witnessed during the day they'd passed in Woods Rest. As the children slowly opened up—as they silently watched the adults, wincing at any motion but relaxing as they received only kind words and touches—the older children began to speak in whispers, as if they hadn't known they had the skill.

It was midafternoon before they came to a cluster of ramshackle wooden buildings. Jo slowed as she approached a crossroads in the trees. To the left, a rutted, weedy road ambled into darkness. To the right, the road was better kept. Sunlight shone on the center of the road, a few cottages crowded into the space, and a lopsided inn had its door standing open.

Jo halted, and Dustan dismounted and gave Rose his hand as she slid to the ground. She stretched her stiff muscles. Dustan took Jo's reins and tied her at a post. She whickered in protest.

"We have to keep up appearances," he whispered into Jo's ear.

A few minutes later they were sitting at the wide open window in the inn's front room, looking out at the road and having tea with bread and cheese.

"I keep thinking about the looks on their faces, Ladi and the others," Dustan said. "I wonder how their day is going."

"I can't imagine it going badly," Rose said.

"You performed a miracle, returning them."

Rose wanted to deny it, but it warmed her heart to hear his words. She looked down and took another bite of bread.

Jo whinnied, and Dustan looked to where she stood beyond the porch. She snorted, dipping her head, and stamped a hoof. Dustan leaned out the window and listened. A moment later, Rose heard the clatter of horses.

Dustan sat back. "Guards, I think." Rose's throat tightened, and she swallowed the lump of bread. Dustan reached across the table and took her hand. "They can't see us. Just stay calm."

The clattering grew louder. At a cottage across the road, an arm reached out to pull shut the shutter over the window. The hoofbeats slowed. Six guards in the castle uniform rode into the crossroads, weapons shining in the bright daylight, and pulled their horses to a stop to dismount. A young one gathered the reins of the horses as the others spread out and began knocking at the cottage doors. One guard headed toward the inn. The innkeeper stepped outside.

"On orders of the king," the guard said, "I'm looking for two people, a man and a woman." He fumbled with a paper and read a description of Rose—long dark hair, fair skin, green eyes. And

Prince Dustan, last seen with short dark hair and brown eyes, rumored to be a fairy. Would they suspect they had found her?

The innkeeper shook her head. "Haven't seen anyone like that," she said. "Just a merchant yesterday, and these two today." She gestured at the window where they sat.

The guard turned to them.

"We live in Woods Rest, my sister and I," Dustan said. "We're going to Knotty Knob to see some goats."

The guard turned back to the innkeeper. "I'm sorry, ma'am, I have orders to look around."

She led him inside.

Rose's anxiety lessened. She pinched off another bit of bread.

"Don't they know about your illusions?" Rose whispered.

"Maybe some," Dustan said, "but our skill with herbs has grown. One benefit of being trapped in the caverns all these winters."

Someone shouted. At the cottage across the road, a brawny guard emerged dragging a young woman, followed by what looked like her mother and young brothers.

"Her eyes are brown," the mother said, reaching for the guard's arm. "That doesn't match at all."

The guard shook the mother off. "She has to come with me," he said. "Won't take long."

The girl's eyes were round with terror. In the center of the road, the young guard holding the horses stood motionless and stared.

Wouldn't someone help her? Rose had never seen the guards act like this. Back in the castle, Adela would order the guards around. And sometimes Avianna would see what she could get away with, taunting the ones who stood at attention. Rose was used to guards who jumped to attention if she needed anything. They'd never have dared touch her, or even looked twice at her. But out here they could do as they wished. The villagers were too scared to stop them. And there'd be no reprisals. Rose's heart raced, but now she was angry.

The guard dragged the girl toward the horses as tears streamed down her face, and suddenly Rose remembered King Murkel dragging her across the sandy beach, and how there'd been no one to help her. Rose was out the door before she knew she was standing. She reached the horses as the guard turned to lift the girl on.

"Let her go," she said, stepping between the guard and his horse.

The guard turned to her. "Get out of my way or you'll be next, only it'll be a whipping for you."

"You work for the king," Rose said. "They don't pay you to harass the peasants. Let her go."

The guard turned to Rose, and the moment his grasp loosened, the girl tore herself away and ran back to her cottage. The guard cursed, turning after her. Dustan had followed Rose out and stood a few paces off but within her sight—his muscles were tense.

"Rye," said the one holding the reins. "Let's just go."

Rye turned back to Rose, his face reddening under his tightly cropped hair. This close, he towered over her, and she could smell sweat and leather and the horse against her back. Rose braced herself, staring back into his piglike eyes.

The guard looking around the inn exited and came toward them. "There's no one here," he said.

Rye snorted, glaring at Rose so that she feared he'd hit her, and then what would happen? But Rye merely pushed past her to mount his horse. The other guards were returning. Rose stepped back. The guards mounted and wheeled about, talking. Two headed east and the others headed north on the forest road.

As the clatter of hooves subsided, villagers emerged from their homes. Dustan tried to lead Rose back to the inn, but the mother whose girl she'd saved intercepted them as her boys swarmed around Rose's skirt.

"Oh, thank you, miss," the mother said. "I don't know how you were so brave."

"Nor do I," Rose said. "Do they always behave like that?"

"You've never seen them?" the woman asked, and Rose remembered that she was a peasant now.

"I keep her hidden when they're about," Dustan said.

"It's always the same," a man said. "Taking things, sometimes only your food or your chicken, sometimes your daughter for a spell." He spat in the dirt.

"Where are you headed?" the mother asked.

"Knotty Knob," Rose said.

"For the meeting?" the man said, lowering his voice.

"What meeting?"

The man glanced at his neighbors before continuing. "There's a meeting at Elder Kendall's barn, two nights from now. We're tired of this, the guards and the taxes. We could use some brave folks like you." His gaze shifted from Rose to Dustan.

"Thank you for telling us," Dustan said. He put his arm around Rose and led her back to Jo, and the villagers dispersed. Dustan paid the innkeeper and had her wrap their food. A few minutes later, they left the crossroads behind.

Now that the moment had passed, Rose saw how badly it could have gone. She could have been arrested, or gotten Dustan into a fight that got him killed. She began to shake and put her hand on Dustan's back to steady herself.

"I'm sorry," she said.

"Why?"

"They could have taken me, too, or you. I could have gotten us both in trouble. I just couldn't stand by while that poor girl . . ."

"I know," Dustan said.

"I just got so angry," Rose said. "It was like when I saw Oleander with Bluebell. I was out in the road before I realized it. I'm not used to being angry."

He laughed. "You get better at it." After a moment, he said, "What do you think of this meeting?"

Rose had been too upset to think of it, but now the villager's words came back to her. "He said, 'We're tired of this.' What do you think he meant?"

"I don't know. Maybe a rebellion."

A rebellion. The word resonated within her. But Rose knew they shouldn't get involved. It would only draw attention to them. They had to distance themselves from the castle and from Oleander's court.

Jo stumbled over a rock and Rose tipped into Dustan. He reached back and found her hand, putting it on his side. "Don't be shy about hanging on if you need to."

"You too," she said, before realizing the reply made no sense. But he squeezed her hand before letting it go.

The meeting. Rebellion. The words kept repeating in Rose's mind. She could hide in the woods with Dustan, but then nothing would ever change. Not for her, and not for any of the other peasants who suffered under the king. She and Dustan could leave Sylvania. If it came to it, Dustan could hide them on a ship to get them away. But most of the peasants didn't have that option. They needed a rebellion to be free.

"What do you think of a rebellion?" she asked Dustan.

"Against your king? I'm all for it."

"And we're headed to Knotty Knob. We'll be there in time for the meeting."

"Yes, we will."

"Then maybe we should attend."

Chapter 23

✍

A MURMUR OF VOICES DRIFTED FROM the dimly lit barn as Rose and Dustan approached in the darkness under the low-hanging branches of oak trees. A horse tethered to the fence snorted. A woman arrived on foot, nodding at them as she walked to the barn door.

Dustan dismounted and reached to lift Rose down. He looked at her in the darkness. "Are you sure you want to do this? We'll draw attention, being strangers."

"You said it seemed like a rebellion. I want to find out more." She couldn't explain the burning in her chest. Since she'd learned of the meeting, the pull to go had only grown. Before, she had always tried to hide, to avoid drawing any notice. But now something compelled her into the open.

Dustan nodded. He looped Jo's reins over her back and gave her a warning look. She snorted and lowered her head to the grass.

As Rose and Dustan slipped through the open barn door, the murmuring resolved into words.

"I'm not a traitor," said the man closest to the door. "But this king lets his guards do as they will. It's not safe for any of us, and our hard work is rewarded with theft and arson."

" 'Tis the same anywhere."

"Not in Norland." The speaker had darker skin than the rest of the crowd, like Ladi's.

"Oh, Norland! Your grandfather never should have left."

Several in the crowd laughed, and the Norlian man smiled.

As Rose and Dustan sat on a bench, a woman stood.

"There's no reason we can't aspire to something better," she said. She spoke quietly, but the crowd stopped laughing. "Norland's a good model, with King Amare's People's Congress. There are many more commoners than courtiers in Sylvania. The lords in their manors do nothing to serve or protect us. Why should they rule?"

The crowd grumbled in agreement. The woman continued. "With the king removed, that would be a start. We could install a People's Congress to review the laws, to levy fair taxes, and oversee the guards."

The woman spoke treason, of course, but her words made sense. What gave the king the right to rule, when he did it so poorly? A congress made up of the people would surely be better. And, Rose couldn't help but think, if the king were not ruling, if there were a People's Congress, as the woman said, surely they wouldn't care about finding ex-princess Rose.

"What should we do, Kendall?" someone asked the woman. "We'll never have the fighting skills to match the king's guard, much less have as many weapons. Should we take the manors first?"

Another person spoke. "Attack a manor, they call on the castle, and the castle guard comes. It's all the same."

The whole room was quiet.

Kendall stepped toward the front of the audience. "You are right that we'd never match the king's firepower. We're here to find a solution."

"We need to trick 'em," someone called out. "Take out the guards one by one, till they're scared to leave the castle."

"They'll just send bigger numbers of troops and more firepower."

"It'd take time, but we could do it."

Voices rose, some agreeing, some in protest.

Rose grew uneasy. She remembered the attack by the guard she'd witnessed two days before. The guard, Rye, abusing his position and threatening an innocent girl. He deserved to be removed from the guards and more. But not all the guards were like Rye. The young guard holding the horses' reins had tried to persuade Rye to leave the girl alone.

A dog lolled at the feet of one of the peasants in the barn, like Aid would have. Rose had named Aid after the guard Aidan. Aidan had always been kind to Rose, and he had a family. And what of Kate's poor son, Burne, who shouldn't have been a guard at all, but who had been forced into it simply because he was a boy and old enough?

Rose found herself on her feet. "Who are the guards?" she said. All the faces turned to her. "They're peasants, your own sons, taken away to the castle and made to serve. They're not all brutes."

"But the ones who are—"

"They turn 'em mean," someone said.

"My son would never behave like those guards," said one woman, and as Rose turned to her, the woman's neighbor rolled her eyes. "I raised my son better."

Kendall was biting a fingernail, staring hard at the floorboards. "They're always strangers when they come," she said, and the voices quieted again. "I've never recognized one. When they come through, they are always strangers."

Rose sank back onto the bench. Her whole body was shaking. Dustan squeezed her arm.

"Thugs, more like," someone said, but this time, no more voices rose in dissent. Everyone waited on Kendall.

"It's as if they segment them by their home town," she continued. "What do you think would happen if a guard came face to face with his mother in the crowd? Or his sisters? You think he'd act as badly as they usually do? I think it would sober him up, snap him out of the trance they've put him under. Our sons are somewhere. If we could find them and turn enough of them to our side, we'd be able to stand up to the king."

"So how do we find them?" someone asked.

"Go to the castle," Rose said. Her words were met with a deep silence.

She'd never thought about how the castle guards were organized and trained, but now she could picture the guards training on the plain outside her window. She could see the young faces that lined the castle walls, and the older, hardened faces that stood nearer the king. She slowly stood again. "The castle, that's where most of the guards are, especially the young ones who are serving their time. You'd be sure to find the boys you know."

"How'd we get in?" Kendall was studying Rose, and she hoped she hadn't said too much.

"You could get them out," she said. "They always send the new ones first, to assess any situation." Her voice faltered. "They're expendable."

"So we trick them, make them think there's an attack," Kendall said. "Then we don't fight. Convert them to our cause."

"That's mad!" someone said. "We'll be shot."

"It's true it's a risk. A crowd can quickly turn violent."

"And how would we find anyone we know?"

For a moment, no one spoke.

Then to Rose's surprise, Dustan stood beside her. "I can help."

Every eye of the two dozen men and women sitting on benches and hay bales turned on Dustan.

He hesitated. "Some of you may remember the old fairy magic," he said at last, nodding to the older folks in the barn. "It is seldom seen these days, but it still exists."

Somehow the space became even more quiet. Rose could barely breathe. What was Dustan doing?

Dustan held up a finger and became still. His hair shimmered, darkening to a deep blue. A few people whispered. The blue faded away. Dustan walked to the front of the room. "The fairies use moonflower for calming. It could prevent violence, giving us time to act and to reunite families in the crowd. If we could surround the troops, we could calm them from the outside in."

"How'll we get close enough?"

"There's this," Dustan said. He reached into his pocket and tossed something into the air. A sparkling dust drifted down. Rose had seen the dust before—in the gardens, the day she'd talked to Dustan all afternoon. He'd walked around her, the air had shimmered just the same way, and the castle guards and Adela had failed to find her.

A gasp went up from the crowd. Dustan was shimmering, as was Kendall, standing beside him at the front of the room. Rose could halfway see through the spell. To the people in the barn, the two figures must be completely invisible. But the barn wall behind them remained visible. Maybe her searchers that day in the gardens had looked right at her and seen only an empty bench.

Dustan stepped forward through the screen he had created, causing the crowd to gasp again as he appeared before them. "If we had enough, we could hide a crowd. There's also a sleeping spell we could use, but it doesn't last very long."

Throughout the barn, people began talking. Kendall called for order, and the group began to plan. Dustan looked over at Rose, and he gave her the smallest of smiles. Tears sprang into her eyes. He'd exposed his identity, and shared his magic with humans, people he didn't even know. She knew he'd violated her trust in the past. He'd had her under a spell, controlling her. It had been wrong. But perhaps he had changed.

Chapter 24

ℒ

BEFORE THE SUN HAD CLEARED the horizon the next morning, Rose and Dustan were headed back into the forest. All day they hunted for the items he needed to aid the rebellion—the seeds, roots, and leaves required to work his magic. Now Rose pushed aside the ferns, scanning the vines and dead leaves underneath as she inhaled the pungent scent of the forest floor. She hadn't had much luck gathering moonflower seeds. Hopefully Dustan was faring better. Across the clearing, Jo eyed her. When the horse caught Rose looking, she snorted and went back to nosing through the leaves to nibble grass.

Rose pushed herself up on her knees and sat back on a rock. She'd given up on this clearing, but now that Jo had found something to eat, she didn't want to move on. Each time she moved, the horse let out an exasperated snort and followed her. Rose could only imagine what orders Dustan had given Jo before he'd left.

And where was Dustan? It had been hours since they'd dismounted and picked their way into the forest. He'd shown her the moonflower seeds to look for. When she'd questioned how far she should go from the spot, he'd looked confused and then tried to suppress a smile. "I think I'll be able to find you," he'd said, before disappearing in the trees.

She was tempted to move delicately and to brush away any footprints she made, just to thwart him. Only she didn't want to get lost in the forest.

Rose thought over the plans made at the meeting. Kendall and the villagers were spreading the word about the rebellion throughout all the villages of the kingdom, a peaceful rebellion that would change Sylvania from a kingdom ruled by a tyrant to a land ruled by its people, all without a soul being harmed. It wouldn't have seemed possible, but Dustan's optimism was catching, and perhaps with his help, the peasants would succeed. The people would gather in Woodglen in a few days' time to enact the plan.

Jo looked up. Rose heard only the songs of the birds throughout the treetops, and the whisper of the wind far above. But a moment later she heard the soft crush of footsteps on leaves. Dustan emerged from the trees.

"Are you all right?" He came toward her and offered her a hand.

"Yes," Rose said. He pulled her to her feet. "I didn't have much luck."

"Don't worry, I found plenty," Dustan said. "Moonflower can be tricky to spot."

Jo let out a whinny. She stepped backward to the base of a tree she'd already grazed at and nosed aside a dead branch.

Dustan walked over. "Good job, Jo," he said, kneeling down and reaching beneath the branch to pinch off several pods of moonflower seeds. Rose closed her eyes and lowered her head into her hand.

Dustan stood. "There's another clearing nearby, at the edge of a creek. It would be a good spot to camp." Rose forced herself to look up. "Will you walk?" he asked.

"Yes." There was no way Rose was taking a ride from Jo.

Dustan took Jo's reins and led her into the trees, and Rose followed. The ground sloped down, and a few minutes later, through the trees came the rush of a creek. The trees opened onto a grassy bank, the air beside the tumbling stream fresh and cool. Overhead, the sky was fading to a deeper blue. Dustan took off Jo's halter and the saddlebags, and she began to pull at the grass.

"We could have a campfire," Dustan said. "It might get chilly when the sun goes down."

He was just making conversation, Rose knew, but she wished he'd stop. She felt so useless.

Dustan was watching her. "Do you remember how to split wood?"

"I thought I remembered doing it, but I didn't believe it. I never held an axe in my life."

"You did, though. You were quite good at it."

"I was?"

"You can be good at anything, Rose. They just didn't teach you much at the castle." He stepped closer. "Be kind to yourself. You're new at this."

He seemed to know her thoughts.

"Can you show me again?" she asked.

"We'll have to wait until we have an axe. But help me gather firewood."

Rose followed him out into the trees, scanning the ground for broken branches. Soon she had an armful. She listened for the creek and followed the sounds back to their campsite. Dustan was laying the fire on a muddy patch close to the stream. He'd placed smaller bits in the middle, with larger branches forming a tent above. Rose studied the structure so she could repeat it. She expected him to use fairy dust to ignite it, but instead he gathered dry moss and showed her how to make a spark with rocks to light the moss.

They poked twigs into the glowing moss, lighting them, and a few minutes later, the fire was crackling, just as the light began to fade from the sky. The sounds of the fire stirred Rose's memories. She had never camped out by a fire like this in her life, but it felt familiar. The memory must be from her time with Dustan, the time she'd spent enchanted by his spell.

Dustan passed her slices of bread and cheese from his pack, and then removed some dried figs and began to cut them with the knife he carried. He passed her pieces as he cut them and ate every other one himself.

"Fairies don't eat meat," Rose said.

"No, not much anyway. It's hard to eat animals when you know what they're feeling."

"They tell you?"

"Sort of. It's more like we feel it. It's stronger if you get to know them."

"Do they all speak different languages? The dogs, and birds, and others."

"They do, but that's not how fairies communicate with them. It's more of an understanding. Just putting the words out in thoughts, in your own tongue, but willing them to reach the audience. It's hard to explain. We don't learn to do it, it just happens. It's stronger in some."

"You do it well."

"Yes."

"You knew Aid. Before we came out of the fairy tunnels."

"Aye. He was on the beach that day." Dustan looked down. "The day I first saw you."

Rose swallowed hard.

"Where did he come from?"

"He was a stray. He wandered onto the castle grounds, following the scent of the kitchen. I'd put the guards to sleep, so he was able to get in. As everyone began waking up, I had to leave, and I asked him to watch out for you."

"I don't think they let me keep him."

"No, he went to live with one of the villagers. A guard. Aid found us again later, when his guard tracked us to the cabin. He warned me in time to hide you."

"Aidan," Rose said. "The guard. He was always kind to me, and he took the dog. And when I woke, I didn't remember anything. But I named the dog after him."

"What else do you remember?" Dustan asked cautiously.

Now was her chance. Rose swallowed her fear. "You came to my room," she said.

"Yes."

"How did you do it? With all the guards?"

"I had a ladder up your tower. I hung it from your window the night of the supper party, while all the guests were out in the gardens. It's fairy thread. We make it from spiderwebs with a spell. It's hard to see but very strong."

As he said it, memories of the ladder came to Rose. "What about Adela? She was always with me."

"I gave you a potion. You put Adela to sleep. I waited for you to use it, and"—he paused—"when you seemed ready, I let myself in."

"Ready?"

Across the fire, Dustan looked down again. "You wished for me. You . . . you were in bed."

Rose felt her face flush with heat. "Did we . . . ?"

Dustan kept his face down, and Rose suspected he was embarrassed. But she had to know the whole story. She kept watching him, waiting for an answer. "We made love," he said. "And again in the woods. Those were the only times."

"In the woods?"

"You climbed down the ladder with me. We went to my campsite."

The tent where she and Aid had spent the night. She'd been right that Dustan had been there. And she'd been there before, too.

"Did I like it?" she blurted out.

"You seemed to," he said. "But the spell—"

"That would make me like it?"

"Yes."

"But it's gone now?"

"Yes. I have no effect on your feelings."

Rose stayed silent. She wasn't so sure he was right.

He reached to put another branch on the fire and rested his arms across his knees, and his chin on his forearm, as he stared at the flames. Rose studied his face in the shining light—his real face, not the fairy illusion he wore. His eyes were liquid pools in the firelight, his lips perfect.

She tried to remember the time they'd spent together, and making love to him, but the past felt dead. Maybe that was for the best. She didn't need it confusing her. It hadn't been real, but this was—sitting by the fire, with Dustan being honest with her. He'd helped her rescue the children from his own mother, and now he was helping her people fight the king. And he hadn't so much as touched her, nor even looked at her for more than a moment.

Why? Because he didn't want her anymore? He'd come to her in the first place only to seduce her for a child. And he seemed to be helping her now as penance for lying and using a spell on her.

But he had loved her. He'd said so. She imagined herself across the fire, sitting beside him, leaning in to kiss those perfect lips, how warm they'd be, and welcoming. And her heart, already working overtime, gave a new kind of flutter.

Dustan raised his eyes to hers, and her heart pumped harder, heat again rising to her face. But all he said was, "We should get some rest."

Dustan rose and went to Jo's saddlebags, which he had leaned against a tree. He pulled out the blankets and bedrolls and spread them on the grass close to the fire. Rose couldn't look away from him as he moved. What would it feel like to touch him? To lie with his arms around her? Her thoughts kept her awake long into the night.

Chapter 25

✍

WHEN THEY'D GATHERED ENOUGH PLANTS to make the spells, Dustan and Rose headed back to the cart track and made their way south. They were to meet Kendall in the woods near Woodglen, where villagers from across Sylvania were gathering in secret. Rose shuddered at the thought of being so near the castle. Maybe she could stay hidden in the woods.

It was a long day on Jo's back, but they reached Woods Rest by nightfall. To most visitors, the village would give no hint that a rebellion was brewing. But Rose noticed extra people loitering in the square, and campfires burning behind the homes. From towns all over, people were coming.

Aid dashed up the lane to meet them before Jo had even neared the stone house. In little over a week, much had changed. Maryanne came to greet them with Young Amare, and they took Jo to the shed in back. Children's voices rang throughout the house, and scampering feet went up and down the steps, carrying extra pillows and blankets as visitors found places to sleep.

Travelers filled the grass alongside the back garden, resting on blankets or eating. On the back stoop, Liza and Jane dished out stew into an odd assortment of bowls. After surveying the scene, Dustan turned to Rose.

"I'll find a spot out here. Find me if you need anything." And with that, he walked into the crowd. Rose watched him go. She wished they could be back in the woods, just the two of them, talking over a campfire.

"Rose." Ladi appeared by Rose's side, and Rose took her hand and squeezed.

After a pause, Rose asked, "How are things here? All seems well, but . . . How are you? And Kitty?"

Ladi sighed. "Kitty throws herself into it, taking care of everyone. Stops her pain, I think. I try to help, but 'tis hard. I can't stop seeing her face, mine who didn't make it."

Rose squeezed Ladi's hand again. She wasn't sure how else to say it, but she whispered, "How have things settled with the children?"

Ladi seemed to get her meaning. "Amare's attached to Maryanne," Ladi said, "and to baby Jacob. That boy follows her around, holding the baby." She smiled. "Liza tries to help, but you can tell she only sees Aislinn. She and Jane take their girls out in the woods to play, sometimes all day. I think Liza and Jane halfway want to be fairies."

"What is Jane's daughter's name?"

"Murielle."

"And the middle three?"

"Deka, Ebele, and Jelani. Ended up naming them all after the Norlian royal family. They're very quiet, as if they never stop being scared. They follow Amare, so 'tis like Maryanne's mother to them all."

Ladi was silent after that, and Rose didn't ask anything more. She wished it could have been different.

"I make it sound all bad," Ladi said after a bit, shaking her head. "There's joy now, too. Always somebody needing something, some way to help out. And I know the truth at last."

Ladi wanted to hear the details about the rebellion and how they planned to avoid violence. When Rose explained Dustan's ideas and the seeds and such that they had gathered, Ladi nodded, sighing.

As Rose finished describing the plan, she yawned.

"You'll sleep in the kitchen?" Ladi asked, leading Rose back into the house.

"Unless someone else needs it," Rose said. If her pallet were taken, she could find Dustan in the crowd and sleep beside him on the ground, as she had the past few nights.

But Ladi responded, "No, the visitors all settled in the yard."

Disappointment filled Rose. After the past few days of talking to Dustan by the campfire, sharing meals, and sleeping beside him, being without him felt empty. Ladi went out the back door, leaving Rose alone. From the doorway, Rose scanned the crowd and found Dustan talking with some peasants. She watched him, willing him to look up, but he didn't.

On her small pallet in the kitchen, Rose looked at Aid, snuggled against Mouser on the floor, and sighed. The door opened. Rose sat up and pulled aside the curtain. It was Ladi again.

"I'm not the one you hoped for," Ladi said.

Rose bit her lip and looked down. "I'm sorry."

Ladi's head tilted, curious. "How's it stand between you?"

Rose considered. "He's not behaved the least bit inappropriately."

"You wish he would?"

"Oh, Ladi," Rose said. All at once, the words came flooding out. "It's just I can't stop thinking about him. I want to be near him all the time. And when he's near, I look at him and want to touch him. It happened the past few days. We've been in the woods, gathering herbs for his spells, and it's just been the two of us, talking. And we'd sit by the fire at night." Rose stopped herself from raving on.

"Could it be a spell?" Ladi said. "Making you want him?"

"I've wondered that myself. It feels so strong. But he's promised me there's no spell, and I believe him." After a moment, Rose asked, "Did you need something?"

"I been thinking," Ladi said. "I'd like to go. With you, to Woodglen. Don't have a reason. I don't know what help I'd be. I'd just like to do something."

"I'm not sure what help I'll be either."

"You know the castle. That might come in handy."

Rose shuddered. "I've been pushing aside the memories of life there. I hope I don't have to go near it. Or see the king."

"Well, we set off tomorrow. Let's get to sleep."

ROSE WOKE AT SUNRISE, AND half the yard was already clear. Travelers left in twos and threes, hoping to avoid the attention of any guards on the road.

Ladi poked her head into the kitchen. "Rose. Come look."

Rose turned away from the window. Ladi led her through the house, her steps quick. She pushed open the front door and led Rose out.

Ladi pointed. A scrap of birch bark rested on the top step, weighted down with a stone. "Wasn't there last night."

Rose reached for it. "There's writing. Can you help me read it?"

Ladi unfurled the bark and leaned in close. "The fairy queen planned to come after you. But there was resistance. The fairies heard what you did and fought the queen. She's still trying."

So the fairies were resisting, too. "I'll tell Dustan."

Back inside, they prepared to leave. After bowls of hot cereal, Ladi and Rose set out, with Aid trotting at their feet and Dustan behind them.

"I think I should return Aid to his owner," Rose told Ladi.

"He's not yours?"

"He was a stray. I remember now. He followed me into the castle and I liked him. But Adela, she was my warden, she had a fit when I tried to keep him. I was under Dustan's spell, and I think the spell made me braver. Before, I never defied Adela's orders. But Adela got rid of the dog, and Aidan took him. Aidan's one of the oldest guards, but he's not hard like most of them get."

"So you named the dog after Aidan?"

"I didn't know it. Aidan was in the company that tracked me and Dustan, and Aid was with him and warned us, and Dustan asked him to stay with me. He knew Aid could guide me to safety. Dustan never expected Aid to guide me back to him."

"And to the children."

"Yes. But Aidan has a family, too. They must miss the dog."

From up ahead, a bird whistled, a long, strange sound.

Rose and Ladi stopped.

"That's the signal," Dustan called behind them. Someone up ahead was alerting them to hide if they could, to avoid suspicion. Dustan peered up the road. "There's time. Quickly, over to those bushes."

They stepped off the track and made their way through the branches toward a spot with thick bushes. They hunkered down, out of sight of the road, and waited. A moment later, they heard the tramping of hooves. Rose peered through the branches and watched the flash of riders pass through the trees. It was a large contingent, dozens of men. Fewer to encounter at the castle.

Before nightfall they neared Woodglen, where the road left the forest. As soon as the trees cleared, Rose looked for the spires of the castle. For a brief moment her spirits lifted when she didn't see them, as if all the upcoming conflict might simply be avoided. But the branches separated and the tall, stone towers appeared. The sight of them against the orange sunset filled Rose with dread.

The road meandered alongside the forest. Tents stood among the dark trees, and the farms outside the town had campfires blazing. As the light faded, they happened upon a drunk man, slumped on a crate at the side of the road.

"Can you direct us to Kendall?" Dustan asked.

The man sat up, the fog clearing from his eyes. "Welcome," he said. "Over by that big oak, then straight back into the trees."

Dustan turned to Rose and Ladi as they walked on. "Kendall is organizing the crowd, finding those who'll stand in front, the ones with a son or husband in the guard. And we'll have people on both sides, ready to sedate the guards with moonflower dust. But I'll have to manage the hiding spell myself. I should check in with her."

"We'll be fine," Rose said. "I'm going to look for Aid's family in the village."

"I'm afraid I must rest," said Ladi.

Dustan pointed to a massive rock in the field. "Put our things behind that rock, and I'll find you there. We should be safely out of sight in the darkness."

Once they'd made camp, Rose continued along the lane and into the village. Aid trotted beside her. Rose had always longed to visit this place. She'd seen the rooftops from her window and wondered about the people here. She glanced up. The castle towers loomed near, the top turrets glowing in the final light of sunset.

The village buildings were shabby, with patched roofs. Paint peeled on the signs of the shops. People walked about, carrying blankets or pots of food, and the smell of the day's catch drifted up from the docks. How different would the scene be if no rebellion were coming?

She came into the square, where cobbled lanes outlined the village garden in the center. The trees were still majestic, even if the railings and benches had fallen into disrepair, and the flowers grew wild and weedy. She passed the dry goods store and the milliner's.

One shop sign had a sprig of green leaves, and something clicked in Rose's memory. An herbalist's shop. Stone steps led to the door, with a railing that curved outward, opening onto the square. A child might climb the steps on the outside of the railing to swing under it. She could feel herself doing just that.

She stood outside the shop for a long time as Aid sniffed around the barrels and plants near the door. There were no lights inside. She couldn't bring herself to knock.

Finally Rose continued through the town. No one would recognize her as the former princess of the castle. Dustan had maintained her disguise of brown eyes and curled hair. And everyone would assume she was simply one of the many visitors in town that night. Villagers greeted her with a nod or hello. Yet she felt like an imposter. She was finally free to mingle with the villagers, but she began to feel lonelier than ever. After so many winters of imagining a trip to the village, being in the village felt strange.

Now Aid led the way, sniffing the sides of the road. He led her past the garden and down a lane lined with row houses. His ears perked up as he approached a door, then scratched. He barked once.

A chair scraped across the floor inside, followed by footsteps pounding. The door swung open and children spilled out. "It's Muttonchop!" one of them cried, and they fell on their knees as the dog jumped on them, licking their faces.

Aidan appeared behind the children. His head tilted as he looked at Rose.

"I found the dog in the woods," Rose said. "When we got to the village, he knew where to go."

Aidan nodded, still looking at her. She hadn't disguised her voice, she realized with a lurch in her stomach. Did he recognize it? She thought about revealing her identity, asking him to join the rebellion, but she didn't dare risk it. As the children headed back inside, Muttonchop followed them, casting one glance back at Rose. Aidan thanked her and closed the door.

When Rose returned to their campsite, she found Ladi and Dustan roasting potatoes over a low fire. Dustan shared the plans for the next day's maneuver. The first fireflies of the season drifted across the grass, and the damp odor of hay drifted up as evening deepened. Other travelers had surrounded the spot, making places for themselves to sleep. Rose hoped they'd quiet down soon, but the nearest group passed around a flask, sharing gossip between villages.

As Rose settled next to Ladi, words drifted over from the neighboring campfire. "Whoever took her from Murkel," a man said, "he must've had mighty powers. Like a sorcerer."

Rose wanted to sink into the ground. They were talking about her.

"Or a necromancer," someone responded. A collective shudder ran through the group.

"Or maybe he was just a fisherman," someone added, and the group chuckled.

Of course the kidnapping of the princess was still recent news. The reward had tripled in size. In the woods and in Knotty Knob the past few days, it had been easier for her to forget who she was, the princess with a price on her head. She'd been just another peasant in a plain dress.

"Imagine selling your own daughter," a woman said. "Serves him right the shells were all fake."

"She's better off without that Murkel. Who ever heard of Merlandia, until he showed?"

"Who ever heard of Skye, for that matter? She might be no better off."

"Whoever took her, it wasn't the one who left her dress in the waves. He's bound to be better than Murkel was."

"Imagine selling your daughter to such a one."

Ladi and Dustan had gone silent, watching Rose. She tried to smile at them, but the conversation made her embarrassed. And part of her wanted to march over and set the people straight. Her disguise had made her feel safe, but now it rankled. Why was she hiding? She'd done nothing wrong.

She'd feared being sold again, and being trapped. But all of the villagers feared the king. That's why they'd gathered to fight. They had as much to lose as she did.

She turned to Dustan. "I want you to remove this disguise."

"Are you sure?" he asked, looking in her eyes.

"I'm not scared anymore," she said, though she wasn't sure it was true.

"Very well." Dustan leaned toward Rose and rested a hand gently on her head. He whispered a few words. She felt a tingling. He flicked at the ends of her hair, once again dark and swinging over her shoulders. "Dark hair, green eyes," he said. He closed his own eyes and went still, and Rose watched as his curls darkened and straightened, until his hair stood in points all over his head, and the freckles faded from his face. He reached up to brush his hair flat, and the familiar motion made Rose smile. Dustan smiled back, that lopsided grin that was like a present to her.

"So this is the real Dustan at last," Ladi said.

Chapter 26

❦

EARLY THE NEXT MORNING, ROSE and Ladi were hidden on the wooded slope overlooking the road, like most of the rebels. Rose held still, her hand pressed against the rough bark of a tree. Sunlight dappled the ground around them, warming away the morning chill. The roadway below was flooded with sunshine.

At the base of the hill gathered the families of men in the king's guard, hidden from the road behind a fairy spell. And Dustan, she knew, stood on the road with a handful of the bravest volunteers, out of sight, ready with a supply of moonflower dust. Rose shifted, trying to find them, but between the spell and the branches in the way, they were impossible to see.

A runner had gone to the castle a few minutes earlier, crying about a bear who was tearing apart the storage barn where the brewmaster made the king's ale. Now hoofbeats drummed and, through the trees, six guards appeared, thundering down the road, some with pistols in hand. They slowed to question a villager who stood in the road in front of the hidden group.

Rose clutched the tree, straining to hear as the guards circled the villager. Had Dustan gotten close enough to enchant them with his moonflower?

"What do you mean, no bear?" one of the guards yelled, and the horses pranced. Another guard lifted his hand sharply. A middle-aged woman moved forward, and the air shimmered as she crossed Dustan's spell. Had the guards been watching, they'd have seen her appear in midair. She chugged up the incline to the road.

"Arley!" she called. "Is that you?"

The people on the slope were silent as they stared at the scene below. The guards turned to the woman, looks of surprise on their faces. The horses shifted nervously before settling down. The voices were too quiet to hear. The guard who'd raised his hand to strike the villager slid off his horse to face the woman. She pointed a finger as if lecturing him, and then turned to all the guards on their horses. Rose caught the words "I didn't raise—" and "Is that the kind of king—" The guards' heads hung down. Her lecture done, the woman stepped back. Another villager hobbled out from the woods and up the slope, and another guard dismounted and went to greet the person.

As Kendall appeared, all the guards dismounted. They turned to her before four of them led their horses off the road. Arley and his mother stayed. The sixth guard turned his horse back to the castle, remounted, and thundered away. He'd gone to draw out more guards.

Rose again scanned the road for Dustan, but he was hidden well.

A few minutes passed before Rose could make out another cloud of dust down the road. The ground shook under the faint pounding of hooves, and rows of mounted guards appeared. This time it wasn't a few fresh-faced youths, but the main company. The leader and his underlings stopped where Arley and his mother still stood in the road.

"Guard, get back on that horse!" the leader bellowed.

"Colonel, with respect sir," came the reply, but the rest of it was too low to hear.

"Your duty is to the king!" the colonel said.

This time, Arley's voice rang out clear. "Nay, it's to my country, as is the king's duty. But he sends us out to pillage towns and hurt our own people. We do not serve Sylvania when we serve this king."

The colonel drew his pistol, and the crowd gasped. Rose held her breath, craning to see with everyone around her. The harsh lines of the colonel's face slackened, and he chuckled, lowering his pistol. The moonflower had reached him. The horses around the colonel stamped in confusion. The colonel waved a hand lazily, his horse out of line.

A lieutenant barked an order.

The colonel responded, "I said, let 'em go!"

The moonflower was reaching more of the colonel's men. The entire squad of leaders became disordered, the men swaying on their horses. Behind them, the main company awaited orders, some looking at their neighbors and whispering.

Several people along the roadside walked forward through the spell and up to the road.

"Riley!" one called.

"Alton!"

"Holden!" A young woman, leaning back to support her pregnant belly, walked out.

Heads turned in the rows of guards. One man dismounted, giving the reins to his neighbor. He emerged from the company to take an old woman's hands. She shushed him as he pointed her back to the safety of the woods. The pregnant woman embraced her husband at the edge of the company.

The lieutenant called for order, but most of the leaders had dismounted. Kendall now held the colonel's pistol and directed someone to lead the colonel away. One by one, more of the people approached the road. Horses stepped sideways as the men in the company scanned the woods, confused and pointing each time a new person appeared out of thin air. Soon the retinue of guards had dissolved into a crowd of reuniting families.

Someone shouted and a handful of guards, still mounted, wheeled their horses around and forced a path through the crowd, and the small group galloped back toward the castle.

A cheer rose up from the people hidden in the woods, and they surged forward down the hillside. Guards leapt back in surprise, and the horses whinnied. Rose and Ladi let the crowd sweep them along.

A few minutes later, Rose was in the throng on the road, pushed this way and that as she tried to find Dustan. The bright sun made her squint. All around her, cheerful voices talked and people hugged. Before she could move very far, a bugle blew. The crowd turned toward it. Kendall was climbing onto a boulder in the field alongside the road. She stood over the crowd, and everyone drew closer and quieted.

"Many of the king's guard are here," she said, "but there are more. The king will not accept a loss of power. Guards, gather in your companies and have your leaders come to me."

"Will we storm the castle?" someone shouted from the crowd.

"We may have to wait the king out," Kendall said. "We don't have the means to knock down the castle walls. But we have more people than the king does, and now we have firepower as well."

The crowd began to murmur. Near Rose, a woman said, "My sister's there, in the kitchen." She turned to Rose and asked, "What if she's trapped?"

Rose wanted to say something reassuring, but the words stuck in her throat. She knew better than anyone that the king wouldn't hesitate to use his servants to save himself. Once he found out about the rebellion, he'd hold them hostage in case he could use them to help himself escape.

"We have to get them out," Rose said.

"But you heard," the woman said. "We cannot get in the castle."

"I can," Rose said.

"You can?"

"I must go now, before it's too late." Rose scanned the people around her. She would never find Dustan in this crowd. She turned to the woman. "You must go to Elder Kendall, the woman who spoke. Tell her to find Dustan. Tell him Rose went into the castle. Can you do that?"

"Yes," the woman said, staring at Rose.

Hopefully the woman would follow through with her instructions. Rose pushed her way through the crowd in the direction of the castle, until she reached roadway that was clear. She picked up her pace once she was alone on the road and ran until her sides ached and she slowed. But the woman's voice echoed in her head, worried for her sister, and Rose pushed herself on. She wouldn't give in to her own fear, which simmered just below her thoughts. If she could keep her head clear and focus on running, maybe she could fend off the fear.

As the castle towers came into view, Rose thought over each entrance, wondering which to try. The outer wall only had a few gates, but there were inner gates as well. All would be guarded. And if she gave herself to the guards, how would she help the servants?

The beach. But the rocks that bordered it were treacherous. She'd never been able to sneak away from it. Sneaking onto it would be no easier. The village had boats, but once on the beach, she'd have to get through gates into the gardens. And knowing the king, as soon as he learned of the rebellion, his best shooter would be stationed in a high tower, ready to shoot anyone who approached.

Rose stopped to catch her breath. The crowd of villagers had disappeared behind a bend, and she could no longer hear the murmur of their voices. She squinted up at the castle towers, finding the one she'd been locked in for so long. A breeze blew, flapping the flags that waved from the spires.

Dustan's ladder. The memory of it came back to her, her memory of going down it with her arms around him, and later climbing back up by herself. He'd been beneath her, of course, but still she had climbed it. Would the ladder still be there? How long did fairy thread last? Could she climb it again?

She quaked at the thought, but she had to do it. If the people decided to march on the castle, or if the king realized he was trapped, he would turn to violence. She thought of Kate and Maybeth in the kitchen. She couldn't let them come to harm.

Rose ran. The road was deserted, but the thought of a guard finding her spurred her on faster. Finally the castle walls came into view. The road curved around a tower. Just beyond was a gate. She veered off the road, making for the grove of trees at the base of her tower. She didn't slow until she was hidden by their branches.

Rose panted in the shade. Her sight adjusted to the dimmed sunlight, and another memory of the night she'd stolen out with Dustan returned. They'd descended the tower into the tree closest to the wall.

She approached the giant oak tree. The lowest branch was just at her shoulders. She reached to pull herself up, but her foot caught in her skirt. She gathered the skirt, tying it up, and tried again.

It took all her strength but she pulled herself up to the lowest branch, hooked her legs around it, and pushed herself over the top. She hung onto the tree's trunk and, wobbling, slowly stood. She reached for the next bough to steady herself. She glanced around.

The ladder was gone.

Rose took a deep breath and let it out, trying to relax. She stared at the tree trunk. At the sides of her vision, the ladder appeared, swaying in the breeze. It had simply gotten loose and drifted away from the tree.

Rose broke a branch off and used it to catch the ladder and pull it to her. Once she had it in hand, she felt steadier. She tugged on it, then hung on it with all her weight. It held.

She began to climb.

She didn't look down or think. She just climbed, one hand over another. And the rungs were there, one after another, though she couldn't see them. Her feet found each step without fail. She emerged from the top of the oak tree, bumping against the stones of the tower, and the breeze blew her hair. She didn't look anywhere but at her hands. Sooner than she'd expected she reached the top, and only then did she remember that her window would be locked.

As she hung there, outside her window, she considered. Would anyone be in her rooms? She'd have to risk it. She carefully reached down and took off a shoe, put it over her hand, and slammed it into the glass of the nearest pane. If any of her former ladies-in-waiting were in her bedchamber, they'd probably run, shrieking that the castle was under attack. Rose knocked the shards of glass from the edges of the pane. After dropping the shoe inside, she felt with her hand for the window latch, which she unfastened. The window swung open.

Now came the worst part. Rose caught hold of the window's edge and pulled herself toward it, taking the ladder with her. She counted to three and let go of the ladder, moving her second hand to the window and pulling herself halfway in. Her feet left the ladder and it swung away. She kicked at the air, and for a moment she imagined herself falling, but her body rested securely on the window ledge. She wiggled herself over it and into the room.

The two rooms were deserted and the door shut. Rose lowered herself to the floor, careful of the broken glass, and looked around. The bedchamber was as she remembered, with the bed made up and the trunks standing by the wall. And in the sitting room, the empty chairs waited. The rooms were just as she'd left them on that terrible day when they had taken her to King Murkel—someone must have returned the trunks after Murkel left them on the beach. Had someone missed her? Why had they kept her rooms like this?

She sat to put on her shoe. The king had probably kept her room ready in anticipation of catching her and housing her until he sold her again. She had no interest in the room that had been her prison. She stood, walked to the door, and paused to listen. The castle was quiet. She slowly opened the door, but no sounds came from below.

She crept down the stairs to the first landing without incident. Of course, no one would guard an empty tower. But she couldn't be spotted now, or they'd cart her off to the king. At the second landing, she turned away from the corridor she used to take, out to the parlors and gardens, and instead she entered the narrow, unlit staircase she'd never been allowed to use, though her mother had often taken her that way. It led down to the kitchen.

Roses padded down the steps. She heard voices below, and the smell of Kate's biscuits wafted up. Rose came to the entrance and peeked in. Servants filled the kitchen. The cooks and maids and footmen were sitting idle, the young ones on boxes and barrels, the older ones at the crude wooden table down the center of the room. Kate bustled at the ovens.

Rose stepped out from the stairway. A ripple of surprise went through the room.

"It's the princess," someone hissed.

Kate turned, holding a pan of biscuits. "Rose!" She dropped the pan and rushed forward. Her arms engulfed Rose, pulling her into a soft hug that smelled of butter and flour.

After a moment, Rose pushed Kate gently aside. "What's happening?" she asked. "Are there guards nearby?"

"He's out by the pantry," Kate said. "Guarding the food from the pirates. Wherever did you come from?"

All the faces in the room watched her.

"What pirates?" Rose said. "I've come from the village."

"Is it true that everyone is killed?" someone asked, a sob in her voice.

"Killed?" Rose said.

"They invaded the village—pirates from Sarland. We've got to stay in the castle."

"Those are lies," Rose said. "That's what they told you?"

"They said ships landed and pirates overran the village," Kate said, "burning and looting, and that we had to stay shut in the castle to wait them out."

"It's a lie," Rose said again.

Everyone was silent.

"There are no pirates. The village is fine. The guards have put down their arms to rejoin their families, all but a few who remain loyal to the king. The people want peace, and a fair way to rule themselves."

There were a few gasps.

"We need to get you out," Rose said, talking over their murmurs. "The king will use you for ransom. Are all the gates guarded?"

"There are guards at the outer gates only, and with the royal court, and at the doors of the treasury. We thought the rest were out fighting."

"There is no fighting. Everyone out there has turned." Rose listed the castle's outer gates in her mind. "Which gate would be easiest to sneak out? The north?"

Kate nodded. "That's the closest."

"We'd have to overcome the guards," one of the footmen said. "And they have muskets. They'd see us coming."

Rose grasped for an answer. If she appeared at the gate, it would distract the guards. But they'd still see the servants. But if she approached from the outside . . . . "I can distract them. I'll arrive at the gate as if I've just escaped the village, so their attention will be on me. You could come from behind."

The footman stood, looking around, and a handful of the bigger, tougher-looking servants also stood. "We could hide behind the stables and wait until they're distracted. We'd have to be quiet."

"We'll need some rope to bind them," another said.

"But how will you get out, m'lady? And how did you get in, for that matter?"

"I can't explain," Rose said. "Only it won't work for this many." Rose pushed aside the queasy feeling that came when she imagined trying to get back onto the ladder from her room.

"You must rest a moment," Kate said. She turned to the footman and the other servants. "Gather your supplies. Be ready to go." She turned to Rose. "I know there's not time, but at least tell me you've been well."

"I have," Rose said, and she blushed before she even said his name. "I've been with Dustan."

Kate waited.

"He was one of the princes—"

"I know who he was," Kate said. She seemed to be weighing her next words, when one of the kitchen maids approached, looking shyly at Rose. It was Maybeth. Rose smiled.

"M'lady, where've you been? Prince Murkel said you weren't with him, but we all saw you leavin' to be bonded. Did you find out about his gold?"

"Hush, child," Kate said.

But Rose put a hand on Kate's arm. "I don't mind. Murkel was a liar. He's a sea monster. I didn't know about the gold, but he tried to drag me into the water. Prince Dustan rescued me."

Several of the staff had gathered closer, and a few sighed. But Kate scowled. "Dragged you into the water?"

"He ripped off my dress and pulled me into the waves. And once he was wet, he had a giant tail. He lives at the bottom of the sea. He was going to keep me in a cage of air down there."

Kate clutched her chest, and Maybeth's lips parted as she stared at Rose in horror. "But Dustan came in a boat, and the birds and fishes helped."

"The birds?"

Rose blushed again. "Dustan is a fairy."

Kate tightened her lips, shaking her head. "I knew there was something about that one."

"Dustan was lying, too. He'd come to seduce me. But he's changed. He helped orchestrate the rebellion. He's out there now."

"He's a fairy?" someone asked.

"Yes." Rose noted how easily the villagers accepted the notion. Perhaps they'd been raised with stories of the fair folk, or even remembered them, as Old Synne did. Isolated upstairs in the castle, she'd not heard those stories, except what she remembered from her mother.

Kate took Rose's arm and led her away from the others. "Your mother spoke of fairies," Kate said. "I always wondered . . ."

"My father?" Rose asked.

Kate nodded, and Rose nodded back.

"We'll speak more when we're out of here safely. Tell me more about this rebellion. After we escape the castle, then what?"

Rose described what she'd seen. "I don't know how they'll subdue the king, but there's enough people to overcome him."

"Lock him up, I say," Kate replied.

"It's hard not to pity him. For so long I thought he was my father."

Kate's face reddened in anger. "Kindness is in your nature, Rose, but don't you pity that man. If you knew."

"Knew what?"

Kate hesitated and then spoke. "Your mother hated him. They forced her to bond with him, and soon she was expecting. I always thought she might've run, if not for that. You were born moons early, a full-sized baby, and with those eyes. Many suspected that the king was not your father and gossiped about it, and word got back to him.

"I don't think he believed in fairies, but he was quick to see that others did, and if others thought you were a fairy, there might be profit in it. He didn't do anything at first. But then people began visiting the castle, strangers, and you were always paraded in front of them. Your mother hated it, and it began to worry her. She realized it was more than the king suddenly being proud of a daughter he'd never much cared for.

"One of the visitors talked in the pub. That's how she found out. The king had offered to sell you. He was telling 'em you could see fairy ways and find their gold, and had magical powers, but they wouldn't appear until you were grown. The day she found out, your mother took you and tried to escape. She took a horse from the stable. She'd been a good rider. The king sent his dogs after her, and they scared the horse and it threw her. That's how she died, broke her neck with you cradled in her arms.

"And the bastard went on trying to sell you. Didn't you ever wonder why he never picked a suitor? All those rich princes. But they wanted proof, proof that you could find them gold and do magic. And he had none, so they went away. He sold you the first moment he could. So don't you feel sorry for that man." Kate clamped her mouth shut and turned away, the anger simmering in her eyes.

Rose sank onto the nearest bench. Her mother had died because of the king. She'd always known the king was greedy, but she'd kept trying to love him. Now she didn't want to.

WHEN ALL WAS READY, ROSE climbed back up the tower steps and walked into her old room. She turned her focus to what she had to do next. Without a glance back, she hoisted herself onto the window ledge and found the ladder. Soon she was back on the ground outside the castle walls. She paused to fix her appearance. After walking so many leagues and sleeping on the ground, she hardly needed to muss her hair and clothes. She already looked like an escaped captive. She took a deep breath and ran to the gate.

The two guards were startled and gripped their muskets, stepping in front of the wooden doors. One called to her to halt.

She stopped in the road, panting. "I've only just escaped," Rose said, hysterics creeping into her voice. "It's me, Princess Rose."

The guard came forward and looked closer. He called to his companion.

"It is," the other said. "Forgive us, your highness."

"Come quick, m'lady, let me help you." The guard took Rose's arm and urged her toward the gate. As the door swung open, the guards inside turned to face them.

"Look who we found," the guard holding her said, and all of them turned to Rose.

What story had Murkel told—that Dustan took her?

"He's had me trapped," she said, her voice breaking. "I couldn't get away!" She blubbered on about being a captive, hysterical enough that it wouldn't matter if her words didn't make sense. She had to keep the guards distracted. She ignored the motion behind them.

Three of the guards were grabbed around the neck. The fourth twisted away from his attacker, pulling his pistol, but the footman's band outnumbered the guards. One man went for the pistol arm, keeping the firearm pointed at the ground, while another caught the guard's free hand and yanked it back before he could find another weapon. The guards, trapped in choke holds, clawed at their captors, until one after another slumped to the ground. Rose had stepped back, but now she darted forward to slide the weapons out of reach of the guards who were still fighting.

Once the entire band turned to the final two guards, the struggle ended quickly. Soon all four guards were lined up, sitting against the castle wall with their wrists and ankles tied and rags over their mouths. A few stared up at Rose in confusion.

The servants began gathering the weapons.

"I'll go to the kitchen," Rose said, "and let them—"

Voices shouted from around the corner. Everyone stopped.

"It's more guards," the footman whispered. He reached for one of the muskets, fumbling to ready it. "Arm yourselves."

Rose grasped for a better solution and found nothing. The voices grew louder. Suddenly she knew what she had to do. "Wait," she said to the footman. "I'll stop them. Get the servants out." And she ran toward the voices.

Chapter 27

✍

ROSE INTERCEPTED THE ARRIVING GUARDS before they reached the castle gate. As she'd hoped, after the fuss of discovering who she was, all of them turned to accompany her into the castle. Now, as she approached the dining hall, surrounded by guards, Rose remembered entering weeks ago, on the night of the supper with the three princes. The pathetic Prince Herbert flashed into her mind. What if her father had chosen him? Would Dustan still have rescued her?

The king bellowed for wine, and she trembled. She was back in the castle, her prison for so many winters. What if the rebellion failed? What if everything went back to the way it had been before?

It wouldn't, she told herself. And if it did, she'd find a way out. Or Dustan would find her. She had to believe in him. And in herself.

The guards nudged her through the door.

One of the guards had hurried ahead and was speaking in the king's ear. Below the dais, the tables stretching the length of the room were only half filled with courtiers, and already people were turning to see her. A murmur spread across the space.

The king stood, and the look of concern that fell across his face almost could have fooled her. "Rose," he cried, stepping toward her. "My eldest daughter has returned. What have they done to you?"

Rose went forward and tried not to cringe as he embraced her. "I'm fine, Father. I escaped."

"Your hair!"

"It will grow back."

"What happened to you?"

"Prince Dustan took me. He guarded me constantly, never letting me out of his sight. But we got caught up in the fighting and I got away."

"Did the pirates hurt you?"

"Are there pirates?" Rose asked, and she lifted her eyebrows and placed her fingertips over her open mouth. "There were guards everywhere, and I couldn't tell who was who."

The king spoke loudly, his voice booming over the assembly. "Rose has escaped the prince and the pirates. Thank the skies."

Rose swayed on her feet. "If you please, sir, I'm very tired."

"Of course, of course." The king clapped his hands and pointed at a guard, who came forward. "Escort the princess to the nearest parlor. Take all of them. Ladies!" He gestured at the table where Rose's former ladies-in-waiting sat.

The ladies stood. They wore their fine dresses, their hair coiled atop their heads, but their faces looked gaunt with fear. They clutched each other as they moved. Rose followed the guard out and down the hall.

She entered the parlor. The ladies filed in after. When they were all inside, the guard closed the door. The lock turned.

Rose looked at the ladies in silence. They stared back. She couldn't think how to begin.

"Where's Adela?" Rose asked at last.

"Adela." Avianna snorted. "Turns out she had a secret beau. Soon as you were gone, she was off to be with him. Good riddance, I said."

Elspeth pursed her lips. "You just hated her, ever since she caught you tumbling Prince Murkel and took away your privileges."

Avianna sniffed, closing her eyes. "Well it's not like I hurt anyone."

Elspeth turned on Rose. "Was it Prince Dustan who had you this whole time?" Rose couldn't stop herself from blushing. "So it *was* him! He kidnapped you!"

"Rescued me, more like," Rose said. She cast an eye at Avianna. "You liked Murkel, but he is a monster. Really—a scaly tail and everything! It appears when he enters the water. Merlandia's under the ocean."

Avianna's jaw dropped.

Elspeth smacked her arm with the back of her hand and grinned. "A sea monster! And you tumbled him, Avi."

"He didn't look like a monster. Or feel like one."

Elspeth turned back to Rose. "So you liked him? Dustan?"

"Very much."

"Did the pirates get him?"

Rose looked at the women around her, some trembling with fear. "There are no pirates."

"No pirates?" Avianna said. She almost seemed disappointed. No doubt she'd been fantasizing about what she'd do in the hedges with a Sarlian pirate.

"There's been a rebellion," Rose said. "The villagers have overthrown the guards. All that's left are the men guarding the castle."

No one spoke at first. "What do you mean?" Elspeth asked.

"The guards in the village put down their weapons. They won't fight for the king anymore. Soon he will not be the king."

"You mean they'll come here and take us?"

"They won't hurt you."

"But what'll happen to us?" Elspeth asked. "If we're not allowed to live here?"

"Don't you have a home to return to? A manor in Sar Bay?"

"Won't the rebels go there?"

Avianna butted in. "And not all of us have families to return to."

Rose hadn't considered this. But she'd gotten by, and she'd had no skills when she left the castle. "Don't despair. It's harder out there, but it's brighter, too."

"But what'll we do?"

"Wait'll you see what it's like. It's different, you'll have to work at something. But it's good. It's better than sitting all day in the castle."

They stared at her without smiling. Tears caught in Avianna's eyes.

Rose tried another tack. "Just wait. The houses are small and the clothes not so fine." She lowered her voice. "But the men are so handsome. And there are so many."

A quiet hush of whispers rippled through the group and she knew she had their interest. "Rugged men, not like the ones in the castle. Maybe they dress plain, but there are hard muscles under those plain clothes."

Avianna blinked, biting her lower lip. "Doesn't matter how he dresses when his clothes are off."

"And it might be easier to get *our* dresses off if they weren't so complicated," Elspeth added, looking down at her corseted bodice.

Avianna began fanning herself.

"The men I've met do things," Rose continued, "like chop wood and build you a fire, things the courtiers wouldn't even be capable of. Men who can take care of things."

"This one time," Avianna said, "I came across one of the gardeners, he was kneeling in the dirt, pressing plants into the garden, and his hands were covered in dirt. I just couldn't stop looking at his hands. He tried to apologize. But I pulled him into the greenhouse with me." She fanned herself harder and her eyes sparkled. "The fingerprints he left on me . . ."

The other ladies hung on her words.

Rose waited for Avianna to finish recounting her jaunt with the gardener before she spoke again. "There's freedom outside the castle. Women aren't treated like possessions. They can do things."

"You like it better," Elspeth said slowly.

"Well, she never much liked it here," Avianna said, snorting. She looked at Rose.

"What was there to like? Clothes and jewelry? At least you had a friend," Rose said quietly.

There was silence.

Someone shouted outside the tall windows. The women raced to look. People dashed across the courtyard—villagers, from their dress. And they had muskets.

Outside the castle, a peaceful change had taken place. But Rose was still inside and she knew the king would fight his way out. He might try to take the court ladies with him, using them as shields. Who knew what he was capable of?

The group of villagers had passed, and the courtyard became eerily silent.

Rose unlatched the closest window and pushed it open. "I think we'd be safer out of here," she said. "When it comes to it, the king won't protect us. Who will come with me?"

To her surprise, Avianna stepped forward first.

"What about our things?" someone asked.

"There's no time," Rose said. She grasped the window frame, stepped onto the ledge, and lowered herself out into the courtyard. She turned to help the others down. Their dainty shoes slipped on the hard cobblestones. When they were all out, Rose led them toward the nearest gate, unsure what she'd find.

They'd made it a dozen paces when a shout came from behind them. The women turned. Guards had entered the parlor. The king was at the window.

"Stop," the king demanded. "Get back here!"

Rose turned away and kept walking. She could hear the others behind her.

A shot exploded.

She froze.

Someone near her whimpered, and Elspeth gripped her arm.

As she turned, two guards climbed out the windows. The king stood in the center. One guard stood by his side with a musket pointed in the air.

"What will they do with us?" Elspeth whispered.

Rose stared at the king, her anger rising. He'd taken her mother, ruined her childhood, and threatened her into submission. She was done with it.

"They only have three muskets," she said. "There are more of us. We can overpower them."

"Us?" Elspeth said. "But we're women."

"Exactly. Look at them. They're not even training the weapons on us, now that we've submitted. Get close and get the muskets out of their hands. Quickly." Rose began walking back toward the window.

"Split three ways," Avianna said, following. "Rose, rush that one by the king."

The pack of women closed the distance to the guards. A skirmish broke out as the ladies grabbed at the muskets, and the king shouted in surprise. Rose dashed forward at the guard in the window, who stared open mouthed at the melee before him. The king was still shouting.

Rose grabbed the guard's legs and pulled. He fell into the courtyard. Before he could catch himself, Elspeth had wrested the weapon from his hands.

The guards were down. Avianna sat atop one, pinning him to the cobbles. The other was held by six hands. And the one who'd fallen was still in shock on the ground. Rose stepped back as the king came out the window. She reached for Elspeth's arm, pulling her back. Elspeth held the musket carefully.

"Rose, I don't know how to use this," Elspeth said.

"I do."

Rose turned. Dustan stood at the edge of the courtyard, a throng of rebels behind him. Several had weapons, their guard jackets hanging open to show they no longer obeyed the castle. Dustan's gaze was on her.

The rebels moved forward. The king had paused by the window, and now Dustan looked to him, with the crowd behind him, and Rose turned to watch. Rebels reached for the captive guards, pulling them to their feet.

"Rose," the king said. "I had men searching, as soon as I found out about Murkel. I was so worried. Tell them to let me be."

She stared at the king a moment, willing herself to feel pity, but none came. She shook her head slightly. The rebels surged forward to seize the king.

He sputtered, struggling as they bound his hands, his face turning a mottled purple. "You damned bastard fairy!" he shouted. "I should've given you to the first one who wanted you."

Dustan glared at the king with a murderous look. Rose lifted her chin and turned her back on him.

The king continued to hurl insults at her as they dragged him away. Rose waited, knowing he'd be gone in a moment, and that the people would decide his fate as he'd once decided hers. He began to shout at the people, cursing the rebels and calling for guards.

A cry went up, and voices shouted. But before Rose could turn to see the commotion, a shot fired, and all went silent. She turned. The king's body sprawled on the cobblestones with blood pooling beneath his head. One of the rebels held a pistol out, and another helped a young woman who'd fallen beside the king. The fingers of the king's bound hands slipped from her clothing where he'd grabbed her.

The king was dead. He couldn't hurt anyone anymore.

Dustan stood beside Rose. She lifted her face to his.

"Are you okay?" he asked.

"I think so."

"Why did you go? When I heard that you were in the castle, I was frantic."

Rose began to shake. Now that it was over, all her strength seeped out and left her quivering. Dustan touched her arm, but she couldn't stop shaking. His arms enfolded her.

"It's okay," he said. "It's over. You're safe."

"I couldn't find you," she said into his soft shirt, "and if I waited, the king might've done something. All these people . . ."

He held her, his hand rubbing her back, until her shaking subsided.

"But how did you get in?" he asked after a minute.

"I came up your ladder."

His arms loosened and he stepped back to look at her. "I'd forgotten it," he said.

"It seemed strong."

"It is. Fairy threads don't fray easily." And his arms tightened around her again.

Chapter 28

✄

DUSTAN AND ROSE STOOD IN the courtyard as it emptied. The king's body had been removed.

"They're going to the dungeons," Dustan said, loosening his grip around her. "To free the king's prisoners."

Rose looked up. "Poor things."

"Most of them. But not all. Murkel's down there, remember?"

Rose shuddered slightly, and Dustan pulled her back in.

"I must make sure they don't let him go. Will you stay here?"

Rose had faced the king. She could handle Murkel. She shook her head no.

She and Dustan followed the rebels out of the courtyard and into a passage of the castle, then down into darkness. The heavy stone walls closed in, empty of hope, and Rose found herself clutching Dustan's hand as they descended. The dread returned, just as she'd felt as a child, the time the king had locked her here.

The flickering flames of a torch anchored in a wall sconce lit the confined space. A small crowd had gathered in a corner, at the only cell not yet open.

"Water," came a rasping whisper.

"He always wants water." A man wearing the castle livery stepped from the crowd and headed for a bucket against the wall.

"Wait," Dustan said.

The servant looked up and stopped.

Dustan approached the cell, drawing Rose with him. Inside, a figure sat slumped on a bench. He was shriveled, like a husk of corn that had missed the harvest. Thin hair streamed over his shoulders, brittle and straight.

"He's not human," Dustan said. "He's from the sea. And he's a danger to us as long as he has the power of the sea."

The shriveled form shifted, its head tilting up. His eyes were sunken but recognition spread across Murkel's face.

"But if he's too long away from water, he'll lose the ability to change form. He'll no longer be a threat."

"So we keep him here?" the guard asked.

"Yes. It shouldn't take long. It might already be too late for him now, but give it another week to be sure. And no water."

Murkel lurched toward the bars, and Rose jumped back. Dustan didn't even flinch. Murkel's thin fingers gripped the metal and he tried to scream, but all that came out was a hoarse cry.

He was pathetic. But Rose thought of the prison he'd made for her under the water, and the terror she still felt chased the pity away. How would the people of Merlandia feel when they learned their ruler was exiled on land? Maybe they'd celebrate.

ROSE AND DUSTAN CAME UP from the dungeons into the daylight. They walked together out of the castle. Everywhere Rose looked, people celebrated. She kept remembering that the king was gone, that she no longer had to hide, but she couldn't believe it. She had no idea what came next.

When they reached the village, they were swept into the celebrations. Kate and Maybeth and the other castle servants had shared the news of Rose's role in freeing them, and word had spread that the princess was alive, and that she'd returned to fight the king.

Rose thought her role had been embellished a bit, but she couldn't dampen the villagers' enthusiasm. She ended up staying in one of Woodglen's inns, with Ladi beside her and Dustan in the room down the hall, courtesy of the innkeeper.

Now Rose fidgeted in her bed, but sleep wouldn't come. Faint sounds of revelry drifted up from the pub beside the inn. Light diffused into the room, outlining Ladi's recumbent form. All the lanterns along the village lanes had been lit in celebration. Ladi's breathing had settled into the steady pattern of sleep.

Rose turned over, willing herself to sleep. Instead she remembered the scene at Murkel's cell, and climbing the ladder to the tower window, and being led to the dining hall during her brief return to imprisonment. So much had happened in one day. Sleep wouldn't come. And the more she tried to sleep, the more awake she became.

She rolled to her other side. Was Dustan awake? She imagined him coming to check on her, but he wouldn't, not with Ladi sleeping beside her and the door locked. As long as he knew she was safe, he would stay away. But the look in his eyes today, when he'd found her in the castle—his eyes had said something his lips never would. And the feeling of his arms around her . . . did he want to come to her? Was he lying awake, too, hoping she'd come to him? The thoughts wouldn't leave her be.

She could go to him.

But what if she went and he didn't want her there?

She'd lose her mind with wondering. She had faced her worst fears today—the castle, the king, the dungeon, and Murkel. Surely, she could face Dustan. Rose sat up, reaching for her shawl. She wrapped herself in it, quietly stood, and tiptoed to the door.

All was quiet in the corridor. She crept toward Dustan's room. She gave a tiny knock and listened. There was no response. Slowly she pressed the latch, and she sighed with relief when it clicked. She eased the door open.

His room was dark, with the curtain drawn against the light

from outside. No sound came from Dustan until he whispered,
"Rose?"

"Yes."

"Are you all right?"

"Yes." She stood in the doorway, unable to move.

"Come here," he whispered.

She could see him now, leaning on his elbow, his chest bare and
his eyes rimmed with sleep. She closed the door behind her. Tentatively, she stepped toward him. When she was beside the bed, she
didn't know what to do.

"Can't you sleep?" he asked at last.

"No."

"Are you scared?"

She only shook her head.

He hesitated. "Do you want to sleep here?"

Rose nodded.

He moved to make room beside him, and she lowered herself
onto the bed, casting aside her shawl. His bed was warm, and he
pulled the coverlet over her. She could feel the heat of his body, just
a hand's width away from her. He didn't move.

She didn't dare look at him. She inched herself toward him
until his body touched hers. She rolled to her side to fit her back
against him. His arms closed around her, warm and strong, and he
sighed away any spaces that had remained between them, sealing
their bodies together. She closed her eyes, soaking in his presence,
wishing they could stay like this always.

He was silent, and she thought she'd lie awake all night, con-
scious of being in his arms. But she was safe, and Dustan was with
her. She drifted into sleep.

WHEN ROSE WOKE, SHE WAS alone. Morning light glared in the
windows, and the pub outside was quiet. Would Dustan return?
Thinking of him by her side filled her with peace. It felt so right.
Did it feel that way to him, too?

He hadn't returned after ten minutes. Rose sat up and looked around the small room. A wash basin stood in the corner, and her shawl had been folded and draped over a chair. Beside her, the sheets were rumpled. She was tempted to lean down and sniff them. Something green poked out from under Dustan's pillow. Rose reached for it and pulled, drawing out a velvet scarf. It was her scarf. She'd worn it the night she'd left the castle with Dustan. She'd never put it back on, after they'd made love.

And he'd kept it.

People moved in the hallway outside the door, talking as they made their way to the staircase. Soon she'd be trapped in Dustan's room, in her nightgown, with everyone awake in the inn. Rose pushed the scarf back under the pillow. She retrieved her shawl and crept back to her room. Ladi was just stirring. If she had noticed Rose's absence, she didn't comment.

Dustan didn't appear all through breakfast.

Ladi wanted to walk in the village. After casting one last glance around the inn's common room, Rose agreed to go, too.

"Castle's empty," Ladi said as they made their way along the lane. "Guards who wouldn't back down are all taken. They've organized into peacekeepers now, the guards who rebelled."

Rose pulled her attention back from scanning the village lanes for Dustan. "I wonder what will happen to the castle," she said.

"Kendall has a plan, I heard," Ladi said. "'Course the Council of Villages will decide, but it was a good plan. Sell tours to visitors to bring wealth to the villages. Serve meals for the poorest in the dining hall. Breed the horses. You didn't want anything from in there, did you?"

"No. There was nothing of my mother's left." The two women turned onto the lane that led to the village square.

"How is it with Dustan?" Ladi asked. "You spend time with him yesterday?"

Rose swallowed. Had Ladi heard her sneaking to Dustan's room? But then she recalled Dustan finding her in the castle courtyard in the heat of the rebellion. "When he found me yesterday, he put his arms around me. It felt so right, Ladi."

"You love him," Ladi said.

Rose remembered that once she'd been sure she loved him. The spell had made her love him. But the spell had been broken and everything had become confused. Now she thought about him constantly. Was that love? She wasn't sure what love felt like.

"But he might not love me," was all she answered.

They emerged from the lane into the square, the cobblestones shaded by the towering trees of the village garden in the center. Rose looked for the herbalist's shop, the one she had spotted on her first walk through the village. She looked again at the curving steps.

"You want to go in," Ladi said. Rose stopped walking. "You look at that shop every time we pass by."

"It's just that it's familiar, but I can't remember why."

"Well let's find out," Ladi said, taking her hand and leading her to the steps.

As they opened the door, it brushed against a bell inside. Rose gazed at the bundles of dry herbs hanging from the rafters, reminding her of Synne, and she wished something would spark a memory.

There was some shuffling in the back room, and a hunched woman with gray hair appeared. "Good day," she said. She stopped and stared. Her voice came out in a whisper. "Rose?"

"You know me?" Rose said.

The woman hobbled forward and grasped Rose's hands. "Grace used to bring you to see me. But I haven't laid eyes on you since she passed. I'd recognize those eyes of yours, though." She smiled. "Who is your friend?"

"This is Ladi."

"And I'm Nell," the herbalist said. "Come in, come in, and I'll make us some tea."

Nell led them back into her living space behind the shop and set about boiling water.

"Please, would you tell me what you remember about my mother?" Rose asked.

"She was so kind," Nell began. "She first came to see me when I was ill, but then she kept coming. We talked about everything."

"Everything?" Rose asked.

"She told me her secret," Nell said, looking up from the stove. "I suppose you know your father was a fairy?"

"Aye."

"Your poor mother. Well, the king is dead. I never thought I'd be glad of someone's death, but . . . . Nothing to do about it now." Nell shook her head. She continued talking, telling them of the times she remembered.

Rose sank into a reverie, thinking of her mother as Ladi asked Nell about her work. The morning drifted past. Was Dustan back at the inn? Rose waited for the other women to pause in their talk. "I might head back," she said. "I don't want to interrupt your chat."

"You go ahead," Ladi said. "I'll follow in a bit."

Rose hugged Nell, promising to visit again. She exited the shop, breathing in the warm air as noon approached. She slid her hand down the railing as she descended the curving steps, pretending she could remember playing there as a child. Doves poked about on the grass of the village garden, and overhead, birdsong filled the trees.

In front of Nell's shop, Rose hesitated. She'd go back to the inn. But if Dustan wasn't there, she could try the stables. Or the pub. Was she being pitiful?

As she stepped forward, a woman in a dark cape pushed past her. Rose stumbled, and hands caught her. An arm encircled her waist and dragged her backward. She tried to scream, but a hand clamped over her mouth.

Chapter 29

ᐄ

THE MAN HOLDING ROSE YANKED her into the alley beside Nell's shop. The caped woman appeared, blocking the exit. Adela.

Rose felt a moment of relief before she realized Adela's face was pinched, calculating.

"Be a good girl, Rose, and don't make a scene," Adela said.

The hand eased off Rose's mouth. "Adela! What are you doing?"

"People need a way to make a living, Rose." Adela's voice spewed bitterness. "I waited thirteen winters to make my fortune off you, and the gold turned into pebbles the day you disappeared. Reginald and I have nothing. We need shells, the gold kind."

"I don't have any coins, Adela. You know that."

"You may not *have* shells, but you're still *worth* shells. And now that the king is out of the picture, it might as well be me who profits."

Rose's chest tightened. Adela was kidnapping her to sell her again. She sucked in a breath to scream, but Reginald's hand re-covered her mouth, pulling her head back against his body. Adela removed a vial from her dress.

"You're not the only one with potions, princess," Adela said, dripping a clear liquid from the vial onto a kerchief. Rose struggled against the arms that held her. Adela came toward her, holding out the kerchief.

Please, Rose thought, sending her prayer out to anyone who might hear. Please help me.

A sharp, sweet smell filled her lungs, and Rose's vision blurred. She felt herself sag in Reginald's arms as the fumes penetrated her senses.

"Not too much," Reginald muttered.

As Rose felt herself losing consciousness, Adela shrieked. There was a fluttering, and a curse, and the smell disappeared. Rose gasped for clear air. The flapping around her intensified. What had they done to her? Reginald's hands still bound her, but Adela was dancing, flailing her arms. Abruptly, Reginald cursed and dropped Rose. She fell to the ground.

Rose tried to crawl forward and became tangled in Adela's legs. She kept going, knocking Adela over. Blood streamed down Adela's face. Her hat looked like a fat dove, and it was moving. Rose was hallucinating. She gripped the corner of the building; she was almost out of the alley.

"Rose!" Hands were on her, gentle this time. "Get the peacekeeper!" A different arm encircled her waist, pulling her up and out of the alley. Rose sank onto the steps of Nell's shop. Ladi was holding her up.

People were shouting, rushing toward them. Everything was a commotion. Rose focused on not being sick. Ladi was talking. Slowly Rose's head cleared, and her vision returned. She slumped against Ladi.

"What happened?" Ladi asked.

Rose looked at Ladi. "It was Adela."

"Guards have her and the man, over there. What'd she do?"

"She was going to sell me again." Rose felt Ladi's arm tighten around her shoulder. "She had a potion that made me faint. I couldn't get away. If you hadn't come . . ."

"We heard a scratching at the window."

Nell hobbled up. "It was the birds who saved you. When we came out, the birds were diving into the alley."

"The birds?" Rose asked.

"The air was thick with them."

Rose looked across at the garden. The doves had settled on the grass, but instead of poking about, they watched her. A row of sparrows lined the nearest bench, and on the tree limbs, starlings and ravens gathered. Every bird in the garden stood watching her.

Thank you, Rose thought, sending her message out with her whole heart. In answer, the doves turned back to the grass, pecking for food, and the sparrows flitted up into the leaves.

After the peacekeepers had taken Adela and Reginald away, Ladi helped Rose stand and stumble back to the inn. Rose fell into her bed and drifted to sleep.

ROSE WOKE ALONE AS GOLDEN rays of the setting sun pierced her window. The world had quieted, though the suppertime noises of clanking dishes and talking guests drifted up from the dining room below. She still felt slightly sick.

The door opened and Dustan looked in. When he saw Rose awake, he came in, shutting the door behind him. He sank onto his knees by her bedside. "I should've been there," he said, his face stricken.

"You can't always be there," Rose said.

He rested his forehead on his arm on the edge of the bed. "Tell me what happened," he said, his voice muffled.

"The birds, Dustan. They heard me."

"You called to them?"

"I didn't mean to. I just asked for help."

"Thank the stars they heard you. I wish I'd been there."

"I'm not your responsibility. You have your own life to live."

"You don't understand," he said. When he looked up, his eyes shone with sadness.

Tentatively she slid an arm from the blankets and placed her hand into his. It was warm and dry, like the leaves on the forest floor in the autumn sun. He squeezed her fingers, and tears welled in his eyes.

"I thought I'd never see you again," he said. "I didn't deserve to. I wanted to accept the fate I deserved, but I couldn't stop thinking about you. I thought if I returned to you, you'd see nothing in me. I'd be a stranger. Worse, a stranger with a guilty secret."

Rose's heart quivered at his words.

"And then you appeared, a shining star that illuminated the dark fairy underworld. You endangered yourself to rescue those children. I knew I didn't deserve you, but I hoped . . . ." His thumbs rubbed her hand, but he looked everywhere other than at her face. Rose waited. He blinked away his tears. "It's been so hectic, the rebellion, and the magic. I—"

The door opened and Ladi entered. Dustan smiled at Rose. "You should rest now," he said, "after what you've been through." He placed her hand on the bed and stood. "I'll go to my room. Just come if you need me." He nodded at Ladi and left.

Ladi turned the lamps low and stretched out on her own bed.

Rose stared at the ceiling. The queasy, dizzy feeling had subsided. Dustan had said he hoped—for what? She recalled his words. He couldn't stop thinking about her. He'd called her a shining star. She'd gone to Dustan last night, and he hadn't sent her away. Did she dare go again? If she didn't, she wouldn't sleep. She'd lie awake as she had the previous night. Tonight, she was resolute. She would go to him. And she would discover what was between them.

Chapter 30

ⵥ

ROSE SAT UP. HER HEAD was clear and the room was steady. "Ladi?" Rose whispered.

"Mmm?"

"I'm feeling better. Not sick."

There was silence.

"Ladi?"

"Mmm?"

"I'm going to Dustan."

"Mmm-hmm." Ladi was still, her eyes closed.

Rose crossed to the door, wrapping herself in her shawl, and let herself out.

Down the hall, she quietly pressed the latch of Dustan's door. She eased herself in. Dustan stood at the washbasin, drying his face. Rose had a moment to notice his bare chest in the lamplight before he lowered the towel and saw her. Tension sparked in the air, as if lightning might leap between them. She closed the door.

He didn't speak, just lowered his arms and waited, never taking his gaze off her.

Rose approached him, scared to speak in the heavy silence.

"Dustan," she whispered at last. She looked into his eyes, and he stared back into hers. "What is between us?"

His lips parted, but he only shook his head slightly.

Rose wetted her lips. "I want to be with you. When I think of this ending, this time with you, of everything returning—I don't want to lose you."

"You'll never lose me."

"I can remember now, the times we spent together. They seem faded, like someone else's story. I don't want to think about them. I want to be with you now, in this moment, making new memories. And it seems I shouldn't, that I'm not supposed to trust you again. But I do."

Dustan dropped the towel he was holding, and his hands came to rest on her arms, holding her gently. "Rose," he said, "I will never be dishonest with you again. I swear it on every tree in the forest."

She couldn't help herself. Her fingertips reached for him, grazing over the taut muscles of his chest. His hands held her more tightly, but he didn't move toward her. She placed her hands flat on his skin and leaned in to kiss him.

When their lips met, her whole body felt it. Her knees almost gave out, but Dustan's hand came around her back just in time. His kisses were what she'd been missing, what she'd been waiting for all these weeks. She barely noticed her shawl slipping to the floor.

Her fingers moved across his skin, as if she were touching it for the first time. She pressed her body against his. She couldn't get close enough. She abandoned his lips to try kissing his neck, and he copied her, still holding her tight. And as he kissed his way down her neck, her body responded.

"Dustan," she gasped. He stopped immediately. "No," she whispered. "Don't stop."

"Would you like to lie with me?"

She nodded.

He moved to blow out the lamp, then returned in the darkness and led her to the bed. She pulled him down, and as she grabbed the blankets to cover them, he didn't leave a gap between their bodies.

"Is this okay?" he asked.

In answer, she turned toward him and began to kiss him again.

ROSE SNUGGLED AGAINST DUSTAN'S CHEST. He pulled her arms around him and stroked her hair. Being with him felt so right, not just when they were kissing but all the time. At meals, walking . . . she wanted to see him every day, to wake by his side. She believed she could trust him. But even if it were another spell, she would stay.

When the sunlight woke her, Dustan was gone.

Chapter 31

꧁

WHERE HAD DUSTAN GONE? ROSE basked in the warmth of the sheets, trying to catch the scent of him. But as the minutes ticked past, she became restless. Maybe he meant for her to leave as she had the previous morning. Slowly she rose and pulled on her nightgown, wishing he'd return. Why had he left? After last night, she knew he cared for her. But she'd thought he'd be there in the morning. She opened the curtains, letting in the sunshine, and pulled her shawl around her. She was on the verge of leaving when the door opened.

Her breath caught when she saw Dustan. He clutched a bouquet of straggly wild flowers, and his hair was flat, though threatening to return to its usual crest on his head. She thought he must've tried to look special, and she didn't know why, but it excited her.

"Wherever did you find those?" she said, nodding at the flowers.

"In the village garden."

"Why did you go to that trouble?"

"The flowers are traditional, for my people." His hands clutched at the stems. "It is important." He stared down at the bouquet. "After last night."

"Dustan, what are you trying to say?"

"I planned to bond with you once, but it would have been a sham, a life-bond exchanged for fairy gold and you coerced by a spell. When I saw you again, when you came to the fairy realm, I didn't dare to hope that you'd give me another chance. But last night I held you in my arms. Have you forgiven me?"

He'd spoken of the life-bond. "I think I had from the moment I saw you again."

He stepped toward her, looking into her eyes. "Then will you be my life-mate?"

Rose stared, too surprised to speak.

"Not like the king wanted, but a true life-bond in the old ways," he said, his voice shaking, the words bubbling out too fast. "We can live in the village, or the forest, wherever makes you happy. I've talked to Kendall about the gardens at the castle. I'll find—"

"Dustan," she said, putting her hand on his arm. "Yes, I will be your life-mate."

He hesitated for a moment, as if he didn't believe her. He moved forward, and she stepped into his arms, where he crushed her against him, one hand wrapped around her head, the one with the flowers tight on her back, embracing her in the morning light.

When at last he let her go, the flowers stood half smashed in his hand. He held them out to her. "Gillyflower for a happy life, daisies for loyalty, iris for faith, sweet pea for bliss. There are more I was supposed to gather, but it was all I could find in an hour." He smiled his familiar smile.

Joy welled inside her. She would see that smile every day.

"I found one of the village elders. She said we could come, if you agreed. Unless you want more time."

Rose's mind reeled. She'd be Dustan's bride at last. Maybe she would never be safe from enemies. But Dustan would always be near, and they would fight their enemies together.

"Aye, let's go now. Let me dress and find Ladi." She tore herself away from his gaze.

The next hour was a blur. Ladi accompanied them to the village garden. Under an oak tree filled with birds, the elder read the bonding rites and before her, Rose and Dustan made their vows. Dustan produced two rings when asked. Rose had forgotten all about the rings. As he slid Rose's onto her finger, it felt like part of her hand. Maybe it was enchanted.

After the ceremony, they were on the street in the sunshine again, and the whole world looked vibrant. Ladi left them to visit Nell, and as the door to Nell's shop swung closed, Dustan tugged on Rose's hand. She looked up to find a sly grin on his face.

He leaned close to her ear. "I've never made love to my bride before," he whispered.

"Only to other people's?" Rose asked, grinning. Dustan shook his head, smiling, and clasped her hand. They raced back to the inn.

The innkeeper looked up when, laughing and out of breath, they came in the door. They tried to smother their laughter as they walked past the woman, but it escaped again as they hurried up the stairs, tripping in their eagerness. And then they were locked in Dustan's room.

Dustan closed the curtains, but the bright sunlight radiated through the thin material, bathing the room in a dim brightness. He turned to Rose and stopped.

She was breathing hard, from running up the stairs or from what was to come, she didn't know. When he didn't move toward her, she moved closer until she stood in front of him. She began to undo the buttons of her dress. He stayed still, but she felt him respond, as if the whole room pulsed with desire.

She reached for him. He let her kiss his face and tug at his shirt, but he didn't move to help her. But she could see his eyes burning. Something restrained him, his passion held in check. She tugged him toward the bed, sitting, leaning back, and pulling him over her.

When at last they'd both found release, she stilled beneath him and opened her eyes. He knelt over her, panting and watching her face. She smiled a lazy smile up at him.

He exhaled and smiled back. He laid down beside her and wrapped his arms around her, and pushed his damp face into her neck. "I love you," he said.

And then he fell asleep. Rose held him until she too drifted off.

They spent the rest of the day in his room. And the night that followed.

A BIRD WOKE HER. ROSE felt for Dustan beside her, but the bed was empty. Rose squinted at the window, where the bird perched on the sill under the open sash. A cool breeze blew in the smell of the sea. The bird hopped forward, chirping again. It was a wren with a striped face and tiny tail. And it was looking at her.

Chapter 32

THE WREN CHIRPED AGAIN AND looked to the door. Dustan stood in the semidarkness with his hand on the latch, fully dressed. Rose awakened fully, pulling the bed sheets to cover her as she sat up. Dustan let out an exasperated sigh.

"Dustan, what's going on?" Rose asked.

"I had a message. I have to go."

"Go where?" Rose began hunting for her clothing amid the rumpled sheets.

"It's nothing. Just stay in bed. I'll be back before the sun is up."

The wren launched itself from the windowsill, circled the room, and landed on Dustan's shoulder. It emitted a stream of chirping as Dustan tried to turn his ear away. Rose climbed from the bed, pulling her underclothes on.

"What is it saying?"

Dustan glared at the bird before turning to Rose and huffing out his breath. "It's my mother," he said. "She's on her way."

Rose trembled. His mother who'd imprisoned him? Not to mention all the human children whose lives she'd stolen. What wouldn't she do?

"You can't go," Rose said. "She could kill you."

"She won't kill me," he said. "Besides, if I don't go, the whole village could be in danger."

"Then I'm going, too," Rose said. She picked up her dress from the floor. "I won't lose you again."

"You won't lose me. I don't want you to get hurt." His voice pleaded, asking her to comply.

But the bird let off another volley of chirping. When it ended, Rose waited.

"Fine," Dustan said. The bird lifted off and swooped out the window. "She thinks you should come."

"Of course I should."

Dustan ran his hand through his hair. "I know you're capable. I'm just scared of what she might do."

"Whatever Oleander does, we'll face it together."

As dawn approached, they left the inn as silently as they could. Outside, the streets were quiet, the air, cool. Dustan strode toward the main road by the forest, and Rose followed. As they left the village, Dustan stopped. Rose scanned the horizon. The cart path was empty, and the few farmhouses were quiet. The first light of dawn touched the edge of the forest.

"Stay close," Dustan said, taking her hand as they turned away from the castle and moved onto the forest road.

For a few minutes, they walked in silence. Dustan's thumb grazed over the ring on her finger as he squeezed her hand, but he focused on their surroundings. The sky lightened. Birds began singing in the forest, and squirrels appeared on the grass, searching the ground in their frantic way.

They were climbing a rise when Dustan stopped. The sun broke over the horizon, casting a pink light on the forest. The birds' singing had quieted, Rose realized. Dustan stared ahead down the road.

Someone was riding toward them. Her hair blew sideways in the breeze that rose with her coming. She seemed larger than a usual person, or maybe it was the size of her horse, which Rose instantly recognized as Redbud.

Oleander.

A row of riders followed behind the fairy queen, barricading the road. A whip hung from her hand, and sunlight glinted off the curves of her armor. Armor that, Rose had time to think, seemed a little too shapely for a battle. Had Oleander timed her appearance with the sun's for dramatic effect? The riders behind her moved forward with impassive faces.

Dustan stepped in front of Rose.

Behind the riders, more fairies appeared over the crest in the road. First came guards holding bows, but behind them was a throng of unarmed fairies, old and young. Was this their whole army? Maybe Oleander would use magic to attack.

The queen halted fifty paces from Rose and Dustan. "There is my wayward son," she called, speaking into the air so her voice carried.

Immediately Rose detested the contrived voice and words.

Oleander's face snarled. "The dungeon wasn't good enough for you? I'll have to come up with something better, a punishment you'll share with Larch, when we find him."

"Why do you seek to punish me?" Dustan said evenly, looking to the crowd behind the queen. "For speaking the truth about the humans? You've—"

"Seize him!"

"Let me speak," Dustan said, and his words boomed in the air like thunder. Had he used magic? The riders who had stepped forward, dark-haired men on either side of the queen, stopped.

"The queen lies to you! She keeps you in the dark. I am not insane." He paused just long enough to add force to his next words. "I've spent weeks in the human world. They're not evil. They're just like us."

A murmur rose in the crowd, spilling over the voice of the queen as she tried to respond.

Dustan turned to Rose, leaning close. "I need you to do something," he whispered.

"Anything," Rose said.

Dustan turned back to the crowd. "I propose it is time for a new queen," he said.

"That's treason," Oleander said.

"Not if the people will it," Dustan replied. "You know the rules." To Rose's surprise, Oleander didn't reply, only glared at Dustan. Behind her, the fairies whispered.

"Brothers," Dustan said.

The men on horseback around the queen shifted uncomfortably.

"None of you have formed a life-bond." There was no response. "I am youngest," he continued, "but the only one with a bride."

A bride? Rose thought, and all at once she realized he meant her. Did he think—

"A bride?" said the queen as she gestured roughly at Rose. "This is not a fairy life-bond. No bond with a human counts."

"Aye, I think it does," Dustan said. "Our laws speak only of love."

"So you could bond with a pig, and call her your bride?"

"I've not bonded with a pig."

"How will she be queen, if she can't see our magic?"

"But she can. She is half fairy and has mastered the sight."

The crowd stirred.

Mastered? Rose thought.

"Mother," Dustan said, and his voice was quieter. "I hear that you don't want to accept this. But it is not your decision."

"I am still queen."

"That is the question we now debate." He raised his voice to address the fairies. "I propose a different queen, one who rules in love, who respects freedom and peace, who bridges our world with the human one, so that fairies may come and go with no fear, as it was in the old days."

"It was as he says," someone cried, and the crowd turned. A tiny fairy, leaning on the arm of another, raised her hand.

"Thistle," murmured voices in the crowd. Rose remembered Old Synne's friend.

"We were free to live in the sunlight," Thistle said. "And the humans were friends."

"Stop this." Oleander turned Redbud to face the guards behind her. "Remove her."

The guards shuffled uneasily. "That's Thistle, your highness," said one. "She made the medicine that helped my sister."

Redbud danced as the queen tugged on her reins, turning this way and that. Oleander dug in her heels, and Redbud leapt toward Thistle. The panicked crowd scattered from the horse's path, but Thistle stood firm, stretching taller where she stood. Redbud shied away from Thistle, and when the queen dug her heels in again, the horse reared up. The queen held on, but she lost her seat, and when the horse bucked a third time, Oleander fell to the ground.

Dustan moved to stand over his mother. "Who would like to be free?"

The crowd clamored in agreement. He turned to the guards. "What say you? Is your loyalty to one cruel woman, or to your people?"

They shook their bows in the air, shouting in support.

"My brothers," Dustan called. The men on horseback looked at the ground. "Do you have any complaint?"

They did not reply.

Dustan took Rose's hand and lifted it in the air. "Rose was a princess, imprisoned in the castle here in Woodglen. She escaped and left that life behind. She lived as a peasant, rejecting riches and status. She feared the king, but when her people were in danger, she risked her safety to help them. She entered the castle and gave herself up. She led a rebellion against the old king. She is honest and kind, brave and resourceful. She does not seek to build her own power or to dominate others."

As he described her, she certainly sounded impressive, Rose thought.

Thistle stepped forward. Something sparkled in the air before her, and when she spoke, her voice had been magnified. The whole crowd attended her words. "The fairies have always had a queen, though the role has changed over time. Prince Dustan puts forward his young bride, Rose. She has demonstrated that she is brave and caring. Though she's but half fairy, she has mastered the sight. What do the fairies say?"

A ringing cry went up, like singing and shouting blended together.

Oleander lay crumpled on the ground, glaring at Rose.

"Shall we let her rest in the dungeon?" one of the armed fairies asked.

Dustan turned to Rose.

Had she just become the leader of the fairies?

The guard seemed to be waiting for her to speak.

Rose cleared her throat. "If she does no harm to any fairy, or human, she may live free." The guard extended a hand and helped Oleander to her feet, and she immediately reached for a pouch hanging at her waist, but the guard stopped her and removed it.

"Perhaps someone should keep an eye on her," Rose said quietly. The guards led Oleander away.

The fairies cheered before her. Rose gazed out at the faces, some laughing and talking, others watching her shyly. Dustan grinned beside her.

"Dustan, I don't know how to be a queen," Rose whispered.

"It's simple, really, for the fairies. Nothing like the human version," he said. "Wait here a moment." He moved across to Thistle and spoke to her.

Thistle and the other elders began to direct the crowd back to the trees. Birds swooped through the air, welcoming the fairies back to the outdoors, and many fairies faced the sunrise or looked overhead at the wide-open sky before turning to the forest. Dustan returned to Rose's side.

"The simplest things have been kept from the fairies for so long," Rose said. "Freedom to walk outside—just as it was with me. Maybe I can understand them after all."

Chapter 33

&

ROSE AND DUSTAN NEARED THE cabin as the sun neared the horizon.

Rose had been nervous about being a fairy queen, but Dustan explained that the role was ceremonial. The queen welcomed each season at the festival, began the dancing, and blessed the new babies at their first full moon. It was only his mother who had used the role to increase her power. It struck Rose how much Oleander acted like the worst of humankind, though she seemed to despise humans.

Once her duties were clear, Rose grew more comfortable walking through the fairy tunnels. Guards no longer prevented the fairies from traveling in and out, but they kept Oleander in her rooms. She couldn't seem to behave herself for more than a day, and Rose refused to let her endanger anyone. Oleander griped about being a displaced mother-in-law, but the council Rose had appointed to resolve conflicts agreed with Rose.

Kendall now chaired the Council of Villages, which presided over Sylvania, with each village having a representative on the council, as well as a local authority and guards for keeping the peace. Rose talked with Kendall about creating a liaison position for the fairies to have representation on the Council. The Council planned to open the castle to visitors as a source of public revenue. Adela and Reginald had been put to work there and were locked in the dungeon every night. Every time Rose felt guilty about making anyone sleep down there, Ladi reminded her of what Adela had tried to do.

Murkel hadn't caused any trouble since he'd been released from captivity. Dustan had been right—he could no longer form a tail. He now wandered the village, looking for handouts and reminiscing about his days as a king.

Ladi and Nell had quickly made friends among the fairies, who shared their love of herbs. Ladi had decided to stay in Woodglen as Nell's apprentice.

And Snowdrop had found Rose's father, Birch. He shared with Rose the story of how he'd met her mother—Grace had been walking in the gardens when she visited Sylvania to arrange her lifebond with the king, and he'd seen her. Birch had been sent by Oleander to bring back a child, but he had fallen for Grace and stowed away on the ship taking her back to Sarland. By the time they'd reached shore, they fallen in love. She'd kept seeing him, sneaking out at night to meet him, until she'd been caught and shipped back to Sylvania in a hurry. Birch had followed, but Oleander found him and threw him into the caverns as a prisoner. When he'd finally been freed, he'd headed straight to Woodglen to ask about the young queen and learned she had died.

He'd never known she'd been pregnant with his child.

Still, despite being with Dustan, and getting to know Birch, and hearing stories about her mother, it was hard for Rose to be away from the sun. Many of the fairies were building lodgings in the trees around the fairies' vegetable gardens and the clearing where they danced, and Dustan promised Rose that they would, too. But first, they needed a honeymoon. Rose had long dreamed of seeing new places. The cabin was the first stop-off on their tour of Sylvania.

Now, as Redbud entered the clearing where the cabin stood, the huge oak shimmered in the sunset, its branches spreading over the roof. Dustan and Rose dismounted and let Redbud roam free. She began nosing through the grass in the clearing. Dustan climbed the porch steps and opened the door—reassembled from the pieces left after the guards had hacked into it, weeks before. He disappeared inside.

Overhead, the branches swayed in the early summer breeze, and Rose breathed in the deep scent of the forest. How much her life had changed. At the start of the spring, her only happiness had been hearing a bird sing from inside the walls of the castle gardens, or having a day when she wasn't criticized or punished. Now every day brought joy, whether it was walking through the forest or helping with chores or laughing with new friends. She was free. And it wasn't just her own freedom she could celebrate, but that of the whole kingdom.

For so long, she'd had no choices. Her dreams had focused only on finding freedom. Then she'd met Dustan and experienced more in a moon than she'd ever have imagined—escaping the castle, experiencing love, and heartbreak, and finding the courage to fight against injustice. When the tumult of the revolution had finally cleared, her dream of freedom had been achieved, and Dustan was by her side.

Now she had endless choices and she didn't know where to begin. She and Dustan could live where they chose. They could start a family. She could help him in the fairy gardens. He'd once told her he was a gardener, and he'd spoken the truth. He oversaw the communal plots and orchards where the fairies grew vegetables and fruits. Or, she could find another vocation and apprentice to learn. Dustan had suggested weaving or needlework, but she never wanted to see such a project again. Maybe she could be a forester. She'd gotten a lot better at climbing trees and felt at home in their branches, visiting the birds.

When she'd asked Dustan's opinion, he'd replied, "Whatever

you wish," and told her to take her time. That was another reason for the honeymoon—a break to help her find some clarity on what came next.

Rose followed Dustan up the steps and into the cottage, closing the door behind her. Inside, she stood in the semidarkness as he lit a fire in the hearth, a fire that crackled with multicolored sparks and warmed the hearth stones immediately. The trunk of the tree gleamed in the firelight, as did the hammock where they'd slept. This time, she did not intend to sleep.

"Are you hungry?" he asked.

"Not for food," she said, and grinned. His look still made her blush, but now she held his gaze.

He smiled and came to take her hand. "I have something to show you." He led her to the trunk of the tree. But he didn't reach for the hammock. Instead, he dropped her hand and climbed. It wasn't hard to follow. The tree had so many knobs and branches that it was easy to find a footing.

Rose cleared the roof after him. Nestled in the branches was a cushion held up on crisscrossed ropes, like the one she'd lain on with him before, although the memory of it was very faint. As she climbed up to it, Dustan was kneeling in the center. She scrambled up from the branch and stood before him.

Up here, in the brilliant sunset, the warm wind ruffled her hair, and her skirt billowed around her legs. Dustan's eyes sparkled as he smiled. She could tell that he knew what she wanted, why he'd brought her here, but as always, he waited for her lead. She smirked back at him. Sometimes, she remembered her life in the castle, and how shocking her behavior now would have seemed back then, and she burst out laughing, and Dustan would hold her until her fit subsided. She would wipe the tears from her eyes and begin to kiss him.

But tonight, she didn't waste time laughing over how things had changed. She untied the sash of her dress, shrugged her arms from the sleeves, and let the dress fall to her feet. Her hair tickled her bare shoulders as it swished in the breeze. She stepped toward Dustan. He rose on his knees, and his hands welcomed her.

When their passion was spent, they lay still. Dustan pulled Rose to him, his arms tight around her. Exhausted, she settled on top of him. He ran his fingers through her hair, leaving them tangled in it, and leaned forward to kiss the corner of her lips.

Overhead, the first stars were out, the sunset drained from the sky.

Rose rested on Dustan and watched as more stars appeared. This was the best part of her new life. At night—and sometimes in the middle of the day—she could curl up with Dustan's arms around her. How close she had come to being sold to one of those princes, or dragged down to Merlandia. Just thinking of it made her hold Dustan tighter, and he squeezed her back. He'd been right in the end. She had followed her heart, and the rest had come out right.

She might not know what was ahead, but one thing was certain. Rose wanted Dustan beside her every night. And he had been, every night since they'd been bonded. With her head on his chest, Rose watched the stars twinkling.

A Note from the Author

✍

DEAR READER,

Thank you so much for reading *The Forest Bride*. When I started writing it, I thought it would be similar to the fantasy romances I'd read, with battle scenes and evil dark fairies, but that didn't end up happening. As you've seen, the battle scene morphed into a nonviolent conflict resolution! I reconsidered and realized I could write fantasy romances that are not "epic" or high stakes. I call this niche "cozy fantasy romance."

I love writing stories in this cozy fantasy world, and I'm hoping other book lovers might enjoy reading them. If that's not you, that's okay. If you did like the story, please consider leaving a review online to help other readers with similar interests find the book. I would really appreciate it.

The next book in the Sylvania series, *The Village Maid*, will be out March 20, 2022. You can subscribe to my email list at https://janebuehler.com for an email when the new book is available. I send only a few emails each year, so I won't crowd your inbox. When you subscribe, I'll send a link to some bonus material. The email list is also how I give away advance review copies.

You can also connect with me online on Twitter as @ephemerily or on my Goodreads author page. And you can email me at jane@janebuehler.com.

Sincerely,

Emily Jane ♡

Acknowledgments

Ø

I'M THANKFUL TO HAVE FRIENDS and family who have always supported me, especially my parents, who've been on board with my publishing schemes since they began, and Darcy, who's always willing to stay home on the weekend if I want to write.

Thank you to all the beta readers of *The Forest Bride*: Yukiko M., Robin H., Charlotte C., Sara B., Dane S., Jen S., Cinnamon F., and Jessica M. Special thanks to Adrienne M. and Angie M. for all their feedback. (It's been a while—if I forgot anyone, please let me know.)

Thank you to Kelly Urgan for her excellent and encouraging copyediting.

Thank you to Cory Marie Podielski for taking on the challenge of creating a cover without any comparable titles to look at, and for being my long-time colleague and friend.

And thank you to all the readers. It means so much to have you reading my stories. We authors couldn't do this without you!

About the Author

EMILY JANE BUEHLER WAS ADRIFT for many years before realizing she wanted to work with words. She published two nonfiction books—one on the science and craft of baking bread, the other a memoir of her bicycle trip from New Jersey to Oregon—before venturing into fiction. She now writes "cozy fantasy romance": lighthearted stories that focus on a protagonist finding their courage and happiness, as opposed to plots with a lot of fighting and darkness. She also copyedits (mostly science papers) and teaches bread-making classes.

Emily lives in Hillsborough, North Carolina, with a bossy cat named Coco. She is looking forward to becoming the weird old lady who walks around town in a reflective safety vest and fit-over sunglasses. Her favorite things include letters sent through the mail, made-in-the-USA knee socks, and very dark fair-trade chocolate. She is passionate about living waste free and supporting local businesses.

Emily publishes fiction using her middle name, Jane.

www.ingramcontent.com/pod-product-compliance
Lightning Source LLC
Chambersburg PA
CBHW050033120726
47903CB00006B/2026